Millie's Encounter with the Parallel World

KERRY TAYLOR

DEDICATION

For my mom, Julia, who read this story first.
My sister, Jenna, who read it second.
And my boyfriend, Dave, who is yet to read it.
Thank you for supporting me.

CONTENTS

Chapter 1   1

Chapter 2   13

Chapter 3   28

Chapter 4   40

Chapter 5   52

Chapter 6   63

Chapter 7   74

Chapter 8   87

Chapter 9   97

Chapter 10   108

Chapter 11   118

Chapter 12   130

Chapter 13   139

Chapter 14   151

Chapter 15   162

Chapter 16   176

Chapter 17   192

1

"Millie! Wake up, you're going to be late for school!"

Millie reluctantly opened her eyes to the bright September morning, her stomach filled with butterflies at the thought of another day at school; she had just started year eight at Farnhall Academy, and the year hadn't gotten off to a good start. Her best friend, Oliver, used to go there too; until he and his family moved to a new house. They'd been inseparable during their first year at Farnhall Academy. Once he'd finished the term, Oliver's parents enrolled him in a school nearer to where they lived. She'd known him since nursery, and they'd barely spent a day apart. Now they spoke most nights on the phone, but they didn't see each other half as much as they used to. Oliver loved his new school; he was making new friends and was happy.

Millie lay staring at the ceiling. After a minute or two she finally sat up to find her cat, Chris, curled up at the bottom of her bed; she stroked his fur while he purred away sleepily. She listened to her mother clattering around downstairs in the kitchen. Millie knew it would only be a matter of seconds before her mother called up to her again, so she climbed out of bed and stretched her arms towards the ceiling while letting out a huge yawn. She walked out of her bedroom onto the landing, dragging her feet along the carpet. As she walked by her sister's bedroom door, she thought back to when she would've burst into the room and dived on her sister's bed to wake her. She wouldn't dare do that now, things were different - Carla was fifteen and was a typical teenager. Carla was too cool to be seen speaking to Millie at school, or even speak to her at home. Oliver had warned Millie that it would happen - when his older brother turned fifteen, they never spoke again. Millie hadn't believed him; she'd thought that they were too close to let an age get between them. Millie wondered whether she would be the same when she turned that age; she made a promise to herself there and then that she wouldn't become the moody spotty monster that her sister had become.

Millie carried on past her sister's room, careful not to wake the beast, and continued down the stairs and through the hallway. The hallway wall was filled with family photos, with everyone looking so happy in them; she could still remember the feelings she'd felt in the pictures - happy and carefree. When these pictures were taken, she had her sister and her best friend by her side.

Millie tore her gaze from the photos and continued into the kitchen. The air was filled with the smell of pancakes and coffee. She sat at the dining table and watched as her mum dished up a plate for her dad while he sat at the table reading the newspaper and sipping his coffee. He was already dressed smartly in his suit and tie ready for work. He worked for an estate agency specialising in commercial property. It was a competitive environment and he was good at his job - he often received praise and made a decent wage; however, he was deeply unhappy and unfulfilled. He'd always wanted to make a difference and do something more worthwhile, but to him this was just a pipe dream. He was caught up in the rat race - his family relied on the steady income that solely maintained their comfortable lifestyle. He would never let on to his wife or children how unhappy he was - their happiness and comfort was the most important thing in the world to him. So, every day he would plaster on a smile and force himself to make the journey to work.

Her mum brought over another plate of pancakes, with a smiley face carved into them. Millie looked up at her and smiled - she knew that her mum was worried sick about her, which made Millie feel even worse than she already felt. She gave Millie a troubled smile and continued to potter around the kitchen. Her mum rarely sat down; she would always say - 'There's always something to do'.

Millie's dad closed his newspaper, placed it next to his pancakes and looked at his wife. "Jane please sit down and have some breakfast."

"I've already eaten," she answered distractedly. "What time will you be home later?"

"I should be home around six." He frowned as she started whipping up another batch of pancakes, "you never sit."

"Well Mark, there's always something to do," she sang in the tone she reserved for her catchphrase.

He looked over at Millie with a raised eyebrow; they smiled at her predictability.

"Don't forget it's date night! I've booked a table at Gino's for eight," she reminded him.

"I know, I haven't forgotten."

Millie sat in silence as she ate her pancakes and tried to believe that the day ahead of her would be better.

A thud above their heads interrupted her thoughts - Carla was up. It was like time stood still - they all sat motionless staring up at the ceiling; listening and waiting for It to make Its next move. When they heard Carla take her next step, Jane worked quickly to make up a plate of pancakes; Millie shifted uneasily in her chair, and Mark immediately rammed as many pancakes as he could into his mouth. He stood quickly and grabbed his coat in a hurry to avoid 'morning Carla', which was marginally worse than regular Carla. He kissed Jane goodbye then went over to Millie, he gave her a kiss on the forehead and placed a hand on her cheek.

"Keep your chin up love, today might be better."

Millie smiled and hoped he was right.

They could hear that Carla had made her way from her bedroom and had started to descend the stairs. Mark said his goodbyes once more before he left the kitchen and made his way through the hallway towards the front door, and unfortunately intercepted Carla at the foot of the stairs.

He smiled cautiously, "Erm, bye Carla. I'll see you later honey."

"Mm-hmm," Carla grumbled, as Mark edged past her and left for work unscathed.

The scuffing of Carla's slippers on the floor grew closer as she approached the kitchen. It appeared in the doorway looking disheveled - barely resembling Carla.

"Good morning darling," Jane sang.

Millie diverted her gaze, careful not to make eye-contact, "Morning Carla."

"Mmmmmm," Carla groaned.

Carla slumped into a chair at the table and Jane immediately presented her with pancakes. Millie watched the scene across the table, she felt like she was at the zoo watching the keepers feeding the lions - throwing the food the lion's way and trying not to get their arm bitten off. Carla began to fill her face like she hadn't eaten in a week.

"Are you still OK to stay in tonight to look after Millie while dad and I are at the restaurant?"

"Ugh, can you stop asking me questions! I've only just woke up!" she roared, she picked up her plate and stomped back upstairs. "Yes! I said I was staying in to look after her so that's what I'm doing!" she shouted from the top step, before pounding across the landing and slamming her bedroom door.

Jane looked at Millie with a look as if to say - 'What did I say?' Millie shook her head in silent response. They suddenly fell into a fit of childish giggles at Carla's dramatic reaction; stifling their laughter with their hands to prevent Carla from hearing and angering her more. Jane cleared her throat and regained her composure.

"You'd better start getting ready, you don't want to be late."

And just like that - the butterflies were back.

• • •

Millie approached the school gates a few feet behind her sister and her friends. They hadn't spoken a word to Millie during the walk from the house to the school, except for the three words Carla would say every day once Jane had waved them off - 'Walk behind us!' Having completed her verbal contract with their mother to ensure Millie got to school safely - Carla ditched Millie the second that they walked through the school gates. Millie watched as the stranger that used to be her sister walked away and left her standing alone; the further away she got the more she resembled the Carla that she once knew. She watched as Carla chatted away with her friends happily, before she disappeared into the crowd. Millie wondered what it was about her that made Carla dislike her so much; she decided that now was not the time to wonder about the relationship with her sister - she needed to stay focused and alert. She'd started the day with hopes that today would be better but walking through the school gates with her sister tended to knock any positive feelings out of her most days. She made her way towards the far block for registration; she kept her head down and walked quickly. As she weaved her way through the groups of friends forming to catch up with the events of their weekend, she mentally prepared herself for a day the same as the days before.

After registration she checked her planner to see what class she had first - Art - her heart sank. It wasn't that she didn't enjoy the subject; she used to love Art when Oliver was in the class with her - it was one of her favourite subjects. There were three reasons why Millie now dreaded Art, and their names were Jamie, Mora and Jenna. Jamie and Mora had been the school bullies for as long as Millie could remember; but until now, they'd never bothered her. This year they had recruited their newest mean girl – Jenna. Jenna was new to the school; she'd started at the beginning of term and had no problems fitting in. She was Jamie's cousin, and therefore gained an automatic entry into their club. Millie only had two lessons with all three girls, which was when they were most brave and when they bothered her the most.

Since Oliver had left, she felt all too visible; especially to Jamie, Mora, and Jenna – it hadn't taken them long to notice Millie's vulnerability, and had decided that she would be their target. The first week at school they'd convinced the whole class to pretend that she was invisible - it lasted three days. Word spread to kids outside of the class, and then the whole school got involved in giving Millie the silent treatment; even her handful of friends were too scared to speak to her. Carla even committed to ignoring her at home, which she thought was hilarious; but that was the only positive part of it for Millie - Carla not barking at her for three days. But things were getting worse - she'd had to change her mobile number because the girls at school had gotten hold of it and had been harassing her at all hours. Millie suspected that one of her friends had been forced to give it over.

Millie sat alone at her desk in Art watching the door; waiting for the girls to make their fashionably late entrance. It was 9:15am and she was hoping that they hadn't come into school, or decided to be rebels and skip the class, or all three of them had been hit by a bus. When Mrs Carpenter looked disappointedly at the clock, got up from behind her desk and closed the door - Millie finally relaxed.

"Good morning everyone, today we're going to pick up where we left off last week-" The door flung open and slammed against the wall - cutting Mrs Carpenter off mid-sentence. Mora and Jamie strolled in arrogantly, closely followed by Jenna, who looked moderately embarrassed. "Girls, you're fifteen minutes late," said Mrs Carpenter, already defeated.

"Soorrryyyyy Mrs Carpennntttterrrr," they drooled in unison as they walked at a casual pace towards the back row of desks, directly behind Millie.

Mrs Carpenter began her sentence again, trying to disguise her anger and failing with her clipped and shrill tone, "As I was saying! Today! We're going to pick up where we left off last week! Get your sketch pads and anything you need from the supply cupboard!"

Millie wasn't the only one they'd gotten to - at the beginning of term, Mrs Carpenter had been a completely different person. She was usually bubbly, enthusiastic and patient, it had only taken a few short weeks for the girls to break her. They disrupted every class and were late most days, and through all of the tellings-off, threats, and detentions; they still managed to keep that cool calm exterior that got under any teacher's skin. Millie felt a connection with Mrs Carpenter - they both dreaded the moment Jamie, Mora and Jenna walked into a room. The others in the class were different - there was an excitement in the air when the three of them entered the classroom, and when the entertainment arrived, they all wanted a front row seat.

Millie got her sketch pad and a few pencils from the cupboard and went back to her desk. She listened to Mora moaning behind her - telling Jenna and Jamie how her dad had told her she couldn't go out Saturday, but she'd be sneaking out to meet them anyway. She told them how much she hated her parents for never allowing her to go to any parties - even though she went anyway without their permission. Millie couldn't help but roll her eyes at the conversation behind her. Mora went on for twenty minutes and showed no sign of stopping. Millie started to feel at ease - it seemed like she was the last thing on their minds; they were distracted by Mora's problem - judging by their empathetic advice.

She carried on with her sketch and let her mind wander - she hadn't spoken to Oliver in a few days and she missed him. Even though Oliver and his parents had moved, at the time it hadn't occurred to either of them that he would've had to change schools — it'd come as a shock when he broke the news to her in the summer holidays. She'd relied on Oliver too much and had forgotten to make any other friends; now she was starting from scratch, like others had in her year group a year ago when they'd arrived at Farnhall Academy. Millie planned to see if he was free to hang out after school, or the weekend, and go to the cinema or bowling.

Millie felt excited at the thought of some well overdue quality time with Oliver, and before she knew it the bell was ringing to signal the end of class. It suddenly dawned on her that a whole forty-five minutes, from the time they'd arrived, had gone by without

Jamie, Mora or Jenna even looking in her direction. It crossed her mind that they may have been pretending that she was invisible again - but this felt different. They had gone through a whole class without even thinking to bother her; maybe this was the start of something, she thought, each lesson she'd get less and less hassle.

Even Mrs Carpenter looked relieved as realisation hit that there had been no drama caused by them. "OK, good lesson guys, see you all Wednesday."

Millie put away her sketch book and pencils, packed away her things and put on her jacket. They slowly filtered out of the classroom into the corridor, joining the sea of kids that flooded out from surrounding classes. As Millie walked amongst the crowd towards the exit, she started to notice the unnatural silence forming behind her. Her heart dropped as she knew instantly something wasn't right. She turned to face her classmates that had fallen back in a huddle behind her, which was headed up by Jamie, Mora, and Jenna. Millie stared at the crowd in confusion, trying to piece together what was happening. The crowd suddenly erupted into a fit of laughter.

Jamie fought to get the words out, "You've... got... something... on.... your back!" she strained whilst gasping for air in between howls of laughter.

Millie pulled at her jacket to see what was on her back, which only made them laugh harder. As she stared back at the laughing crowd, her lip began to tremble against her will.

Mora pointed at her face and screamed in excitement, "She's crying!"

The group laughed harder. Millie stood opposite them with tears now falling freely down her face as they doubled over with laughter. Her focus was pulled to the only person who was stood upright - Jenna – she wasn't laughing, she was looking down at her feet trying not to meet Millie's eyes. Millie turned and ran down the corridor until she could barely hear the laughter. She ran into the girls' toilets and locked herself in a cubicle.

An hour later, Millie wiped her swollen damp eyes and finally left the cubicle. She turned to look at her back in the mirror - red paint covered the back of her jacket and had smeared onto the tips of her hair. She looked at her blotchy red face in the mirror and didn't recognise the reflection; she was so different to how she used to be.

Unable to face the rest of the day, Millie snuck out of school, and by 12:00pm she was home. After listening to Millie's explanation, Jane went ballistic giving Millie a lecture on how 'Anything could've happened to her walking home alone from school.' Once she'd calmed down, she turned her anger towards the school. Millie sat in her room listening to her mum ranting down the phone to the Headteacher. She felt sorry for him - it sounded brutal. Her parents hadn't yet met the Headteacher at Farnhall Academy, Mr Wright. Millie smirked to herself, picturing their faces if they ever actually did meet him – they'd have a shock, she thought. Mr Wright was the epitome of ridiculous - both as a person and a Headteacher. The thought of Mr Wright made her think of Oliver, and how they always shared a laugh at his expense.

She decided to text Oliver - he always cheered her up.

'Hey! Guess what.... I'm not in school today! Probably won't go in tomorrow either. Fancy skipping school and coming over to mine? My mum will be out *all* day so we can chill and watch films or something.'

'WHHAAAATTT! How come you're off? You sick? I'm not coming round if you're sick!'

'Nope not sick. Just them stupid girls messing with me! You up for it tomorrow then?'

'No are you crazy my parents would lock me in the house until I was twenty-five if they found out! They're still bullying you! You

should just punch them in the nose, you know what people say - violence solves everything.'

'OMG stop being boring and skip one day! Your parents won't find out, promise. I'm not punching anyone, and I'm pretty sure that's *not* what people say.'

'FINE! I'll come round when my parents leave for work tomorrow morning.'

'Yay it will be fun! ☺'

Jane made Millie's favourite for dinner - spaghetti and meatballs. Jane and Mark had postponed their date night so they could have a meal as a family around the table. Millie thought to herself, if this didn't scream pity, she didn't know what did. She sat in silence watching the unnatural scene - her mum and dad with their over the top smiles and lighthearted chit-chat, and Carla was on her best behaviour.

When Carla smiled at her, she'd had enough. "Stop it."

"Stop what?" asked Carla, defensively.

"Actually, everyone Stop it! You're all treating me like I'm going to break."

"I'm sorry love, we're just worried about you," explained Mark.

"Well don't be, I'll be fine!" she stabbed at a meatball with her fork. "Even if I have to transfer to Oliver's school."

Her parents looked uneasy - of course when they'd seen how hard the news of Oliver's move had hit Millie, they'd considered moving her too; but Oliver's school was too far out of the way for either of them to factor into their schedule. It wasn't walking distance, or on Mark's way to work, or even on a route for public transport; plus, they liked that Carla was there for Millie - which would've been fine before her personality transplant.

"If that's what you want, we'll make it work," said Jane, uncertainly, casting a worried look at Mark. He smiled and gave her hand a reassuring squeeze.

Millie felt awful and selfish, she knew how difficult it would be for them. But she felt that moving schools would be the only way she would feel happy again. She caught a glimpse of Carla subtly shaking her head.

She couldn't sit there any longer; it was unbearable with Carla's disapproval and her parents' palpable worry all contributing to her guilt. "I'm going to bed, I'm so tired. Thanks for the lovely meal mum."

"You're welcome Millie."

Mark opened his mouth to call after her, but Jane gave him a look to say - 'Let her go.'

Millie lay in her dark bedroom staring up at the ceiling, with Chris stretched out next to her - purring loudly. He's always so happy, she thought, suddenly feeling envious of his blissful ignorance.

The light from the hallway lit up a sliver of the room as Jane pushed open the door just enough for her to peep in.

"I'm awake," Millie whispered.

Jane walked into the room and perched on the edge of the bed, "You know, I was once bullied."

"You were?" Millie asked in surprise, wondering why her mother hadn't mentioned this before now.

"Yes, so I know how you feel, and I know you'll get through this."

Her mum looked different somehow - there wasn't the pity in her eyes that usually appeared when she looked at Millie lately. She looked strong and knowing, almost like something had shifted.

Millie felt relief wash over her; she hoped her mum would have all the answers and wisdom she needed to put a stop to this stage in her life, "What did you do?"

"Well, it was a difficult time. It was after my parents had passed away. I wasn't as strong and brave as you are. I tried my best to fight, but eventually I gave up." Jane looked away from her daughter, feeling slightly ashamed that her story didn't have a more inspiring ending.

"What do you mean you gave up?"

"I mean I stopped fighting and gave in. I couldn't face it anymore, so I left. So, I understand why you feel like you have to run. But it's always bothered me that I ran, I wish I could go back and face it."

"I don't think I can face it anymore," Millie admitted, feeling exhausted.

"Nonsense, you're tough! We will get through this together. And if it doesn't work out, your dad and I will figure it out and you can transfer schools."

A smile spread across her face, "Really?"

"Of course, we just want you to be happy," Jane reached around to the small clasp of her dainty silver necklace that hung around her neck; she held it in her palm and looked at it affectionately. The necklace was understated, apart from the small single emerald pedant. "My mother gave me this necklace before she passed away. I could always feel her with me when I wore it, now I feel her with me whether I wear it or not; it always gave me strength. It's been passed down the family for generations - I want you to have it."

Millie was touched, she knew how much the necklace meant to her mother, and now how much it would mean to her; she would treasure it and hoped that it would give her strength like it had her mum.

She gave Jane a tight hug and buried her face in her shoulder to hide the tears brimming in her eyes. "Thank you, mum."

Jane stood and kissed the top of Millie's head. She placed the necklace in the jewellery box near the window. "Good night darling," she whispered as she left the room, closing the door behind her.

2

A loud commotion in Millie's bedroom woke her abruptly – half asleep and confused, she lifted herself onto her elbow and looked around the room. In the corner of her eye, she saw Chris stalk out of the room. Hesitantly, she looked over at her alarm clock – 3:00am. She huffed groggily in annoyance and flopped back down on her bed, silently cursing Chris. Now wide awake, she decided to get a glass of water from the kitchen.

She stuffed her feet into her slippers and shuffled out of her bedroom onto the landing - and stopped dead in her tracks. She rubbed her eyes and looked again at the scene in front of her - this must be a dream, she thought. The air was filled with golden glitter, floating from floor to ceiling, never settling. It twinkled in the moonlight streaming in from the window above the staircase. She walked backwards slowly into the bathroom; her eyes fixed on the shimmering haze. Closing the door carefully behind her, Millie switched on the light and splashed water on her face; then held tightly onto the sink for support. Clearly, she wasn't fully awake, she reasoned with herself. Millie stared at her shocked expression in the mirror and told herself she hadn't seen what she thought she'd seen - she hadn't seen a room full of glitter, hovering like dust particles. After a few minutes of rationalising, Millie knew for definite that she was wide awake, and concluded that she must've been dreaming; but just to be certain, she splashed another lot of water on her face.

She took a deep breath and slowly opened the bathroom door - it was still there. There *was* glitter in the air on the landing, but less than before; it was slowly clearing – dissipating into the air rather settling to the ground. Millie took a hesitant step into the glittering mass, and slowly walked down the stairs. The glitter in the hallway hovered near to the floor, creating a shimmering trail that led all the way to the back door, through the cat flap, and out into the back garden. She walked cautiously to the back door, turned the key and opened it. Just as the door opened, she saw Chris bound towards the patch of untamed wild garden - her dad left purposely overgrown for wildlife - and disappear into the long grass. Millie stepped out into the garden and followed him - she walked towards where he had disappeared, all the time looking back towards the house and wondering whether this was a good idea. Millie tried to think logically, there must be an explanation, she thought - maybe Chris was chasing a mouse that had gotten into her room. It wasn't the first time he'd brought a mouse in and then chased it around the house - but never a *glittery* mouse. She knew she was clutching at straws, she needed something logical to keep herself calm; but the more she thought about it, the more her composure slipped. She looked down to see glitter clinging to her pyjamas - she brushed it away; desperately trying to erase the evidence of its existence. Her stomach flipped as she struggled to find a reasonable explanation she could latch onto.

After what felt like a thousand steps, she finally reached the unkempt shrubbery and waist-high grass. There was a small opening in one of the bushes, she knelt and looked through. There was a clear circular path through the grass and bushes, where Chris and other animals had been through frequently. She heard rustling in the bushes and a jingle from Chris' collar - he was still chasing whatever it was that had been in the house. Millie moved further into the bushes curiously, wanting to get a glimpse of what Chris was chasing - but all she saw was darkness. Suddenly fear washed over her, and she jolted away from the bushes. What am I doing, she thought, this is ridiculous - crawling around the garden at 3am chasing Chris around? She was just about to get up off the ground and go back to bed when she saw something in the opening in the bushes, far in the distance. She squinted into the darkness trying to focus her eyes and crawled further into the bushes. Suddenly from the back of the tunnel near the fence came a green pulsing glow. It started as a flicker, then grew bigger, shining through the ready-made path and through the leaves, casting shadows across the garden. She stared wide-eyed, mesmerised; she felt as though she was being pulled towards the light - like a siren's call. The fear flooded her body again, she was just about to turn back when she heard Chris' bell jingle somewhere far in the distance, somewhere further than the edge of the garden. She glanced over to the house - the house was still in darkness; she knew their garden was completely secluded, but she surveyed the area for onlookers anyway - she was completely alone. She plucked up the courage and hesitantly continued to crawl forwards through the dense shrubbery towards the glowing light. As she got closer, she noticed a light dusting of gold glitter along the ground, she lifted her hand to her face - a mixture of mud and glitter covered her palm. For a fleeting moment she felt excitement course through her and continued to crawl eagerly towards the light. As she got closer to the fence it began to shimmer and disappear into the glow along with the bushes. The glow became fog-like, surrounding her; the further she crawled the thicker the fog became. Millie was completely enveloped - she couldn't see a thing that surrounded her.

Millie reached out her hand, blindly feeling her way through the green fog that clouded her vision. The cold damp earth that had been squelching underneath her hands and knees suddenly became solid and warm. She felt as though she'd been crawling for ages - the allure gradually subsided with every second she continued to crawl forwards, leaving nothing but panic. She was about to turn back when her outstretched hand broke into what felt like a different atmosphere ahead of her. The air not only felt warmer than the early Autumn crispness of her garden, but it felt alive with an electric buzz. Millie waved her hand around slowly in the air, enjoying the effervescent feeling reaching from her fingertips to her wrist. She moved forwards, allowing her arm to break through into the atmosphere up to her elbow and waited for the buzz to spread further. She knew if she continued crawling forwards, she would be somewhere else, somewhere other than her garden.

Eager to see what was on the other side, Millie retracted her arm and steadied herself with a deep breath. Reluctantly, she poked her head through the other side, where her hand had just been - her head to her shoulders buzzed pleasantly. She kept her eyes closed - scared to open them. She willed herself to open her eyes - what is the point in doing this, she thought, if she couldn't be brave enough to open her eyes and look. Eventually after a mental tug-of-war, and the buzz had become just a light hum, she slowly opened one eye, then the other.

"Wow," she gasped in awe.

She was in a gigantic forest, but it was like no other forest she'd seen before. The forest was like something only her imagination could create; a fairy-tale – warm, fuzzy, inviting; and enchanting. Everything about the forest was bright and vibrant, she felt as though she was seeing everything in colour for the first time. She realised she was peering out from inside of a tree-hollow, which housed the glow she had emerged from. She pulled herself out of the hollow and did a slow 360-degree turn – taking in her surroundings. The moon was huge, and the stars were bright enough to light up the forest to show its magnificent detail and depth. The trees were thick and alive with creatures. Fireflies danced in the air, weaving in and out of the tall trees and bushes. The grass was vivid green with trails of red and white polka dot toadstools, which led to a stream that meandered off into the distance. She looked further into the vast forest and saw several cobblestone paths with wooden signposts, all pointing in different directions. Lanterns lined the paths - lighting the way in a yellowish tinge, creating intriguing caverns as the paths curled out of sight, deep into the forest. There wasn't a stone out of place - the grass was cut, the trees and bushes were pruned, and the paths were swept.

Millie was pulled out of her state of wonderment by the familiar jingle of Chris' collar. He came into view and sat opposite her near a large bush. She walked towards him casually, she couldn't believe it, she'd discovered a portal; and it led to the most beautiful place she'd ever seen. As she got closer to Chris, she heard rustling coming from inside the bush behind him – he jumped and ran out of sight. The rustling stopped suddenly, but Millie was unable to move - whatever it was sounded large and heavy. Millie's eyes were locked on the bush; she held her breath and waited for whatever it was to go. A branch within the bush snapped as it moved - she closed her eyes and covered her mouth to muffle any sound that might escape. The movement stopped again abruptly, Millie opened her eyes, hoping the creature had moved on. Afraid to move, her eyes searched the bush - suddenly a deep, low, guttural growl broke into the silence. She was completely frozen with fear; her feet felt as though they were set in concrete and couldn't be lifted from the ground. She told herself to run, but it was no use - her feet wouldn't move. The creature's growl continued to rumble and vibrate through the leaves. The rumbling growl broke into a roar as it rushed forwards, braking branches and shaking the bushes violently in its path.

Before the creature came into view Millie jumped to life - she turned on her heel and sprinted towards the dull glow still emanating from the tree-hollow. Her heart pounded against her chest. She hoped that whatever it was wasn't in pursuit; she tried to listen for anything behind her, but her thumping heart was too loud. The green light became brighter the closer she got - she dived headfirst into the light in the tree-hollow and landed amongst the fog on the damp earth, causing a plume of golden glitter as she hit the ground. She crawled through the fog until the bushes around her started to come into view. On all fours she scrambled out of the bushes and into the safety of her garden. She bolted up the garden to the door and through the house, closely followed by Chris. Millie flew up the stairs, trampling on the glitter that now only hovered an inch off the floor. She ran into her bedroom, dived into her bed; threw the bedcovers over her head, and waited for the panic to subside. She strained desperately to hear as her heart thumped in her ears. After a minute or so, her heart had calmed down just enough for her to be able to hear that the house was silent. Sudden shuffling in the next room made her heart skip a beat - Millie held her breath and listened. When she realised it was just Carla, she sighed in relief; she willed her sister to come into her room - she wanted to feel safe. Millie lay in bed in silence – still unable to move from the shock of what she'd experienced. Eventually, from pure exhaustion, she drifted off to sleep.

"Millie! Breakfast!"

Millie woke to her mum yelling up the stairs - a typical morning. She slowly sat up, stretched and yawned. She looked down to the side of her bed to where her slippers usually sat side by side, only this morning the usual baby pink slippers were a muddy shade of brown – one in the corner of the room, and the other on her dressing table. It all came rushing back - the green light in the garden, the forest... the terrifying creature in the bushes. She jumped out of bed, scaring the life out of Chris who had been sleeping happily on the bottom of her bed. Her pyjamas were covered in mud, but no glitter – she quickly changed out of her pyjamas and stuffed them at the back of her wardrobe along with her slippers. Her eyes flicked around the room, checking for any other evidence of last night – nothing unusual. Millie sat on the edge of her bed; a frown etched on her face. She rubbed her head and began to question herself – of course last night hadn't been real, she used to sleepwalk years ago; stress must've brought it back on, she thought. Her concern went to her muddy clothes, wondering how she'd go about getting her pyjamas and slippers cleaned. A clear vision of the sparkling glitter that had filled the air outside her room suddenly came to the forefront of her mind. She ran out onto the landing expectantly - startling Carla - no glitter. She had a logical explanation – she used to sleepwalk regularly; but no matter how many times she recited it; her mind wouldn't accept it. She could still feel the allure of the green light as it streamed through the bushes into the garden, she still felt the electric atmosphere on her skin; but most of all, she could still feel the undercurrent of fear.

Millie pushed passed Carla and ran down the stairs.

"Watch it!" Carla shouted after her.

Millie darted through the hallway and into the kitchen. "Did you vacuum the landing this morning?"

"Morning Millie."

"Oh yeah - morning mum, did you vacuum the landing this morning?"

Jane chuckled, "No, why?"

"No, reason......was there anything on the floor when you got up this morning?"

Jane stopped what she was doing to give Millie her full attention. She placed one hand on her hip while analysing her daughter, "Did you spill something or are you covering up for Chris?"

"No, and no. I - erm - I just thought I heard you vacuuming this morning, thought it was strange that's all - must've dreamt it," Millie said, as she sat down at the table, feeling perplexed.

Jane continued to eye her suspiciously. She tried to act natural and waited for her mum to decide whether she would continue with her questioning. If it comes to it, she thought, Chris will have to take one for the team.

The quizzical look drained from Jane's face as she turned away and continued to potter around. "So, are you going to be OK on your own in the house today? You know you can come along with me?"

Remembering Oliver was coming over she tried to keep the excitement from her voice, "Erm no, I'll be fine on my own."

"OK. Your dad and I are meeting with your Headteacher this evening, it might be a good idea for you to come along and tell him what you've been going through these past few weeks?"

The thought of stepping foot in the school made Millie's stomach turn, "OK."

"We won't be there long, I promise. But it's really important he hears it from you."

Millie nodded and tried to push the thought out of her head. She was spending the day with Oliver, and she was beyond excited; she hadn't seen him in ages, and they had lots to talk about.

She sent him a quick text, 'Will let you know when they're gone!'

Carla entered the kitchen with a face like thunder. Jane quickly made her breakfast, which was put in front of her the second she sat down. Above them they heard Mark make his way from the bathroom and down the stairs - he appeared in the kitchen doorway, spotted Carla and instantly turned on his heel and headed towards the front door.

"Mark, don't forget our meeting with the Headteacher tonight!" Jane shouted after him.

"OK, see you later!" he shouted down the hall before closing the door behind him.

Jane grabbed her coat and keys, she gave Millie a kiss on top of her head, "See you later honey." She looked at Carla and decided against physical contact, "Bye Carla."

Jane left the kitchen and headed out of the house with a day of errands ahead. And just like that, Carla had cleared the room just by her presence alone. She looked up from her breakfast for the first time since sitting down to look directly at Millie. Oh no, she thought, reading Carla's menacing expression.

"So why do you get to stay off school?"

"Them girls have just gotten too much for me to handle."

"Which girls?"

"You know, the girls who've been bullying me? Jamie, Mora, and Jenna," Millie answered, shocked that she'd had to remind her sister.

"Oh yeah," she said, rolling her eyes. "But still it's not fair that *you* get to stay home."

"Carla I'd happily swap places with you if it meant that I didn't have to face them girls again."

"Well if we *did* swap places I definitely wouldn't be as pathetic as *you*." Carla smirked as she got up from the table, her eyes never leaving Millie's. Once Carla was satisfied with the visible pain she'd caused her sister, she turned and left the kitchen.

Millie's eyes started to prickle with tears. How could things have gotten so bad between them, she thought. When did it get to the point where Carla had not only stopped caring, but had wanted to inflict more pain on her? She thought back to when she first started in primary school, Carla had protected her from everyone. She would introduce Millie to all her friends so proudly as her 'Little sister Millie.' Millie sat at the table fighting back the tears. When she heard the front door slam, she picked up her phone and text Oliver, **'OK come over, they're gone.'**

Ding-dong-ding-dong- din-don-din-don-din-din-din-

"OK OK! You're so annoying!" Millie whined, as she pulled open the door to see Oliver's mischievous grin and devilish glint in his dark eyes.

"It was Morse code - to let you know it was me," Oliver said, pleased with himself for annoying Millie within seconds.

"Quick get in someone could see you!" she chirped excitedly, while pulling at his arm. Millie was so excited to see his face she instantly felt better, and couldn't wait to tell him everything, and in particular - about last night.

"*So,* how've you been?" Oliver asked, tilting his head to the side. Millie was about to go off at him for treating her like her family with the pitying looks when he started to smile - he knew exactly how she'd been and knew that she wouldn't want to talk about it. She laughed and gave him a hard dig in the shoulder. "Oh, I've got news! Joe spoke!" Oliver blurted out, rubbing his shoulder. He stared at Millie, eyes wide and mouth open, waiting for her to mirror his amazed expression.

"Huh? So?"

"He spoke to *me!*"

"What! What did he say?"

"'Pass the salt'- but it doesn't matter what he said. It's been two years since my brother last spoke *words* to me."

"Wow, I'm happy for you!"

"Just shows there's hope for you and Carla."

"Yeah, doubt that," she said with certainty, thinking back to her encounter with Carla that morning. "Carla's on a different level. Believe me! I wish *she* wouldn't speak to me for two years."

"*Oooh* that bad huh? Anyway Mills, what's on our agenda for today?" Oliver asked, changing the subject to keep the day as light and as enjoyable as he could.

Millie wondered how to tell him about her experience last night, "OK... are you feeling open minded today?"

"Always."

"Well... I had the strangest experience last night-" she hesitated, unsure how to tell him without him thinking she was a complete lunatic.

"Did Carla laugh in her sleep?" Oliver quipped.

"No," she giggled, "even stranger if you can imagine."

"She was awake!" he feigned shock whilst stifling a chuckle.

"Oliver stop - I'm serious. I'm worried and I know you're going to think I'm crazy!"

His face suddenly turned serious, "OK I'm listening, I won't think you're crazy."

Millie took a deep breath and started from the beginning, "Last night I woke up to Chris going crazy. He ran out of my room, like he was chasing something." Millie paused rubbing her forehead in disbelief at where her story was going. "I stepped out of my room and there was this glitter, everywhere - all in the air, just floating around." She stopped and studied Oliver's face, trying to read his thoughts so far - nothing. "I saw Chris run outside and I just had this urge to follow him. He ran into the bushes; you know that overgrown area in the garden?" Oliver nodded; his expression serious. "Well I followed Chris in there and - wow this sounds *so* crazy I can't even believe I'm telling you this!" She took a deep breath, "I think I went through some kind of portal into some other world! I know it sounds insane, but it was *real*. There was a forest and there were paths lit up with lanterns, and there was this thing in the bushes, and it growled-"

"Thing?"

"I didn't see what it was because I ran. But it *was* real, I know it." She finally stopped for breath after her verbal outburst and waited for Oliver to make the call whether to have her sectioned.

"You were dreaming, obviously," he said, simply.

"No. No, it was real," Millie shot back defensively.

"Was the glitter there this morning?"

"No, it wasn't! *But* my pyjamas and slippers are covered in mud!" she shouted, as if the mud proved it.

"Maybe you were sleepwalking. Remember you used to do that *all* the time when you stopped at mine – it was so weird!"

"Oliver! I wasn't sleepwalking and I wasn't dreaming!"

He looked blankly at Millie, waiting for her to acknowledge that it couldn't possibly have been real. His expression frustrated her so much that she thought she might burst into tears; she felt alone in every aspect of her life. Even though she knew what she was saying to Oliver was hard to believe, she never thought that he would dismiss the possibility of it being real so easily.

Suddenly she felt fueled by determination, "I can show you, come with me!"

Millie and Oliver stood in the garden opposite the shrubbery. Oliver was now concerned; from the corner of her eye she could see his eyes darting from the bushes to her.

"I'm sure it was right there, where that kind of tunnel is," Millie said, suddenly feeling nervous and questioning herself once again.

"OK, go for it," he said, crossing his arms and nodding towards the bush she had identified as the portal to another world.

Millie walked slowly over to the bushes until she was directly in front of the opening. She looked over her shoulder at Oliver, who mocked her by giving her a double thumbs up. She rolled her eyes and turned back to the tunnel. Now more eager than ever to prove Oliver wrong, she dived headfirst into the bushes.

"Oh, and she's in," Oliver commentated.

Millie crawled along the floor following the path that she took the night before - nothing looked familiar, but she kept on crawling. She'd been crawling for what felt like forever and suddenly, she hit the fence - stunned, she stood up and rubbed her head. She looked back over the stretch of bushes towards Oliver - he was still watching, arms folded, and his whole body shaking in silent laughter.

"It's around here somewhere, I must've taken a wrong turn," Millie said desperately, looking around the bushes surrounding her for anything familiar. She dived back under and scrambled around the ground looking for a glow, glitter, a feeling - anything. Millie gave up, she sat on the floor out of Oliver's gaze, feeling ridiculous - then it hit her. Millie jumped to her feet, so she was above the hedge line again.

"Chris! It must've been Chris, I followed him in here!" she shouted, frantically looking around the garden. "Chriiiisss!"

"Chris," Oliver shouted, less enthusiastically.

"Chriiiiissss."

"Chri - I still can't believe you called your cat Chris. Chriiisss!"

A moment later, Millie heard the familiar jingle. The black and white cat appeared at the back door then trotted over into the bushes and round Millie's ankles. She bent down to give him a brief fuss and then ducked under the hedge line to follow Chris' lead. Chris sniffed around the ground and then looked at Millie lovingly - she knew she was going to get nowhere. Millie huffed and sat for a while with Chris, she was dreading facing Oliver - she felt so stupid.

"Everything OK in there?" Oliver asked, concerned.

Millie stood and waded her way through the bushes, "You're right, it must've been a dream. But honestly Oliver it felt so real!"

"Yeah clearly, you've just crawled around some hedges for ten minutes."

Millie looked at the ground embarrassed, she wondered to herself how she could've thought that last night could've been real.

Oliver reached for her and pulled her in for a hug, "Listen, you're going through a lot at the moment, give yourself a break. Could've been some form of escapism or something. But other people read a book or watch a film, maybe try that next time?"

Millie pulled away from Oliver to fix him with a disapproving look. Oliver smirked and messed up her hair, "C'mon we can practice now, what film are you feeling? You got popcorn?"

They sat on the sofa with a huge bowl of popcorn perched in-between them. Oliver had picked the movie, which wasn't to Millie's taste, but still she was glad for the distraction - not only from the humiliation of earlier in the garden, but also from a feeling she couldn't shake. The feeling in the pit of her stomach — that last night hadn't been a dream, despite evidence to the contrary.

"Well that's two hours of my life I'm never getting back," said Oliver, throwing the last of the popcorn into his mouth.

"It wasn't that bad!"

Ding-Dong-ding-dong.

Millie and Oliver froze, 'Who's that?' Oliver mouthed through a mouth full of popcorn - Millie shrugged.

Ding-dong-ding-dong.

Oliver slid off the sofa onto the floor on his stomach.

"What are you doing?" Millie whispered.

Oliver ignored her and continued to army shuffle around the coffee table and throw himself into a theatrical forward roll up to the window.

"Oliver stop it!" she hissed.

He looked back over at Millie and gave her a popcorn filled grin. Millie couldn't help but laugh, she covered her mouth with her hands - trying to muffle any sound. Oliver peeped out of the window - the girl standing at the door suddenly turned and locked eyes with him.

He dropped to the floor, "She saw me, she saw me!"

"You idiot, who is it?"

"I don't know. Some girl - long red curly hair, sound familiar?"

Millie knew exactly who the girl was - it was Jenna. Millie had always envied Jenna's striking red shiny hair which was always perfectly curled every single day. Whereas Millie's hair was blonde, dull, and a mess every single day. She had always wished that she not only had hair like Jenna's, but a beautiful face and smile like hers too. Everything about her was perfect, apart from her personality. "It's Jenna."

"Jenna? Girl who's picking on you. *That* Jenna?" Oliver raged, now standing and making no attempt at being unseen or quiet.

"Yes, *that* Jenna, just ignore it. Jenna's presence had undone all of Oliver's hard work and had jolted Millie harshly back into reality.

Ding-dong-ding-dong. Oliver walked towards the door.

"Oliver no just leave it - she will go," Millie whispered after him.

It was no use; he was already at the door. Millie ducked out of sight - she couldn't believe that they were now coming to her home. A mixture of fear and anger surged through her - fear that things were about to get a lot worse; and at the same time, she felt infuriated.

Oliver opened the door and looked at Jenna coldly.

"Um, is Millie in?" she asked, hesitantly, flushing the same colour as her hair.

"No. Who are you?" he asked sharply.

"I'm Jenna, I go to school with Millie."

Oliver smiled broadly, "Oh yeah, I've heard about you."

"Really?" she beamed.

"Yeah, don't get excited it was nothing good," Oliver shot back, instantly wiping the smile from her face.

Jenna looked down embarrassed. "Oh, well can you just give her a message? I wanted to tell her that I'm sorry for what happened to her the other day. It wasn't right. Nothing they do is right."

"What have you done to stop the things they do if you feel it's not right?"

Jenna stared at him stunned, she hadn't expected the question.

He shook his head dismissively, "Listen, your apology means nothing if you're still going to stand by them, even if you say you don't agree with what they do."

"Can you please just give her the message? I'd really appreciate it."

"Sure."

Jenna looked at the ground and opened her mouth to say something else - he closed the door before she had chance and strolled back into the living room. He plopped on the sofa and sighed as Millie emerged from behind the chair in the corner of the room.

He smiled at her empathetically, "Well, she seems great."

3

Millie stared at the clock on the wall of the Headteacher's waiting room. Jane was sat next to her, absently fumbling with her wedding ring, and basking in the stream of sunlight that flooded in through the single window. Mark sat opposite, flicking through an old magazine, not reading, but keeping himself occupied. They sat in silence, waiting for Mr Wright to call them into his office. The only sounds were the ticking clock, the occasional flick of a magazine page, and the constant tapping of acrylic nails on a keyboard from Mr Wright's PA in the far corner of the room – guarding the door to his office.

The second they'd pulled up in the school car park, Millie felt her stomach flip. It'd felt worse than usual returning to school; after a pleasant day, she'd been caught off guard by reality rearing its ugly head. She'd not only been distracted from reality by Oliver and the portal in her dream; but also, how she couldn't convince herself that it was just a dream. Jenna had also been on her mind - why had she come to her house, and in the middle of the school day, she wondered; was she being genuine, or was it just another cruel joke that didn't play out, and Jamie and Mora had been hiding around the corner.

Millie's overactive mind was silenced when Mr Wright's office door swung open; startling them all, including his personal assistant - who looked to the sky like she was praying for patience. Mr Wright would always do the same thing, fling open his door to punctuate his entrance, and make the grand reveal of himself – he felt he was really something to see. Millie pictured him creeping towards the door, careful not to alert anyone he was about to do it. She felt for his PA who would have to endure this several times a day, and it wasn't something you ever got used to.

"Hi, you must be Mr and Mrs Shepherd," he greeted, while taking his superhero-like stance in his doorway and flashing them a dashing smile before noticing Millie. "Oh, hello there Millie! I didn't know you'd be joining us."

"Erm- yes," replied Mark, still a little shocked by Mr Wright's entrance. "We thought it'd be best you heard it from Millie rather than us."

"Yes definitely," Mr Wright beamed. He was young and handsome, and a terrible Headteacher. He relied on his looks and charm which usually got him what he wanted or got him out of what he wanted. His ambition for the school, which was highlighted on his mood-board, was to have his face plastered across everything possible. Which included not only posters and newsletters, but school planners. He was lucky that the students at Farnhall Academy were smart, which helped counteract Mr Wright's incompetence. "Come on in, but please, remove your shoes."

They exchanged a bewildered glance and looked at Mr Wright's PA questioningly. She gave them a confirming look as if to say - 'You heard him - shoes off.'

Mr Wright's office was truly a reflection of him. It was grand, pristine, and quite literally - full of himself. The walls were the exact powder blue of his eyes, which was safe to assume was intentional. The carpet was cream, and of the highest pile. There was a large mahogany bookshelf in the corner - the shelves were mainly lined with pictures of him rather than books. A matching desk faced the window overlooking the grounds of the school, which also sported a very posey picture of Mr Wright. The main space of the office was filled with a full-sized snooker table, which Millie believed he spent most of his time playing; and the rest of the time combing his hair.

Mr Wright gestured towards two plush cream chairs at the desk for Mark and Jane, while he took a smaller cushioned chair from the corner of the room and placed it in-between them for Millie.

"So," he said, sitting on the opposite side of the desk in his throne-like leather chair. "I hear you're having some trouble Millie. Tell me all about it."

Mr Wright sat back in his chair, crossed his legs, interlocked his fingers at the knee, and squinted his eyes in an attempt to portray interest.

Millie looked at her mum, who mirrored her expression of disbelief. Jane swallowed her skepticism and gave Millie an encouraging nod.

"It started at the beginning of term-"

"What started?" Mr Wright interrupted, feeling as though his voice hadn't been heard in a while.

"Oh, the bullying..." Millie clarified, "it started when Jamie-"

"When you say bullying, what is it that's actually happening?" Mr Wright interjected once more.

Jane noticed Mark's jaw clenching tighter, and the vein at his temple pulsing – tell-tale signs that he was beginning to get wound up.

"Well they-"

"Who are *they*?"

Mark had had enough, "Will you please let her finish a sentence Mr Wright-"

"Please, call me Matt," Mr Wright said, feeling that they were now familiar enough to be on a first name basis; or in a desperate attempt to charm Mark.

The ridiculousness of Mr Wright stunned Mark into speechlessness; he couldn't believe that *he'd* now been interrupted. "I'd prefer to call you Mr Wright-" Mr Wright opened his mouth to speak but was silenced by Mark's raised finger, "and I'd prefer that as the Headteacher of this school you would know what your students were up to and took bullying seriously." Mark was fuming, he fixed Mr Wright with a piercing glare.

Embarrassed, Mr Wright uncrossed his legs, straightened his tie, and pulled his chair further towards his desk to enhance his focus - knowing his charm was going to get him nowhere with this issue. Mr Wright cleared his throat, "I apologise-"

"I think we would like to hear what *you* will be doing about this, *and* about the repercussions for the girls who have made my daughters school life near unbearable."

During the drive home, Jane listened as Mark ranted about Mr Wright's incompetence. Millie sat in the back not hearing a word, she was too busy mulling over the agreement between Mr Wright and her parents. Mr Wright planned to call in the girls' parents to discuss their behaviour; they would be spending time in isolation as punishment to think about their actions. Her parents had thought this was a step in the right direction and agreed to send Millie back to school the next day. Millie wasn't so convinced that this was the right approach, she felt it had the potential to backfire. In Millie's eyes the only solution was to expel them from school, then ban them from the village since they now knew where she lived. She hoped that moving to Oliver's school was still on the table - since her parents had considered this as an option Millie had felt lighter, she could see a potential light at the end of the tunnel - an escape.

The early evening sky was a dull steel blue with the promise of a storm. As they pulled up on the driveway of their quaint home, the first drops of rain hit the windshield. They lived in Farnham - a small village in Surrey with a few shops, a library, and a post office in the town centre. Oliver used to live in the next street, before he moved to Guildford, which was half an hour's drive away. Oliver's parents had loved living in Farnham and had only moved to lessen their commute to work. Millie and her family had always lived at 62 Sandmere Crescent, and Jane's parents before them. The house was charming and picturesque, with the luxury of being detached and secluded. It was the perfect location - the people were friendly, and it was generally a good place to live.

Millie walked into the house first ahead of her parents and went straight up the stairs to her bedroom. Jane sat at the kitchen table while Mark made them both a cup of tea. She watched her husband fumbling around the kitchen, trying to busy himself.

"She will be fine, trust me," she said in a soothing tone.

"Will she? How can we keep her in that school when we're relying on that ridiculous Headteacher to sort this out? Sorry - *Matt!*"

"Mark, I don't want her running away from this, I really think we need to try and work with him. I want Millie to learn to stand up for herself, and not accept being treated this way," Jane explained, anxious to make this right for daughter, and to encourage her to be bolder than she was.

"She's thirteen, she'll have plenty of time to learn how to stand up for herself. She relied on Oliver for so long and now she's alone. And she's changed — it just seems as though all the fight has been knocked out of her — I really think we need to consider moving her."

Millie lay on her bed with Chris and tried to make out the hushed conversation between her parents downstairs. Failing to hear anything, she gave up and began to wonder what tomorrow would bring. She wiped away a single tear that escaped from her eye and breathed in deeply in an effort to lighten her mood. Why was she being so negative, she thought - perhaps Mr Wright wasn't as useless as everyone thought he was. She reconsidered the thought, and decided it was a little too optimistic - he definitely *was* as useless as everyone thought he was, but with her dad breathing down his neck she hoped it would force Mr Wright to do his best to put a stop to the bullying. Millie went over to her jewellery box on her dressing table near the window, which overlooked the back garden. She opened it and reached in for her mother's necklace - it was so beautiful, the emerald sparkled as the light from the lamp hit it. She put the necklace on and placed her hand over the emerald – holding it close to her heart. She gazed out of the window at the garden, and over to the wild patch that she had crawled through earlier that day. She began to giggle to herself, she pictured Oliver's face – his expression changing from amused to concerned. Just then she received a text - she flopped onto the bed, sending Chris into the air, and picked up her phone as Chris landed; unbothered, he settled back into the same spot on the bed.

'Hey, today was fun! My highlight was you diving into the bushes then hitting your head on the fence! Lol! How did it go at the meeting with Mr 'Perfect' Wright? I hope you got me a signed picture?'

'So much fun! Let's just pretend that didn't happen, OK? It went alright I suppose, they're being punished and I'm going back to school tomorrow. So, looks as though I'm staying at Farnhall Academy! Fun times. No sorry I forgot to get your picture…. next time I promise!'

Millie grinned at her phone, after trying to be more open-minded about the meeting, she was seeing things more positively - Oliver's light-hearted conversation helped too.

'Ahhh that's not good, it would've been great being together again every day! But hey, this might work out! When you say punish, I hope you mean you get to cover them in paint too… using paintballs! Ahhh Mills, fail! Well I hope you at least gave him my love!'

'Paintballs! You're harsh,' Millie scolded.

'I wasn't talking point-blank; they could have a head start to hide first! Anyway, tell me how Mr Wright's hair looked…and don't leave out any detail,' Oliver joked.

Millie laughed out loud, she cast her mind back to when Oliver used to get into trouble at Farnhall Academy; he'd always get out of it by complimenting Mr Wright. He would never question Oliver because his ego was just too big to believe that the compliments were anything other than sincere. For the first time in a while she was feeling positive and uplifted.

She heard Carla shuffling around in her bedroom next door and suddenly felt an overwhelming urge to speak with her sister - she missed her and craved her company. Millie took a deep breath to gather her courage – she put her phone down next to Chris and boldly made her way to Carla's bedroom. She stood at the door hesitantly, listening to the rummaging behind the door, her fist hovering inches away ready to knock. With one last steadying breath Millie knocked the door - the room fell silent. Suddenly the shuffling inside the room continued - rushed and erratic.

"One second!" Carla shouted, before stubbing her toe - "Ouch!! Hold on, one minute!"

Millie stood patiently outside the door, wondering what Carla had in her room that was so secretive. Just then the door flung open, Carla stood in the doorway out of breath and with a sheen of sweat on her forehead.

Seeing Millie, she visibly relaxed and looked at her with disdain, "Oh it's just you - what do you want?"

Millie opened her mouth to talk, but nothing came out. She was strangely taken aback by Carla's response to her presence. It wasn't as though this was an unusual response for Carla, but Millie had thought that maybe her deliriously positive mood would somehow influence Carla, and naively expected a warmer response.

"Well?" Carla asked impatiently.

"Erm... I just wanted to talk..." she said, hopeful, while Carla looked at her perplexed. "Can I come in?"

Carla rolled her eyes and without a word pushed her door open further in silent invitation.

Millie couldn't believe it; she hadn't been inside Carla's room for what felt like years - the toys were now replaced with masses of clothes and posters of her favourite bands. Everything looked so different, but still felt familiar. She looked over to the corner to where they used to play with the dollhouse they'd shared, it'd been as tall as them just a couple of years ago. It still stood in the corner, barely recognisable with handbags hung from the chimneys, and outfits piled on top of the roof. The memories flooded back in Millie's mind - of happier times with all the laughter and excitement.

"So...what did you want to talk about?" asked Carla in a way that told Millie that she wouldn't be welcome in her room for very long, and bringing her back from the fuzzy nostalgia of her memories.

"I just wanted to talk about us, what happened? You never want to be around me, and you only spend time with me when mum makes you."

Carla studied her sister, searching for words.

Suddenly Millie saw a vulnerability in Carla that she had never seen - she looked uncomfortable, like she was fighting with herself whether to open up or remain closed.

Carla opened her mouth, then quickly closed it again. She felt angry with herself - she knew she'd let Millie in briefly, and now she would have to let it out - "It's not just you it's *all* of you! Mum and dad treat you like you're so special - I'm completely ignored! They never ask how *I'm* doing or make *my* favourite meals for dinner." She paused to catch her breath, "You're *clearly* the favourite! Do you think it's easy-" Carla stopped mid-sentence, staring at Millie's neck.

Millie quickly covered her necklace with her hand.

"What's that?" Carla asked urgently.

"What's what?"

Carla swatted Millie's hand away, which had been covering the emerald stone hanging from the necklace her mother had given her.

"See," Carla said, defeated. "You're the favourite."

Millie looked at her empathetically. It hadn't occurred to her that Carla would care that their mum had given her the necklace; she hadn't known how Carla had felt until then, but still she scolded herself for being so careless. Carla's demeanour suddenly shifted – her vulnerability slipped away, back behind her hard teenage-mask she always wore. It was a shift so subtle that only those closest to her would've seen it. But now Millie knew that Carla was hurting and covered it up with a mask that only she knew Carla wore.

Carla grabbed her sister by the arm and dragged her to the door. She flung Millie out onto the landing, sending her flying into the banister, and slammed the door behind her.

Millie's mind raced as she lay awake watching the minutes tick by - 2:45am. She couldn't shake Carla's pained words, she wondered how long her sister had been feeling this way. The worst of it was - it was true - not that their parents preferred her, but that she was treated differently. More so now than ever she hated Jamie, Mora, and Jenna – they were the reason, she thought, if they hadn't started bullying her then their parents would still treat them the same. It wasn't just Carla it annoyed; Millie didn't like being treated *special* either.

She reached down the bed for Chris and found that he wasn't in his usual spot - curled up at the bottom of her bed. She only then realised her door was closed - she always left it ajar for Chris to sneak in after his nighttime antics. Millie was about to get out of bed to open her door when she saw a small flash in the corner of her eye at the window. She sat up and shuffled to the top of her bed, further away from the window, all the while keeping her eyes fixed on the spot where she'd seen the flash. The rain beat hard on the window, and a flash of lightning lit up the room - she breathed a sigh of relief as she realised the flash had been from the storm. She had no idea why she was so on edge – the storm hadn't been much of a surprise – it'd been brewing all day; and she was never usually nervous of thunder and lightning. She pulled herself together, peeled away from her headboard, and shuffled to the edge of the bed to open the door. Another flash pulled her attention to the storm outside – the rain pelted on the glass; the wind swept the drops diagonally across her window. As she watched the storm, her nerves irrationally turned to fear - she moved towards the edge of her bed to close the curtains. Suddenly, a bright gold emanating orb appeared at the corner of the window. Millie froze - she watched in amazement as the orb danced across the outside of her window. The rain blurred her view, but she could see that the orb was no bigger than an apple, and it was beautiful. Slowly, she moved towards the end of the bed, closer to the ball of light at her window - it darted off out of sight into the darkness. She ran to the window but couldn't see a thing through the torrential rain; her eyes searched the sky frantically. A sudden creek outside of her bedroom door snapped her back into the room. Something stood quietly on the outside of the room, the floorboards strained as they struggled to hold under the heavy weight. She knew that this wasn't either of her parents, or Carla; or even human. Millie stood at the window, not moving and barely breathing, hoping she would go undetected. She silently pleaded that Carla and her parents would stay quiet, so whatever was outside of her door wouldn't turn on them - a silent tear rolled down her cheek. A dull green light suddenly burst around the door frame, like a spotlight indicating she'd been detected. Millie stared wide-eyed as a mist began seeping underneath the door. The mist bellowed into the room in rhythmic bursts as the creature breathed at the other side of the door. The creature breathed in deep, taking in Millie's scent before it let out a deep terrifying growl. Millie was petrified - she couldn't move; she stood quivering as tears streamed silently down her cheeks. The growl grew to a deafening roar - she screamed and threw herself into the corner of her room as the door began to bang and shake.

"CARLA!" she screamed as she banged on the wall dividing their rooms, "HELP!! Please help!" The door burst off its hinges, filling the room with a blinding green light -

"Millie! Millie!" Jane shouted as she held Millie's shoulders and shook her into consciousness. "Millie wake up, it was just a nightmare!" she reassured "Shhh it was just a nightmare."

Millie's eyes darted around the room then locked onto her mum.

She clung to her, suddenly feeling safe; relief washed over her as her mother's words registered, and she realised it was a nightmare.

"Are you OK?" Jane asked, holding Millie at arms-length to study her face.

"I'm fine, sorry to scare you mum."

"Are you sure you're OK?"

Millie nodded in response.

Jane hugged Millie tightly and kissed her damp cheek before hesitantly leaving the room.

Millie wondered whether she should speak to her parents about the reoccurring dreams involving green lights and terrifying faceless beasts, and how real it all felt. She decided almost instantly that she couldn't, she'd already given them enough to worry about. She wondered whether it was her subconscious creating the intense feeling of reality. Because deep down, although the dreams ignited a fear she'd never known, she craved it. She craved the fear that made her feel alive, and the possibility of an alternate reality, in a parallel world. The dreams sparked the excitement of promised adventure; Oliver had been right, she thought, her mind was providing an escape. Oliver was the only one she could talk to - he joked a lot, but most of the time he only joked to make light of things - to help her not to worry so much; she knew if she needed him he would be there for her. Millie took a steadying breath before she closed her eyes in an effort to go back to sleep.

"Millie!" Jane called up the stairs. "Time to get up darling!"

Millie was exhausted, she'd hardly slept a wink. She pulled herself out of bed, stretched then headed down to the kitchen.

Jane stood at the cooker making eggs and bacon. Mark sat at the table reading the paper; and Carla sat opposite texting frantically.

"Morning love," said Mark, as Millie sat in her usual seat.

"Morning dad, morning mum, Carla."

"Good morning honey," Jane sang.

"You woke me up last night with your screaming," Carla said, in disgust. She crossed her arms and waited for an apology.

"Oh, well it was good of you to check that I was alright!" Millie snapped fearlessly - she was in no mood for Carla; she was tired and feeling volatile and felt she could easily take her on today.

"I knew it was probably just for attention, so I ignored you."

"Stop it both of you!" Mark reprimanded before going back to his paper.

They gave each other a stubborn stare - Carla looked away first, only because she couldn't resist checking the message that had come through on her phone.

Millie sat at the table silently, reeling over her tiff with Carla, and barely able to keep her eyes open. How different Carla seemed from last night to now, she thought, it was like two different people. Before Millie could wind herself up more, Jane placed a welcome distraction of eggs and bacon in front of her. Chris' collar jingled as he trotted down the stairs and through the kitchen energetically. Millie watched him enviously - wishing she had some of his energy. He stretched and yawned before diving through his cat flap and leaving a small sprinkling of golden glitter on the tiled floor that brushed off his tail.

"I knew it!" Millie shouted, startling her family. "Sorry, just thinking out loud," she gave as an explanation as she got up out of her seat.

"Where are you going?" asked Jane.

"Tooooo- get ready for school."

"You've hardly touched your breakfast."

She began to back out of the kitchen, "Sorry mum I'm not hungry."

Jane raised her eyebrows disappointedly then poured herself a cup of coffee and sat at the table. When Mark went back to his paper and Carla went back to texting, Millie turned quickly and ran upstairs to her room.

She picked up her phone and began to text, 'Want to stop over Saturday?'

4

Millie sat at her desk in Maths class watching Mr Greene gesture towards the equation on the board. Mora, Jamie, and Jenna were all in isolation on the order of Mr Wright, as promised. Her day was looking peaceful, unless she bumped into them at lunchtime. However, Millie was too preoccupied to enjoy it. She now had confirmation that she had entered another world. She hadn't dreamt it like she'd tried to convince herself; it was real, she wasn't crazy or sleepwalking. She had two days to plan it. Oliver was staying over on Saturday, and she needed every detail to be mapped out. Before the plan could take any shape, she needed to figure out how to get *into* the other world. She couldn't face another incident like yesterday. If this didn't work, Oliver would definitely think she was nuts. Millie thought back to Monday night - *the* night. She'd followed Chris into the portal, but it hadn't opened when Oliver was there. Millie needed to keep a close eye on Chris, he was obviously going in and out of the portal regularly, and he'd also managed to avoid the creature from the bushes. The thought took her back to the nightmare last night, her heart began to pound. She pushed the memory away, reminding herself that last night had actually *just* been a nightmare. The faceless creature hadn't found its way out of the portal and hadn't been standing outside of her door. Even though it had been a nightmare, Millie knew that reality wouldn't be much different from the portrayal her subconscious had concocted of the creature. She knew that the smart thing to do would be to never visit the other world again, but curiosity had already gotten the better of her. She ignored the fact that the creature she *had* encountered sounded just as dangerous as the one in her nightmare. She snapped her thoughts back to the plan before she could talk herself out of it. Once she figured out how to get into the portal, she needed to figure out how she would convince Oliver to go with her into the other world. At first he would think she'd lost her mind; but if she managed to convince him that there was a portal in her garden, and it wasn't a dream, or all in her head - would he be too frightened to go with her.

"Millie! Can you tell me the answer?" asked Mr Greene, crossing his arms in expectation.

"Erm, five?" Millie guessed, her face flushing red.

He stared furiously at Millie. "Jack, any idea?"

Jack glanced over at Millie apologetically before responding, "You would use Pythagoras to find the hypotenuse."

"Thank you, Jack," he said, his eyes still on Millie. "Pay attention people!"

Lunchtime, Millie sat at her usual table with her two friends, Jack and Naomi. She had only just returned to her usual skin tone after the embarrassment in Mr Greene's class.

"I'm sorry about that Millie," Jack said, his face pinched with worry. "I thought about taking a dive but Mr Greene would've gone ballistic!"

"It's OK, I should've been listening."

Millie knew that Jack would never get an answer wrong on purpose. He was ridiculously smart and wanted everyone to know it. He did everything by the book, he'd never had a detention, never been told off by a Teacher; and never scored anything less than an A in anything he did.

"What were you daydreaming about anyway?" asked Naomi, "You were away with the fairies."

"Just planning my weekend," Millie answered vaguely.

She would never consider telling them the details of her weekend plans. The three of them barely spoke about anything other than school, which was limited still to the only two classes they all had together. Jack and Naomi were kind, they had taken Millie under their wing after Oliver had left; but the only reason the three of them were friends was because nobody else wanted to be friends with them. The only thing they had in common was that they had all been rejected by the popular crowd, and any other crowd in-between – they were the leftovers. They weren't friends like Millie and Oliver were friends - Oliver would never stop speaking to her on the order of three horrible girls. He would never throw her under the bus in a Maths class, and he wouldn't be leaving her as Jenna weaved her way in and out of the crowd towards their table.

From the distance Jenna's bright red glossy hair bounced through the crowd, Millie had spotted her a mile away, like a big red warning sign. She had no idea she was heading her way until Jenna was close enough to lay eyes on her destination - Millie. Millie watched Jack and Naomi struggle with their food trays and bags to the next empty table and out of danger.

She was livid, she wondered to herself why she even called them friends. She understood it took a lot of courage to stand up to the girls, and it was her problem to face; but she expected her friends to stand by her side and support her, not run off at the first sign of trouble and hide on the side lines. She looked over to where they sat facing her, watching from the safety of their table, 'Thanks' she mouthed sarcastically.

Jenna was almost at the table. She thought about getting up and leaving herself but decided against it. Jenna was alone and obviously adamant to talk to her, if it wasn't now it would be another time, she thought.

She reached the table far too quickly. "Hi," she said, with an uncertain expression.

"Hi," Millie replied, timidly.

Jenna looked at each chair, and opted to place her hand on the chair to the left of Millie, "Anyone sitting here?"

There *was*, Millie thought, until you scared them away – but decided to reply with a simple, "No."

Jenna pulled out the chair, then decided to leave a gap between them, and pulled out the next one over.

They sat in awkward silence for what felt like hours, when in fact it was about thirty seconds. Millie glanced over to Jack and Naomi. They were on the edge of their seats, waiting for the scene to unfold.

"How are you?" asked Jenna, finally breaking the silence.

Millie felt her throat close, she fought to breathe regularly. Why did Jenna have such an effect on her, she wondered. When confronted with Mora, Jamie, or Jenna she couldn't be herself – an armour surrounded her, completely confining her and closing her in for protection. It stifled her and made her shrink inwards, knocking her confidence. She wanted to be able to control it, she wanted to be open and have a chance to be herself and fight back, the way that she once would have; when she was around Oliver, and knew who she was.

Millie concentrated on not sounding nervous or intimidated before responding. "I'm great!" she shouted theatrically, sounding ridiculous, nervous, and intimidated.

"Good," Jenna replied. They once again fell into silence – looking around the hall, busying their eyes, neither of them knowing what to say next. A further thirty seconds went by, Millie wished Jenna would leave, but she stayed, prolonging the awkwardness. "I was wondering whether your friend gave you my message?"

Millie wondered what she was playing at - she couldn't endure it any longer, "Jenna, why don't you just get it over with? We both know this is going to end up with me being the butt of the joke so stop dragging it out!"

"You think I came to your house and came over here just now to set you up?"

Millie tried to read Jenna's expression for any hint of malice, but only saw sincerity and regret.

"Well can you blame me?"

"I suppose not," Jenna admitted, "I genuinely wanted to apologise, I feel terrible." Jenna looked down at her hands ashamed. "But I want you to know that it wasn't me that wanted to do those things. When Jamie and Mora get together, they're awful – they encourage each other."

"So why do you hang around with them?" Millie asked, baffled.

"Because Jamie's my cousin and I have no other friends. I had no idea what they were like together. I just feel like I've got no other option, you know?"

Strangely Millie's unpleasant feelings towards Jenna began to dissolve and were replaced by empathy. She knew what it was like to have no friends, and to have no choice but to latch onto whoever would accept you. Jenna's friends were bullies and did things that Jenna was ashamed of. Whereas Millie's friends were cowardly and didn't have her back, which embarrassed Millie. They were both in their situations out of necessity rather than choice.

"Yeah, I know how you feel," she said with a glance over to Jack and Naomi.

"Anyway, I just wanted you to know that I'm sorry."

Jenna got up from the table and left. Jack and Naomi joined Millie back at the table the second Jenna was out of sight. Jack leaned eagerly across the table, "What was that about?"

That evening after dinner, Millie watched TV with her family in the living room. Jane finished buzzing around in the kitchen and joined them. Mark was sprawled out on the sofa; he patted the spot next to him as Jane entered the room. She sat next to him and curled her legs underneath herself. Millie looked over at her parents with a warmth in her heart. Jane shivered, she looked around the room and down the side of the sofa.

"Anyone seen the throw?" Jane asked as she continued her search.

Carla was sat in the armchair next to Millie, fully engrossed in her phone, but shook her head in response to Jane's question.

"It's probably in the wash love," said Mark.

Jane settled back in her seat and cuddled up closer to Mark.

Absent in mind, Millie laughed along when her mum and dad did, but she wasn't paying any attention to what was on TV. She was busy planning, she needed to be prepared this time – she had to trial the plan, it had to be perfect for Saturday. Tonight, she would set her alarm for 2:30am - thirty minutes before the time she'd discovered the portal. This would give her time to find Chris and follow him. Across the room, Chris lay belly-up on the ottoman, fast asleep. That's it, she thought, get some rest because we're in for a busy night. Excitement began to rise in her stomach. Time was ticking by slowly and she couldn't wait until everyone called it a night and went to bed. She would set her alarm but knew she wouldn't sleep. Millie tried to control her excitement, she stopped herself from thinking about the night ahead, and turned her attention to what was on TV.

Millie lay awake feeling a combination of anxiety and excitement. She looked over at her digital alarm clock on her bedside table which was set for 2:30am - 11:33pm glowed back at her. She let out a long sigh - this is going to be a long night, she thought. She kept one eye on the slightly ajar door, hoping Chris would soon make his appearance. If she managed to pull this off, she thought, how would she go about getting Oliver to go with her, 'Remember that time I said I thought I'd stumbled upon a new world..', no that's stupid, she thought, 'Guess what - I'm not crazy, follow me!' No that *will* sound crazy at 3am.... 'Oliver quick, I think I heard something in the garden,' then push him in the bushes - no words needed. Just then she heard Carla moving around in the next room, she obviously couldn't sleep either. Carla shuffled around for a few minutes before the house was once again silent.

Millie woke to her alarm. She quickly turned it off before it woke up the whole house and listened for any murmurs from her family. When she was confident everyone was still asleep - she made her move. Silently she slid out of bed and scanned her room for Chris - he wasn't there. Her mind raced, wondering where she could find him.

Millie quickly put on her shoes and crept towards the door; suddenly aware how squeaky the floorboards were in their house. She peaked out through the crack in her door to check no-one was about – the landing was empty and in darkness, she gently pulled open the door. The house was silent and felt completely dormant. She tiptoed past Carla's room, then past her parents' room and paused at the top of the stairs. The house was old, and the stairs were creaky. She thought about sliding down the banister, when a memory suddenly appeared from when she was younger - she'd slid down the banister and flew off the end into the wall in the hallway, sending the pictures flying off the wall. She decided she'd take the safer option and take the stairs slowly. Taking a deep breath, she put one foot on the first step, gently putting all her weight down without a creek - she sighed gratefully. Gradually she shifted her weight down each step - it was painfully slow but necessary to see the plan through. When she got to the middle step, she heard the patter of Chris' paws above her - she had no idea where he'd been hiding. Chris appeared at the top of the stairs, then ran past Millie effortlessly in complete silence, leaving her stranded on the middle step.

"Chrriiissss," Millie whispered after him, desperately trying to get his attention so he would linger a little longer - but he continued towards the kitchen and out of sight.

Just as her heart began to sink a spark of hope hit her as she realised she hadn't yet heard him jump through his cat flap. Hastily she continued down the stairs, as fast and as quiet as she could. She reached the bottom after what felt like forever – she checked her watch – it'd taken six minutes. Millie walked to the kitchen, she stood in the doorway looking for Chris. As she was about to dart to the back-door Chris appeared from under the dining table. He walked lazily towards the door, stopped and sat. He stretched his leg vertically in the air and began to wash. Millie stood patiently waiting for him to finish.

She heard something behind her and turned quickly - seeing nothing, she turned back to Chris who was now licking his paws before rubbing them over his head and behind his ears.

"Come on Chris you're clean, let's go," she whispered, feeling exasperated.

She turned again quickly; now certain she'd heard something. The sound was coming from near the front door. Careful not to wake Carla or her parents she moved towards the door. She could hear it clearly now - there was something rummaging. It sounded small; Millie wondered whether it was something that had come from the portal in her garden. Her heart rushed with anticipation. This is it, she thought, this could be what had been in the house that had caused the glitter. Her imagination ran wild – the possibilities of what it could be were limitless. She was close to the door, but the intermittent rustling made it difficult for her to know exactly where the sound was coming from. She reached the front door and began to lift shoes that had been left on the floor near the coat rack, checking each of them thoroughly. The rustling started again, the sound wasn't in the hallway, but was coming from outside the door. Suddenly the rummaging stopped, plunging the house back into silence. Millie reached for the door handle, knowing she shouldn't open the door but unable to stop herself. Scratching near the top of the door made her pull back her hand. Whatever was on the other side of the door wasn't small as she'd originally thought. Millie began to sweat with panic, her nightmare came flashing back of the creature outside of her bedroom door. She backed away from the door while she pinched at her arm and told herself over and over to wake up. The terror consumed her as the door slowly began to open. She tripped on the bottom step and fell backwards onto the floor. Millie watched helplessly from the floor as the door opened fully.

"AAAGGHHH," they screamed in unison.

It took a while for Millie to register that it was Carla. When the realisation hit that she wasn't in danger, and when Carla had gotten over the shock of Millie lying at the bottom of the stairs at 3am; they stopped screaming and stared at each other questioningly. They looked up towards the ceiling and waited tensely, hoping they hadn't woken their parents.

The light from their parents' bedroom suddenly flooded the hallway, casting a spotlight on Millie at the bottom of the stairs. Millie pulled off her shoes and threw them amongst the pile near the coat rack before her mum came into view.

"What's going on!" Jane shrieked as she rushed down the stairs. Millie jumped to her feet; Carla tried to hide in the shadows by the front door while she pulled desperately at her laces. "Don't you dare try to hide Carla!"

"What's with all the noise?" Mark groaned sleepily from the top of the stairs.

"That's exactly what I'm trying to find out!" Jane shouted up to Mark, "Well?"

"I just came down for some water," Millie answered innocently.

Jane accepted her explanation without question and turned all her attention to Carla.

"I was getting some water too, Millie made me jump, I didn't know she was down here."

Jane stared at Carla, anger now visibly coursing through her, "You came down to get water... fully clothed?"

"Yes." Carla looked at her mum stubbornly, like she would argue blind that it was perfectly normal to get fully clothed, shoes included, to go down to the kitchen to get water in the middle of the night.

"And you needed your keys also?" Jane questioned, crossing her arms.

"Err-errm well, erm-"

"You sneaked out of the house didn't you!" Jane boomed.

"Erm-"

"Do you realise how dangerous that is! Where have you been?"

"Err, well erm-"

Millie stood silently, she'd never seen her mother so angry, and by the look on Carla's face, neither had she.

"Go to your room!" Carla moved faster than Millie had ever seen, up the stairs and into her room. She closed the door quietly, not wanting to make Jane anymore angry than she already was. Jane took a steadying breath and looked at Millie. "Come on, up to bed," she said, ushering Millie up the stairs.

Reluctantly she climbed the stairs with her mum at her heel. Her heart sank as she heard the familiar sound of the cat flap opening and closing.

When Millie got to her bedroom she moved quickly to her window, just in time to see the green glow retracting deep into the bushes.

It was finally Saturday, and Oliver was coming over. Friday had flown by uneventfully. Millie had managed to avoid Jamie and Mora at school, and Jenna had waved at Millie discreetly from across the grounds. She had tried once again to follow Chris into the garden just before 3am and failed – she'd found Chris in the living room sleeping and had poked him awake to his disgust. After following him round two laps of the living room, kitchen and hallway; he'd made his way to the back door, through his cat flap out into the garden. Millie had felt elated that she would finally see her plan through. Her elation was short lived - she'd discovered the door was locked and the key had been removed. She'd searched for the key for half an hour, and to her disappointment never found it.

It was 8.30am and Oliver was due to arrive in a few hours. She had butterflies in her stomach – she'd thought that by this time she would've had her plan perfected and know exactly how to enter the portal. But she was just as clueless as she was a few days prior. She tried to think about the positives and focus on what she did know – there was definitely a portal in her back garden, she had crawled through to the other side, seen its glow when Chris had entered; and had seen the glittery residue from something in the portal through her house, *and* on Chris. She'd noticed a pattern that the portal opened during the early hours and *not* during the day - as she'd learnt embarrassingly in front of Oliver after crawling around the bushes for ten minutes. And for a reason she didn't know, Chris was potentially the key. What was a mystery to her now was where the key was for the back-door. Her mum had taken Carla's keys after she'd caught her that night sneaking back into the house at 3am. Jane had also hidden the back-door key as a precaution. If Millie wanted to see the plan through, she had to know where the key was hidden.

Millie was finishing up her Maths homework, she wanted it out of the way for when Oliver arrived. She didn't want any distractions; the plan needed her full attention and she couldn't have her homework in the back of her mind. After the embarrassment in Maths that week, she needed to be on top of her game in the subject. She was deciphering one of the questions and absently playing with her Perspex ruler when a ray of sunshine flooded in from her window, it hit the ruler and cast a rainbow across the page. She looked out of the window at the beautiful sunny morning, unusually bright for the time of year. She twirled the ruler in the sunlight and listened to her mum clattering around downstairs as she did her early morning weekend housework. It was then that she had the idea - how to get the key without raising suspicions. She scribbled down the answer, closed her books and dashed down the stairs.

She found Jane in the kitchen frantically scrubbing the worktops.

"Helloooo!" Millie chirped.

"Oh, hi love," said Jane, out of breath and wiping the sweat from her brow.

"Why don't you relax mum?"

"I can't darling, there's always something to do," she sang.

Millie rolled her eyes and smiled, "Well at least let me help until Oliver gets here. I can put the washing out on the line?"

"Oh, thank you so much Millie," Jane said gratefully.

Millie pulled out the wicker basket from the side of the machine and unloaded the clothes from the washing machine.

"Do you have the key mum?" asked Millie in her most innocent voice. It wasn't like she was asking for anything sinister, but she still felt devious.

"Oh yes sorry love, it's in my bedside table, in the top draw. Make sure you put it back once you're finished."

Millie's heart jumped into her throat. That's going to make things more interesting tonight, she thought. She now knew where the key was hidden, if she couldn't get it from her parents' room before they went to bed later, she would have to abandon the plan. In Millie's mind, abandoning the plan wasn't an option. Tonight, she would see the plan through and prove to Oliver that there was another world, and that she hadn't dreamt it. A key couldn't ruin this, she would wait for the opportunity, and she would sneak the key back later in the day.

5

Millie had just set her mum up in the garden with a cup of tea and a book after feeling guilty for deceiving her, when the doorbell rang. She ran through the house and flung open the door. She beamed at the sight of Oliver, with his large backpack and grinning from ear to ear.

"Oliver!" Millie shouted with excitement, jumping on her friend and giving him a tight squeeze. "What've you been up to?"

"Same old stuff different day, how's things with you?"

Millie updated Oliver all about Jenna, and about Carla sneaking out at night as they walked through the hallway into the kitchen.

"Hello Oliver, how have you been? How's school?" asked Jane fondly, as she walked in from the garden, locking the door behind her.

Before the move Oliver had been around their house most evenings. Jane saw him as part of the family and missed him nearly as much as Millie did.

"Hi Mrs Shepherd, it's great - thanks."

"Good," she smiled, feeling relieved that he wasn't having as hard of a time as Millie. "So, do you both feel like going bowling?"

They pulled up on the drive after an eventful afternoon of bowling. Millie walked from the car through the front door with her arms held high in celebration - she had beaten Oliver and her mum in both games. She didn't count her dad in the running, none of them were any competition for him, and therefore was in a league on his own. Carla had refused to take part, but was forced by Mark to come along, as she wasn't trusted to stay in the house. Mark also knew that in Carla's view, spending quality time with family was a punishment. Millie couldn't decide who had the sourest face, Carla or Oliver.

"You're such a sore loser!" Millie laughed.

"I'm not. I'm just saying you can't count it as a win if you've got the barriers up," said Oliver matter-of-factly.

"Who scored more?"

"It's cheating if you've got the barriers-"

"*Who* scored more?" she repeated, then waited for his answer.

"You did - but it doesn't count!" he shouted after Millie as she ran around the kitchen, punching the air in another victory lap. "OK, you're unbearable - I'll leave you to enjoy your fake win. Just get it out of your system. I'm going to help your dad set up the bed in the living room. When I come back you better have calmed down."

"Alright deal," she giggled, glad that he was leaving the room as she was running out of steam. As soon as Oliver was out of sight, she sat down in the nearest chair to catch her breath. It had been a great day, even with Carla being there. She hadn't spoken to Carla about the other night for a couple of reasons - she suspected Carla wouldn't tell her where she'd really been anyway; and she knew Carla must've known Millie was up to something and she didn't want to answer any of her questions. Carla had told her parents that she had met her friend Kendall from across the road after she'd received a text from her asking to talk. When Mark and Jane had questioned her about what Kendall had needed to talk about in the middle of the night, Carla kept it vague with – boy troubles. Conveniently, Carla had deleted the messages from Kendall, and Kendall had backed up Carla's story - even though it'd meant she'd also been grounded by her parents for sneaking out in the middle of the night. Millie suspected that Kendall hadn't met Carla at all, and so did Mark and Jane, but they couldn't prove otherwise. Millie admired their commitment to the fabricated story, and the loyalty of Kendall. She was glad that Carla had a decent friend she could depend on. Since letting slip to Millie how she felt, Carla had kept her mask firmly in place. Millie was even beginning to doubt that she'd seen any vulnerability in her sister at all and thought that she'd misjudged the conversation. Either way, Millie knew that if it even existed, she would never see that side of Carla again, and so she was glad that Carla had Kendall to talk to.

A loud bang from the living room caused by Mark and Oliver struggling with the pull-out bed brought her back into the room - she jumped to her feet. What was she doing, she'd been waiting for an opportunity to get the key and this was it, she thought. Her dad and Oliver were occupied for what sounded like a very long time, Carla was shut in her room playing her music loudly, and her mum was cleaning the bathroom. There was no reason why anyone would need the key at this time of an evening. The door was locked, and Jane was sure the key was safe after replacing it herself - this was the time to take it. She moved quickly to the foot of the stairs, careful not to be seen by Oliver or Mark. If they saw her, they would definitely ask for her help, judging by the brief glimpse she caught of Oliver wedged between the wall and mattress and her dad struggling to free him. She ran on her tiptoes up the stairs, grateful for the deafening music blaring from Carla's room. Stopping mid-way on the stairs, she peered through the railings of the banister which circled the landing, her eyes hovered just above floor level. The door to the bathroom was half open, she could just about see her mum leaning into the bathtub scrubbing fiercely. Millie moved smoothly up the rest of the staircase, careful not to get caught in Jane's peripheral view. She reached the top step, her eyes never leaving her mum. She stood on the landing with her back to her parents' bedroom, facing the bathroom. Slowly she began to walk the few steps backwards towards the room. The door was only pushed to, she opened it just enough to slide unnoticed into the room.

Millie turned on her heel and made her move towards the bedside table. Just then, Carla's music stopped abruptly. She heard Carla's bedroom door open followed by her swift footsteps that past the stairs, and headed straight for their parents' room, where Millie was trespassing. To Millie's horror Carla began to push open the door. She managed to duck behind the large armchair near the corner of the room before the door opened completely.

"Carla! What do you think you're doing?" Millie heard her mum ask.

"I can't find my red t-shirt, it must be in your wardrobe," Carla said dismissively. Millie had a clear view of Carla's feet, she watched as they took a step further inside the room.

"Hold on, you don't just go into our room, you ask either me or your dad for permission." There was a long tense silence, "OK?"

"Yessss." Carla turned to walk into the room again, Millie ducked lower behind the chair.

"Carla, hold on please! I'll check Millie's wardrobe first; it'll more than likely be in there."

"It's not I've already looked."

Millie's mouth fell open, she was furious. She couldn't believe Carla would go into her room without asking her, and her mum didn't seem to mind either. She made a mental note never to leave her phone in there unattended again.

"Oh....OK then, be quick."

Carla walked straight over to the wardrobe and began shuffling through the rails of clothes. Millie ducked as low as she could, making herself as small as possible.

"What do you think you're dooooiinnnggg Caaarlllaaa," Carla whispered to herself. Millie froze, it took her a second to realise Carla wasn't talking to her but was mimicking Jane. "You ask either me or your dad for permission Caaaarlllaaa." Millie tried not to laugh at how stupid her sister sounded. "*Ooooh*, it's more than likely in *Millie's* room is it Jane? Liar!" she said as she plucked her red t-shirt out of the wardrobe. Millie watched from behind the chair as Carla's feet turned and left the room. "Fooounnnd it!" she shouted towards the bathroom before slamming her bedroom door and once again blasting her music.

Millie sighed in relief. She came out from behind the chair and dashed to the bedside table. The key sat in the middle of the top draw, next to a phone charger and a photo of Jane's adoptive parents. Millie barely knew anything about her mum's childhood, she sensed it'd been a hard time in her mum's life; a time that she didn't want to revisit. She knew that her mum's biological parents had died long ago, and that her aunt had cared for her briefly. Jane had never spoken about it in depth, or how she'd come to be adopted. Her adoptive parents had also passed away, Mark had only met them once when he and Jane had first started dating, before Carla and Millie had been born. Her mum was raised in the house that they lived in now, it had been left to Jane in their will. Millie had always thought that her mum's upbringing had been a factor when she quit her job as soon as Carla had been born. When people asked Jane whether she missed her job, she always assured them that she didn't, because she never wanted to miss a second of her children's lives.

Pulling her thoughts back to the mission, she grabbed the key and put it in the back pocket of her jeans. She made her way back to the door and peered out cautiously. Jane had her back to the bedroom, dancing with one bright-yellow-gloved hand in the air, and the other scrubbing the sink. Millie slipped out effortlessly and skipped down the stairs feeling pleased with herself - the plan was coming together.

12:30am glowed back at Millie from the clock on her bedside table. She was beyond nervous and no longer feeling excited. She had one shot, and this was it – the pressure was building, and she felt massively unprepared. The key was in her pocket, the alarm was set, she knew the squeaky floorboards by heart; and knew Chris would be nearby. But the important part was the portal, she had no idea whether it would open. Maybe it'd been a fluke when it opened last time, she thought, and now whatever was on the other side had made sure she could never enter again. The growl from her nightmare slipped from the back to the forefront of her mind. It was always there, warning her;

sometimes dormant, sometimes engulfing her thoughts. But no matter how loud it became, she knew it would never deter her. Before she talked herself out of it, she switched her focus to Oliver. He was the next hurdle in the operation – she wondered what she could say to him to convince him to go out with her into the garden. Her mind whirred as she began to concoct a reason for him to go with her, one that would be sure to get him to follow her without question; and without raising suspicion that once again she would be attempting to cross worlds. She kicked off the covers and got up out of bed, she was too agitated to stay still. Millie paced her room under the watchful gaze of Chris, who lay lazily on her bed. She walked over to the window, racking her brain for a plausible story. She rested her head on the glass - her eyes fixed on the hedges. By 1am she decided to try and get some rest, convincing herself she'd know what to do and say when the time came. She took one last glance at Chris and closed her eyes.

Millie woke five minutes before her alarm was due to sound. She looked down to the foot of her bed and to her relief - Chris was still there. Careful not to disturb him she got out of bed, took out the clothes she'd prepared earlier from her wardrobe and got dressed. With her heart pounding, she silently left the room with Chris in her arms and her shoes in one hand. She padded across the landing, now quicker than ever. She'd become a pro - she knew exactly where to place her feet to create the least amount of noise. Chris settled in her arms, quietly purring and enjoying the ride. As Millie approached the stairs, she heard shuffling from Carla's room. She froze and held her breath until the movement stopped. Once she was sure Carla had settled, she was off - stealthily tackling each step. It took her a record breaking four and a half minutes to reach the bottom. Millie stood in the doorway of the living room looking at Oliver, who was spread out on the pull-out bed, fast asleep.

"Oliver," she whispered from where she stood – nothing. "Oliveerrrr," she whispered, this time with more force - not even a stir. She looked over at the clock mounted on the wall - 2:40. Determined, she crept closer to where Oliver was unconscious, "Oliver." This time he rolled over, Millie waited in anticipation, and to her frustration, he settled in his new spot - still asleep. Millie rolled her eyes in annoyance. "Oliver," she hissed, kicking his mattress.

"Huh? What? Oh, what are you doing?" he asked, looking at her confused with half open eyes, his curly hair a tangled mess on top of his head.

"Shhhh! Get up, we need to go somewhere."

"Go where?" he asked, lifting onto his elbow.

Millie hesitated, "To the garden."

Oliver stared at her; a frown etched on his forehead then it faded into realisation. "Oooh you're having that dream again Mills," he said softly, getting up out of bed and taking her arm. "C'mon, put Chris down and I'll take you back up to bed."

Chris jumped from Millie's arms and trotted out of the room.

Millie swatted Oliver away. "No get off! Look what you did, we need Chris! Come on hurry up-" she stopped mid-sentence. "What are you wearing?" she asked, scanning his baby blue pyjamas that featured several cartoon sheep.

"What? My mum got them for me for my birthday. What's wrong with them?" Oliver replied defensively.

"Nothing, they're fine," she said, holding up her hands and giving them one last glance. "Just get dressed, we need to go - now."

"What did you need Chris for?"

Millie sat in the nearest chair to put on her shoes. Oliver stood still, watching her and waiting for an answer.

"I think he opens the portal," she said, almost inaudibly, not looking up from her shoes.

Oliver didn't move, he stood frowning, concern on his face. Eventually he shook his head and began to put on his shoes.

"You're not getting dressed?"

"Nope, don't think this will take long," he said as he strolled past Millie out of the living room into the hallway.

Millie jumped up and tiptoed after him, "Be quiet someone could hear you!"

They walked into the kitchen and were just in time to see the back end of Chris leaping through the cat flap. Millie dashed to the back door and pulled the key that she'd lifted from her parents' room earlier from her pocket.

"You supposed to have that?" Oliver questioned her suspiciously.

Millie ignored him, twisting the key in the lock and opening the door in one fluid motion. She stepped out into the cool night air. She didn't have to look far to find Chris. He was in the middle of the garden, flinging and twisting himself in the air trying to catch moths that flew by clumsily.

She marched towards the bushes. This is it, she thought, this has to work.

"You're serious?" Oliver called from the door.

Millie turned abruptly, she hadn't realised Oliver wasn't by her side, "Stop talking so loud and get over here!"

Oliver pulled the door closed and slowly shuffled over to where Millie stood opposite the bushes.

Suddenly they heard the creak of a window being opened. Millie grabbed hold of Oliver's arm and dragged him behind the wooden bench in the garden. They scanned the house for the window that had been opened - it was Carla's. After a minute, they began to move from behind the bench, when a bundle of tied up sheets flew out of the window they darted back. The sheets unraveled at speed and hit the garage roof. Seconds later, Carla dangled from the window ledge, fully dressed and with a large full backpack. She shimmied down the make-shift rope and landed without a sound on the garage roof. She walked to the edge of the garage towards the front of the house and elegantly jumped to the floor and out of sight.

"Clearly that's not her first time," Oliver remarked.

"Where's she going," Millie asked, rhetorically.

"Don't know, let's follow her," he said, stepping in the direction Carla went.

Millie grabbed hold of his pyjamas top and pulled him back, "No!

We're doing this! Watch!"

Oliver sighed, "Millie this is stupid. C'mon, she can't've gotten far we've still got time!"

"Come on Chris," she said encouragingly, ignoring Oliver and walking towards the bushes, then back towards Chris again when he didn't follow. "Come *on*," she whined. She picked up a stick and threw it into the bushes, Chris flattened to the ground in pounce position then quickly lost interest. "Go on, fetch."

"OK. I think I've had enough excitement for one night," Oliver sighed as he turned towards the house and started to walk back.

"Oliver come back! Oliver!" She turned back to Chris determined, and continued trying to entice him towards the bushes.

Oliver shuffled towards the house. He was worried for his friend and wondered whether he should speak to Mark and Jane. He didn't want to betray Millie's trust, but he knew he had no choice but to tell them. He had seen first-hand that Millie hadn't been dreaming or sleepwalking, she believed this alternate world was real. He could hear Millie behind him desperately trying to get Chris to go towards the bushes. He considered going back for him, but he figured there wasn't much point - Chris would probably be playing in the bushes with or without Millie. He had nearly reached the door when his shadow was cast on the back of the house, large and definite. He stared up at his elongated shadow on the bricks of the house, and at the green-tinged light that surrounded it. Oliver slowly turned, the scene stunned him – Millie stood opposite the bushes, her elated expression illuminated by a green light that beamed hazily from far within the bushes.

Millie looked over to Oliver smugly, then began to jump up and down on the spot with excitement. Relief washed over her, the look on Oliver's face confirmed it all, he could see it too - she wasn't crazy *or* dreaming. His face was lit in the brilliant light, even in its green filter she could see that the usual olive tone to his skin had drained from his face. The thoughts running through his head reflected clearly in his expressions.

"Holy-"

"Can you believe it!" Millie squealed.

Oliver shook his head vigorously.

"See I told you!"

Oliver nodded silently, feeling more fear than the excitement Millie displayed.

Millie had never seen Oliver so speechless, and in a strange way, she felt oddly satisfied by the look of utter shock on his face.

She gestured towards the portal. "Well, come on then before it closes." Oliver didn't move. "What's wrong?"

For the first time since he'd turned around, he looked away from the light to look at Millie, wide-eyed, as if to say - 'What's wrong? Seriously,' although no words came from his mouth.

"Yeah I know it's a bit of a shock - but we need to hurry up before it closes."

"Erm yeah like I said - that's enough excitement for me. Think I'll head back to bed," he said, nodding enthusiastically, happy with his decision.

"Really? Stop being such a wimp!"

"A wimp? Millie, I'm not sure whether you know, but that's not normal," he said, pointing to the light. "And if you've forgotten, you told me something chased you in there."

"I'm not sure if it *chased* me, it just growled at me," she clarified, her thoughts went back to the growl that still haunted her, she pushed it away.

"Oh well, that makes *all* the difference."

"Cool - let's go!" Millie chirped, choosing to mistake his sarcasm with agreement.

"I was joking Millie; I'm not going in there."

She felt exasperated, she noticed the light becoming duller the longer they stood there, "Seriously Oliver, do you want to look back and always wonder?"

Millie held her breath and waited anxiously as she watched her words sink in, all the while keeping one eye on the fading light. She hoped that she'd said the right thing to influence his decision. She willed him to be adventurous and fearless just for tonight. Millie knew he had plenty of positives in his life and would naturally be more cautious, whereas she felt she had nothing to lose.

"If I die, I'll kill you!" Oliver said, with an instant puzzled look on his face. "That didn't make sense, but you know what I mean. I won't be happy!"

"You're not going to die! Just follow me – and stay close," she said, as the rumbling growl filled her mind - she shook her head to shift it.

Oliver had agreed to go with her through the portal, and she was surprised at how she felt. She thought she'd be elated, but she felt terrified; it was almost as though subconsciously she'd been relying on him to pull her back from the destructive path she was insisting on taking. Ignoring the rising fear, she took a deep breath then began to crawl through the hedges, her stomach turned when Oliver followed. Every so often she turned to check Oliver was still behind her, hoping he'd changed his mind and turned back. The light became brighter the closer they got to the mouth of the portal. They were crawling for at least two minutes before the leaves around them disappeared into the light.

"Millie, where are we? I can't see a thing!"

"It's fine we're nearly there, just stay close," Millie answered with a voice as even as she could muster, trying to hide the tremble that gave away that she was concerned. She hoped she was going the right way, it felt as though she'd been crawling for longer this time; and she didn't have the trail of glitter to follow. Just as she was about to turn back to Oliver in blind panic she felt it – the subtle change in the atmosphere humming around her, the slight increase in temperature; the smell of the air – all alerting her that they'd arrived. Excitement and anticipation were once again building and coursing through her, making it easier to disregard the fear she felt. She crawled faster and suddenly - her hand broke through.

"We're here."

6

The hollow in the large tree glowed green on the other side. Millie's head and shoulders slowly emerged from the portal; her skin buzzed as she scanned the area. Although the area looked clear, she couldn't bring herself to step out of the hollow. From within the portal Oliver prodded her back impatiently. A second later he pushed her out onto the ground. He fell out immediately after Millie and landed in a heap on top of her.

"Get off!" she shouted, pushing Oliver and picking herself up off the ground.

She scanned the area again thoroughly, hoping nothing had been disturbed. Oliver slowly got to his feet, his mouth gaped open and his eyes were wide taking in every detail. It was exactly how Millie remembered it - eerily inviting and magical. Although it was the dead of night the forest was bright, vibrant, and alive - every colour was intense and breathtaking. The forest surrounding them was nothing like the forests they were used to seeing, this looked like it'd been lifted straight out of a painting. Although Millie had seen the view before, it felt like the first time. She had the feeling that no matter how many times she saw it, she would still feel charmed and enchanted.

"I really wish I'd gotten dressed," Oliver said, still looking around in awe.

Millie's stomach turned as her eyes fell upon the bushes where the creature had been. With her heart racing and ready to run she moved towards the bushes, she pulled back a branch and hesitantly peered inside.

"Is that where that thing was?" Oliver asked, suddenly behind her and making her jump out of her skin.

"Don't *do* that! You scared the life out of me!" she complained, her hand clutched at her chest, consoling her startled heart.

The question sounded strange coming from Oliver in a non-mocking or humoring tone. She had felt isolated ever since discovering the portal. The only person she'd been able to tell hadn't believed her, and now he did. Once again, they were on the same page and she was no longer alone.

"Yeah, but luckily it's not there now," she answered, relieved.

"Good!"

"Knowing my luck, it's probably in the next bush," she chuckled.

Oliver laughed along uneasily, shifting his eyes to check the next bush. Seeing nothing but an unusual yet harmless purple ladybird, he continued to survey his surroundings. Millie felt lighter, like a weight had been lifted off her shoulders. She had faced the one thing that had been holding her back from fully emerging herself in the adventure. Ever since the night she'd discovered the portal she'd heard the creature's growls not only in her dreams but while awake. Now she stood where she'd been that night, and the creature wasn't waiting for her like she thought it would be.

"This place is amazing!" Oliver said, tearing his gaze away from the deep-blue star-sprinkled sky and looking directly at Millie. "I can't believe you found this! C'mon let's look around!" He grabbed Millie's arm and dragged her towards the meandering cobblestone paths. They approached the wooden signposts eagerly. "So, to the left we have Morendale Village," Oliver read aloud. "Straight ahead we've got Morendale Castle, oooh! Bet that'll be a tourist trap. And to the right is Thatchly Market, hmm - gathering we're no longer in Farnham!"

"There's a sign over there," Millie said with intrigue, as she pointed further along the pathway. They walked along the path in the direction of Thatchly Market. The sign pointed to a deserted path that forked off the path they were on, it ran parallel to the portal, behind the large bushes where the creature had been. Millie read the sign aloud, "120 miles to Hillontropa - these places have some strange names."

They looked down the path into the darkness. The forest surrounding the path was dense and overflowing, making the path narrow. The moonlight was unable to break through the thickness of the canopy, and there were no lanterns lining the path, leaving it in darkness. The other areas of the forest were open and lit brightly by both lanterns and moonlight, making the contrast between the path and the rest of the forest almost like night and day. The odd firefly danced along the path causing the shadows to retract, revealing pockets of the forest that lined the walkway.

"You don't want to go down there," said a voice from behind them. They looked at each other from the corners of their eyes, not wanting to see what was behind them. They stood perfectly still, desperately trying to breathe evenly, and both regretting their decision to venture through the portal. Even though they had no idea what or who was in the forest, or whether it was good or bad; Millie's last experience through the portal, and constant fear, should've been enough to deter her. She'd been reckless in coming back, and thoughtless to have brought Oliver along too. As she stood in the forest in a parallel world next to Oliver, both frozen with fear, she wished she'd listened to him and gone back to bed.

An exaggerated purposeful cough came from behind them, to alert them he was there. Neither of them turned, Millie closed her eyes hoping that if they stayed still long enough, he would leave.

"Wow everyone that comes out of that portal is so rude!"

"Wait," Oliver said, as it dawned on him that others had been through the portal. Intrigued by what had been said, he turned. "What do you mean everyone-" Oliver stopped mid-sentence, unable to speak, he tugged on Millie's sleeve.

From the corner of her eye, Millie could see the shock on Oliver's face. Slowly, Millie turned and was stunned by what she saw. In front of them hovered a fairy, he was around their age and was roughly five inches tall. His clear holographic wings fluttered independently, giving off a fine gold glitter. He wore loose cream trousers and a matching t-shirt; his feet were bare. He had friendly blue eyes with flecks of yellow, and short ginger hair. Millie and Oliver stood frozen in shock. The fairy looked at them offended and confused at their reaction.

Never taking his eyes off the fairy, Oliver reached into his pocket and pulled out his phone, aiming the camera at the fairy.

Millie jumped to life. "Oliver!" she scolded, slapping the phone from his hand.

"What? It's for the *Gram*!"

"Are you serious?"

"Just think how many likes I'd get!"

Millie shook her head disapprovingly and turned her attention back to the fairy who was hovering inquisitively around Oliver's phone in the grass. He edged closer to the phone and kicked it, he flew back quickly like it was going to jump up off the floor and bite him. They watched as he circled the phone, working up the courage before kicking it again. Millie and Oliver exchanged a look, silently agreeing that the fairy was harmless. After a few digs, the fairy floated back up between their eyeline, still staring at the phone.

"I think you killed it," he said to Millie.

"Err yeah," she said, frowning. "Anyway, sorry about that, he doesn't mean to be an idiot." She shot Oliver a sideways glance. "What did you mean before when you said, 'Everyone who comes out of that portal' - have other people been here?"

"Yeah, him!" he pointed over to Chris, who had jumped down from a tree and was sauntering back towards the portal. "No idea what he is but I know he's rude, first time I met him he chased me for hours! Literally hours! I've tried talking to him and he just ignores me, don't know what his problem is to be honest."

"He's a cat," Oliver said. "They don't talk, they chase things."

"*No*, he's a Chris - says so on his badge," said the fairy dismissively, looking at Millie and rolling his eyes.

"*Nooo,* that's his name. He's a cat. They *can't* speak.*"

"Oh, bless him," he said to Millie, ending the debate with Oliver patronisingly, Millie tried to conceal her laughter.

She noticed Oliver's face flush red in anger and quickly changed the subject, "So, what's your name?"

"I'm Whartorlli," he said proudly.

"Stupid name," Oliver muttered under his breath.

"Not as stupid as your outfit!" Whartorlli snapped, leaving Oliver speechless and furious.

"Anyway, I'm Millie and this is Oliver," Millie interjected, to defuse the situation.

"Nice to finally meet you!" he said. "I would've introduced myself the other night but the Chris - or *cat* -" he smirked, "- chased me back through the portal. You must've been right behind me because when I looked back the Chris was with you, over there," he nodded towards the bushes opposite the portal. "I was going to say hello but then Serperus turned up - you ran *so* fast!" he chuckled. "Can't blame you though! But he hadn't seen you, he just smelt you."

"The creature in the bushes!" she said, glancing to Oliver, who was still livid and refusing to look at Whartorlli. "Who *is* Serperus?"

"He's The Queen's most deadly weapon, and acts as a tracker in her Army. You're lucky he didn't see you; you don't want to get caught by him."

"Where is he now?" Oliver asked sternly, trying to keep any sign of interest out of his voice.

"How would I know? I'm here talking to you two!"

Millie grabbed hold of Oliver's arm before he could launch at Whartorlli.

"Can you tell us what's down there?" she asked, nodding towards the dark pathway.

"I can indeed," said Whartorlli, relishing the opportunity to show off his superior knowledge of the area. "Down there is the walkway to Hillontropa."

They waited in anticipation for information that wasn't already written on the signpost.

"What is Hillontropa?" Millie probed.

Whartorlli gave her a sympathetic smile like she should know the answer. "Hillontropa is where Queen Naleem extradites anyone who crosses her - awful place. Probably where *you* would've ended up if Serperus had gotten hold of you, if you survived that is."

"Who's Queen Naleem and why would Millie have ended up there? She hasn't done anything wrong." Oliver said protectively, briefly forgetting his feud with Whartorlli.

"Queen Naleem rules the kingdom, she's very paranoid so most people are wrongfully convicted. And she doesn't like anybody new - and you both kind of stand out." Noticing the confusion on their faces he huffed in exasperation. "You two ask too many questions! Come with me," he said, as he flew in the direction of Thatchly Market. "We're going to see Ophelia. What time is it?"

Millie checked her watch, "Twenty to four."

"Ah perfect, she'll be up."

Oliver opened his mouth to ask another question, Millie caught his eye and shook her head.

"We should follow him," she said, moving to catch up to Whartorlli.

"Fine," he said, lingering behind and dragging his feet. "I'm never wearing these pyjamas again."

They felt as though they'd been walking for hours. Millie checked her watch; it had only been ten minutes. Whartorlli hadn't stopped talking the whole time. Sentences rolled into one another, each with no reference to the last. It was a constant ramble that flitted from bragging to who lived in which house, to random facts - the majority of which were wrong; and then back to Oliver's pyjamas. Whartorlli was relentless, and it was clear to them from the brief time they'd spent with him that he would talk on any subject no matter how little he knew, just for the sake of talking.

Millie thought to herself that it was unusual how irritated he got by questions, considering how much he loved to talk, and even more so if it was a question from Oliver. They continued down the path, stopping occasionally so Whartorlli could give them his full attention when giving them snippets of information. He was like an irritable tour guide who made up facts and passive-aggressively insulted his audience.

"... and here we have Mr Gnomello's house - *silent G* – he's lived here for some years; he was forced to move from Hillontropa when The Queen took over the land. He's just like your kind - but obviously more special," he laughed. "You guys are so basic. Anyway -"

Millie had lost interest; her eyes began to wander the forest. As far as she could see the pathway was lit by glowing lanterns. Paths forked off paths that weaved through the trees, each with a wooden signpost at the start of the new path. Every so often her polite nature would force her to pull her attention back to Whartorlli, and nod in pretend interest. It wasn't that Millie didn't find Whartorlli's stories interesting, but Mr Gnomello's house was the fifth house they'd stopped in front of. The first few stops had been interesting, but after the third stop with a story only slightly varied from the last it was becoming a struggle to pay attention. She looked over to Oliver who was making no attempt to feign interest. His head was back so he faced the sky and his eyes were closed. Millie wasn't sure if he'd fallen asleep or was having an internal conversation to convince himself not to physically assault Whartorlli. She stifled a giggle; she knew Oliver well enough to know that it would be the latter.

"- he has a pet llama, mind you the llama takes *him* for walks if you know what I mean," he said, looking at them expectantly. Millie hadn't been listening, but she sensed it was a moment to laugh, so she obliged. Oliver did Whartorlli the courtesy of opening his eyes to stare at him unamused. "Never mind," he said, rolling his eyes. "Let's carry on."

Whartorlli turned and continued to lead the way, and ramble. Millie thought about what Whartorlli had said earlier - 'He would've introduced himself, but Chris chased him *back through* the portal.'

"Erm, sorry, Whartorlli?" she said hesitantly, breaking the constant flow of chatter.

Oliver looked at her with his eyebrows raised in an expression to say, 'You're brave!'

"Rude. What is it?" he asked, irritated by the interruption.

"Sorry, it's just that you said that you were on the other side of the portal. Were you the one in my house?" She only then noticed the fine sparkling golden glitter that fluttered from his wings.

"I was indeed!" he said, pleased with himself.

"So did Chris bring you through the portal?"

"No! I found the portal, he chased me back through when he saw me in your house and now, he keeps coming *back* here," he said disapprovingly.

"How did you find the portal?"

"Well, one night I was hiding high in the trees, The Queen's Army were out on one of their patrols," he said in a hushed tone, delighted to have been asked about his discovery and relishing in how engrossed they were in his story. "They're very suspicious about fairies, always suspect we're not loyal to The Queen – most of us aren't mind you, so we lay low – or high in our case," he chuckled. "I heard a chase, the usual sound when Serperus is in pursuit through the forest, The Army wasn't far behind. Then Jupiter came running into the opening in the forest below the tree I was in - and before you ask - Jupiter is a peryton." They looked at him blankly. "Oh for goodness sake - he's a stag with the wings of a bird." Shaking his irritation, his eyes resumed the glazed look he'd had while telling the story, like he was far away reliving the night. "Jupiter had his fawn with him, and it was injured. I was about to fly down to help but then a green light appeared from the tree next to Jupiter. I nearly fell off my branch, I was like woah what is *that*! Then, it got brighter and brighter until I couldn't look directly at it. When the light got a little duller, I looked back and Jupiter had gone, ran for his life! Once Serperus and The Army sounded far enough away I flew down – it just looked like a firefly in the tree hollow, a big green one! Anyway, I got closer and then I knew it was something weird! The closer I got the brighter it became, and the more I could just *feel* something different. So naturally I got closer and closer and before I knew it, I was in the light and couldn't see a thing, I was never scared mind you, I just carried on until I was through. The other side felt flat, I had a look around, went through the hole in the bottom of your door and had a look around your house – nothing special through the portal, I was disappointed. Anyway, that was when you followed the Chris through the portal and Serperus was still sniffing around for Jupiter and his fawn." His expression turned quizzical, "Even a run in with Serperus can't keep you lot away huh? Can't blame you, Morendale's a pretty cool place."

Millie and Oliver exchanged a look, Millie knew that he was thinking the same thing. They'd thought that Chris had been the key, but from what Whartorlli had said, they were wrong. Millie hoped that the person they were going to visit could answer their questions, she walked a little faster, eager to meet Ophelia.

They continued along the stone path, a further five minutes had gone by and Millie and Oliver were beginning to get impatient. Whartorlli hadn't stopped for breath during his commentary of the journey. Suddenly he went silent, the silence snapped Millie and Oliver out of their boredom induced trance. Whartorlli floated silently behind a nearby tree.

"Why are we stopping?" asked Oliver.

"Shhh, come over here - quietly."

They looked at each other confused but did as they were told and went quietly over to Whartorlli and hid behind the tree. Whartorlli pointed to the opening in the forest and to their amazement, they saw three semi-transparent women emerging from the trees. Gradually they appeared fully - they were all beautiful. They wore flowy dresses in subtle earthy colours, camouflaging them with the forest. They began to tend to the area – one of them, with a mass of blonde curls lightly stroked the grass causing it to become green and thick, weeds disappeared at her touch. Another reached for a low hanging branch, as she placed her hand on its bark the whole tree sprouted ripe red apples. The third woman, with long glossy strawberry blonde hair and a smattering of light freckles strolled dreamily across the luscious grass, masses of tiny white flowers grew with each footstep.

"Who are they?" asked Oliver, mesmerised.

"They're wood nymphs," answered Whartorlli. "You can see their work everywhere in the forest but it's rare to actually see them, I've only ever seen them twice. Seen plenty of mountain nymphs though – the landscape up there is so open you can spot them a mile away. Never seen a water nymph in my life! They're really rare, ever since the mermaids took over."

"Wow, *mermaids*?" Millie whispered excitedly.

"Yes mermaids, they're half person, half fish-"

"I know what they are, I just can't believe they're real! I'd love to see one!"

"They're not to be trusted – not only are they loyal to The Queen, they're dangerous!" he said in a tone that made Millie feel reprimanded and like a child. "When the mermaids made a deal with The Queen that they'd patrol the water, the nymphs were driven to the far corners of the waters. The areas where the water nymphs have been are amazing - nymphs do a great job nurturing their elements," he said, watching the wood nymphs work in appreciation. He looked over at Oliver, "See the one with the black hair?"

Oliver looked across the opening to the woman with waist-long wavy black hair, who was filling the branches of another tree with red shiny apples with her touch. "Yeah."

"We used to date," Whartorlli said, trying to sound nonchalant.

"Oh, really?"

"*Yeah*, had to let her go though - the other girls got jealous. She was devastated, poor thing."

"Right, didn't you say this was only the second time you've

seen wood nymphs?"

"What can I say, it was love at first sight. You don't have to believe me!" Whartorlli snapped, alerting the wood nymphs of their presence. The nymphs stopped pruning and scanned the trees wildly. As soon as their eyes found them, they darted to the nearest tree and merged back into nature.

"Oh yeah, I saw the love," Oliver laughed.

"Whatever, let's go!"

They weaved in and out of the trees in silence after taking a turn off the pathway. Whartorlli had told them to be quiet while he concentrated on finding the way through the forest to Ophelia's cottage, which Millie thought was rich considering he'd been the only one talking.

"Are we there yet?" Oliver whined.

"Just a minute!"

"We've been walking forever-"

Oliver's complaint was cut short as they navigated around a large oak tree and the cottage came into view.

7

They stood on the outskirts of a white picket fence which surrounded a large garden. In the middle of the garden stood a small unstable-looking cottage. There were several little windows dotted around the cottage and a small red wooden door framed with climbing ivy. The only sign of life was the thin stream of smoke coming from the chimney, indicating that Ophelia was home. The entire garden and cottage was covered by a canopy of cherry blossom trees that looked out of place in the forest. The air where they stood outside of the fence was perfectly still without a hint of wind. They watched as a flurry of pink petals rained down from the draping blossom trees and swirled around the garden like snow. The area beyond the fence seemed to be in its own bubble, filled with a magical haze.

Whartorlli flew towards the gate and stopped just before he crossed over the fence, he looked back at Oliver, "Please don't embarrass me."

"Embarrass *you*? Seriously?"

Whartorlli's eyes hovered over Oliver's pyjamas, he turned to Millie and gave her a pleading look. Trying her best to keep the peace Millie looked at Oliver apologetically before she answered, "Don't worry, I'll keep an eye on him."

Whartorlli sighed in relief, he smiled appreciatively at Millie then turned and flew over the fence into the garden. Millie could feel Oliver's eyes burning into her temple, she ignored him and pushed open the gate. As she walked through the gate she was instantly hit by a pleasant warm breeze. The petals swirled around her like a gentle tornado.

"This is insane! It feels like we're in a snow globe!" Oliver said, appearing next to her with a load of petals caught in his curly hair.

"Come on guys!" Whartorlli called from the door.

They started to walk towards the cottage, Whartorlli shot Millie a look to say, 'Sort him out,' while nodding towards his hair.

Millie giggled. "Come here," she said to Oliver, reaching and picking the petals out of his curls.

Whartorlli knocked the door and waited, Millie and a petal-free Oliver stood behind him. He glanced over his shoulder at Oliver and rolled his eyes before licking his hand and trying to smooth down Oliver's hair.

"Errr, get off that's disgusting!" he shouted, wiping the fairy spit off his head.

Just then they heard a shuffling from inside the cottage.

"Who is it?" came an elderly voice from behind the door.

"It's Whartorlli."

There was a long pause, then from behind the door came an audible sigh. Millie felt bad for Whartorlli as she watched him pretend not to hear the sigh at the mention of his name. She couldn't deny that he was difficult to be around, with his desperation to impress with his intelligence and fabricated date with a wood nymph. But in that instant Millie realised that the reason he was trying so hard was because he didn't have many friends.

"I've got some people here to meet you!" sang Whartorlli, in an attempt to convince Ophelia to open the door.

A second later the door slowly opened, revealing an incredibly old woman. She was about four feet tall - four feet and seven inches if you included the large grey bun on the top of her head. She wore small round bifocal glasses which made her twinkly blue eyes either ridiculously massive, or ridiculously tiny, depending on which section she looked out of. She wore brightly-coloured mismatched clothes and leaned on a knobbly wooden cane. Ophelia gave them her biggest smile, she had no teeth, so her lips curled inwards over her gums. Overall, she had a friendly warm and welcoming face, and she oozed kindness.

"Oh hello! Come on in!" Ophelia said cheerfully, waving her hand in the air encouragingly to emphasise the gesture.

Whartorlli flew straight inside, Millie and Oliver followed hesitantly. The cottage was a lot bigger on the inside, which was deceiving due to its modest exterior. The ceiling in the hallway sloped at different angles and heights. Oliver found a high cove to stand in, so he didn't have to crouch. Straight ahead of them was a rickety open staircase that led to the second floor. To the left of the stairs was a small living room full of an assortment of soft armchairs and sofas that surrounded a crackling fire. In front of the fireplace was a crow, curled up on a rug, snuggled up to a stuffed toy. The crow was wearing a bright pink collar with a small bell. Millie and Oliver looked twice, but after the things they'd seen in the past hour they weren't the least bit shocked. To the right was a tiny sitting room, the walls were lined with bookshelves filled with books. Millie smiled as she thought about the bookshelves in Mr Wright's office, lined with pictures of himself. There were more books on the small dining table in the middle of the room, stacked precariously almost to the ceiling. At the far end of the sitting room, three steps led through an archway down into a cluttered kitchen. Millie instantly felt at home - it was quirky, eclectic and cosy.

"Come in, come in," urged Ophelia, as she negotiated her way around the dining table and into the kitchen. "Take a seat at the table."

Whartorlli sat on a stack of books that were on the floor piled to table height. Millie and Oliver followed Whartorlli and sat at the table, careful not to disturb the wobbling books.

"I wonder whether she's read *all* of these books," said Millie, looking in fascination around the room.

"Well I'd think so, she's about a hundred and seven so she's had plenty of time to read them," Oliver whispered.

"Actually, young man, I'm one hundred and seventy-two next week," said Ophelia, as she appeared in the archway balancing a teapot and cups on a tray. "I may be old, but my hearing isn't."

Whartorlli sat with his head in his hands, mortified.

Oliver flushed bright red. "I-I'm sorry, it was just a joke. I don't really think you look a hundred and seven, I honestly don't think you look any older than eighty...really," he rambled. "Actually, my nan's seventy-three and she looks older than you - not that you look old-"

Whartorlli gave Millie a forceful nudge.

"Have you read all of these books?" Millie asked, cutting Oliver off before he could dig himself a deeper hole.

"Yes, I have, duck. Twice in fact. Tea?"

"Yes please," Millie and Whartorlli answered together. Oliver nodded, scared to utter another word.

Ophelia poured four cups of tea, with a happy grin etched on her pleasant face.

"Ophelia's kind of the Oracle of Morendale. If you think I know a lot, you'll be amazed at Ophelia! She's a master in the art of magic, and she's the oldest person in the whole kingdom," Whartorlli bragged on Ophelia's behalf.

"Thank you Whartorlli, that's very sweet. Now, what can I help you all with?" she said, eyeing Millie and Oliver knowingly. "I can see you two aren't from around here."

"Erm yeah we're from a town near Thatchly Market, just ten minutes away," Oliver lied, not wanting to share too much.

Ophelia's face lit up in amusement. "Is that so, I would've guessed you'd travelled a bit further than that."

"Nope just around the corner really."

Ophelia smiled at Oliver, "I suspect you came from the portal?"

Oliver flushed red and nodded, "Yes."

Millie gave Oliver an encouraging pat on the arm, thinking to herself that he really wasn't making a great impression with the people he'd met so far, which was unusual as most people warmed to Oliver instantly.

"Ophelia, this is the girl I was telling you about. The one I saw here the other day when Serperus was sniffing around!" Whartorlli shouted, barely able to control his excitement.

Ophelia turned to look directly at Millie, "So then, duck, what brings you through the portal?"

Millie told Ophelia about the night she'd followed Whartorlli's glittering trail into her garden and had followed Chris through the portal. She paused as she thought about the reason she could give for her coming back. She knew the real reason was foolish and she couldn't bring herself to say it out loud. She had the feeling that no-one could lie to Ophelia without her knowing about it. So she gathered the courage and continued truthfully, "I wanted to prove to Oliver that it was real and explore and have fun. I know how dangerous it is here, I can *feel* it. But things have been so bad lately I just wanted to get away from reality for a while with my friend." She glanced sideways at Oliver then quickly looked down. "I know it was selfish and reckless of me to bring him here."

Oliver nudged her shoulder playfully; his way of saying – 'It's OK.'

Ophelia listened intently and without judgement. "My duck, I understand that you want to take your mind off things with an adventure, but as you say – Morendale isn't safe."

Oliver watched Millie as she reluctantly absorbed Ophelia's words. He knew her well enough to know that she would keep coming back to Morendale, regardless of the dangers, "Why is it even there?"

Ophelia sighed and took a sip of her tea. "I suppose I'd better start from the beginning," she said, setting her cup down. "Many years ago, the kingdom was ruled by King Kalmin and Queen Rhonell. They were so special and rare that many people in Morendale would say that when they ruled, it was the happiest time of their lives.

"The King spotted Rhonell during one of his trips to the market and fell in love with her instantly, he knew that one day he would marry her. The King visited the market every day; courting Rhonell. She soon became Queen and ruled the kingdom along with King Kalmin. They later had two children, Prince Haiton and Princess Jainella. Queen Rhonell loved the people of Morendale and they loved her. She would regularly take the children out of the castle to visit the people; teaching them that they were part of the community. From her teachings they learnt to use their position for good, and to always consider what's right for the kingdom and its people. The Queen's sister, Umelle, and her daughter, Naleem, was the only family Rhonell had left; and so, The King invited them to live in one of the castle wings. He treated them well and always ensured that they had everything they needed. Umelle, was viciously jealous, and resented that Rhonell had been chosen by The King and had married into royalty.

Ophelia paused and took another sip of her tea before she continued, "In this world there are rare people that naturally harness powerful magic. These people don't need spells and potions or books; it's within them. Rhonell and her family were blessed with this magic. Umelle's jealousy clouded her mind and made her dangerous. Umelle was nothing like her sister, she firmly believed that their family was superior with its magic and should be treated as such. She hated Rhonell's outlook on the people of Morendale and felt that she was wasting her position as Queen.

"One evening Umelle did something unspeakable and unforgiveable. She used her powers to kill The King and Queen. This however has never been proven of course, but those that knew Queen Rhonell well enough would bet their life that Umelle was behind their deaths. Prince Haiton was just a young boy so she insisted on ruling as Queen until he came of age. She instructed The Army to patrol the forests and villages, just to keep the kingdom on high alert and remind them of her ruling.

"Prince Haiton, being the eldest, came into his powers first at the age of fourteen. He hid his powers from The Queen for as long as he could. He knew that she would not only be threatened by his powers but of him taking the throne too. Eventually she discovered his powers and had seen that they'd soon rival her own - the poor boy was never seen again.

"A year or so later, Princess Jainella managed to sneak out of the castle one night, she came to me in a panic. She'd just discovered her powers and was terrified that what'd happened to her brother would happen to her. She feared her aunt and I was scared for her. I respected her mother greatly and I felt it was my duty to protect her daughter.

"I explained to her that I could help her escape and never be found, but she had to be sure that she was ready to say goodbye to Morendale.

"I'd read in books about an alternate world that ran parallel to our own on a different plane. You need strong magic to be able to cross planes, and with her powers being so new I wasn't sure if it would work. We waited until the witching hour; when the veil between planes is at its weakest, and walked deep into the forest, near the peryton territory. I guided The Princess through the ritual and together we managed to create a gateway from one world to another. That was the last I ever saw of her, the people of Morendale suspected The Queen had disposed of her as she had her brother. But of course, The Queen knew better, I imagine that's why she appointed Serperus.

"A few years ago, Queen Umelle passed away. Her daughter, Naleem, now rules the kingdom, she's proving to be even more of a tyrant than her mother."

"No-one knows of the portal other than who is in this room, the portal will only open for those who know of its existence. You can't tell anyone else about the portal, I dread to think what would happen if this knowledge got into the wrong hands." Ophelia fixed them with a stern yet pleading look.

"We haven't told anyone else," Millie said reassuringly. 'But Ophelia, why did the portal open for Whartorlli if he didn't know of its existence before then?"

Whartorlli answered instantly, "I must've heard it somewhere, I couldn't even begin to tell you the amount of dormant knowledge I have stored."

Ophelia looked at him with an amused twinkle in her eye. "I'm not sure whether that's true or not but either way, the knowledge needs to end with us." She looked at Millie, "Duck, we need to make you a memory-loss potion for your cat."

Oliver looked smugly at Whartorlli after hearing Ophelia refer to Chris as a cat. Whartorlli looked straight ahead, refusing to meet his eye.

"But how will he remember me? Or where he lives?" asked Millie, with growing concern.

"Oh, don't worry duck, we can pick and choose what memories we wipe clean. We'll only take away knowledge of the portal."

"You could clear the memory of his name and give him a normal cat name?" said Oliver.

"*Or* we could just clear your whole memory and I could leave you here!" joked Millie.

Whartorlli shook his head vigorously. "I don't think so – he's not staying here!"

Ophelia chuckled, "Now now, that's enough." She turned to the bookshelf and ran her finger along the row of spines, reading the titles to herself absently. "Ah! Here we are." She pulled the book from its tight slot on the shelf and hobbled towards the kitchen.

Sudden squawking pulled Ophelia's attention away from the book. The crow flew in from the other room, squawking loudly. It landed on Oliver's shoulder and pulled at his hair with its beak.

"Aghh, get off!" Oliver shouted, as he shielded himself from the crow.

Whartorlli smirked and watched in delight.

Ophelia hobbled around the table, waving her hand at the crow. "Onyx stop that!"

Onyx stopped and turned to look at Ophelia.

A frown appeared on her face as she stared back at the crow.

"Something's wrong. It's not safe for you both to be wandering around here, not with the patrols. You must go back and forget about this place."

Just then they heard the gate open outside. Ophelia hobbled to the window and peered out. She turned back to them hastily, wavering on her cane and knocking the table, causing an avalanche of books onto the floor. She grasped onto the table for support, suddenly looking frail.

"You need to leave, now! The Queen's soldiers are here - with Serperus," she said, panicked. "Here, go out the back – quickly."

She took them through to the kitchen and silently unlocked the back door. The unstable cottage shook as a fist pounded on the front door. A creature pushed its nose against the bottom of the door and sniffed the air rabidly in the hope of picking up a scent. Millie was suddenly transported to her haunting nightmare - only now, she was living it.

"Wait here until I let them in, then run! You need to get back before the portal closes at dawn."

Ophelia looked distraught and helpless as she hobbled unsteadily towards the front door. Millie and Oliver crouched petrified and waited, Whartorlli peered out from Millie's hair. Ophelia opened the door just a crack; a soldier barged the door open with his shoulder, sending her to the ground. Oliver grabbed hold of Millie's arm as she leaned to move forward towards Ophelia out of instinct. He opened the back door gently and forced Millie outside, then closed the door without a sound behind them. They crouched low to the grass and shuffled towards the gate. As they crawled away, they heard the soldiers tearing through Ophelia's cottage. With every sound that escaped the cottage Millie pictured Ophelia's home being destroyed. Her eyes filled with tears as she visualised the armchairs being ripped, and the bookshelves being pulled down from the walls.

"There's no-one here."

"Serperus picked up an unfamiliar scent leading right to your cottage, Ophelia."

They felt terrible as they overheard the conversation between Ophelia and the solider. Going to Ophelia's cottage had put her in danger; and now they were in danger too. Millie looked at Oliver, she wanted to apologise and tell him what an amazing friend he was and how much he meant to her; but there wasn't time, they had to keep going. They reached the gate which had been left ajar, Oliver crawled through into the stillness of the forest and out of the tainted magical haze of Ophelia's garden. Millie lingered at the gate, she looked back towards the cottage, fighting her instincts to go back to help Ophelia.

"Millie c'mon!" Oliver hissed, reached back into the garden for her.

As he grabbed her arm she turned swiftly, her scent caught on the swirling air in the garden. A second later a deep guttural growl came from behind her that made her blood turn cold instantly. Whartorlli flew up into the trees and Oliver's face turned white in horror as he stared at the cottage, Millie turned - in the doorway of the cottage stood Serperus. He was a powerful and muscular dog, nearly as tall and as wide as the doorway. Instead of fur he had scales like a python - green, black and brown, and the tail of a rattlesnake. His eyes were also that of a snake, bright yellow with slit pupils. He stood rigidly still with his fang-like teeth bared. Millie was frozen to the spot. Oliver slowly reached for her hand and squeezed it tightly. She knew any minute he would pull her into a run. But they had no chance; they would never be able to outrun the beast that stood in front of them. Suddenly Onyx flew from one of the small windows squawking loudly, distracting Serperus. She swooped down at the scaled dog with her sharp beak. Serperus jumped into the air snapping his jaws, just missing Onyx.

With Serperus briefly distracted, Oliver pulled Millie into a sprint towards the trees. As they ran through the forest, they checked behind them frantically for signs of the horrifying dog. Between glances back they searched for the pathway that would lead them back to the portal. Oliver suddenly grabbed hold of Millie and pulled her behind a tree.

"What are you doing we can't stop!" whispered Millie, as she gasped for air.

"Listen," he said, cupping his ear. "They're not following us, but they'll still be looking. We need to get out of here and I don't know where we are."

Millie looked around hopelessly, nothing looked familiar. She checked her watch - 4:45am - they didn't have much time until dawn. They scanned the forest on the brink of panic, they didn't know which direction to go. Defeated, Millie looked at Oliver, feeling deep remorse. With renewed determination he grabbed her hand and made to move, suddenly they were showered in a fine golden glitter. They looked up to see Whartorlli hovering in the branches above them. Millie felt relief wash over her, even Oliver was happy to see him. Whartorlli put a finger to his mouth, signaling to stay quiet, then pointed straight ahead. He darted off through the trees and they followed without hesitation.

Whartorlli kept them away from the path, they weaved in and out of trees and waded through bushes, they turned a corner and Millie saw the familiar hollow which housed the portal; they sighed in relief. Millie looked up at Whartorlli and mouthed, 'Thank you'. He put his thumb up and waved from the high branch. They summoned their last bit of energy and sprinted towards the portal. They had nearly reached the portal when they heard rustling in the bushes ahead of them, Oliver pulled Millie behind him. Piercing yellow eyes stared back at them from between the leaves. Serperus' scaled snout emerged from the bushes, followed by his powerful body. Millie desperately wanted the soldiers to catch up with Serperus, but there was no sign of them. He moved threateningly towards them; slow and dangerous. The scales on his large face curled upwards, crinkling his nose and baring his fanged teeth as he let out a low growl. Oliver searched the floor for anything he could use to protect them. He spotted a heavy looking stick on the ground behind them. He crouched to the floor and edged backwards slowly. As he grabbed the stick Serperus rushed forwards. Millie screamed and pulled Oliver out of his reach. Oliver steadied himself before he swung the stick at the scaled dog. Serperus caught the stick in his jaws with ease and wrenched it out of his hands, pulling Oliver forwards. Millie grabbed hold of his arm, managing to pull him away from Serperus again. They backed away further into the unshielded opening in the forest, putting more distance between them and the portal. There was nowhere to go; they couldn't run and there was nowhere they could hide.

"I'm so sorry Oliver," Millie said, her eyes brimming with tears.

Oliver turned and hugged her. They closed their eyes tight and waited. They heard him padding closer and felt his hot breath as he circled them. They clung on harder, burying their faces into each other. A high-pitched soaring suddenly blotted out the sound of Serperus' snarls. A forceful gust of wind knocked them to the floor. They opened their eyes to find a large stag towering over them. It had wings that spanned across the open forest and magnificent intricate antlers. From Whartorlli's story they knew it was Jupiter. Serperus retreated from the force of his beating wings. Jupiter tucked his wings back against his body. He stood tall over Millie and Oliver; his chest puffed out - warning Serperus. Serperus stared back at the peryton, pleasure almost registering on his face. Millie and Oliver shuffled from underneath Jupiter towards the edge of the opening in the forest. Millie glanced up into the trees, looking for Whartorlli. She spotted him watching from a branch trembling with fear. Serperus growled and lowered himself to the ground before lunging himself at Jupiter. Jupiter leaped over Serperus and kicked out his hind legs, just missing him. He turned and lowered his antlers towards Serperus. He scuffed his hooves then charged. Serperus snapped his jaws shut capturing Jupiter's antler. He twisted his muscular head and flung Jupiter effortlessly to the ground. Serperus turned to face Millie and Oliver, he geared himself up to attack. They shielded themselves and waited for the impact. Suddenly Jupiter peeled himself off the ground. He reared up onto his hind legs and delivered a powerful blow to Serperus' head, knocking him out cold.

In that instant, the forest fell silent and peaceful. They looked at Jupiter in appreciation and awe as he stood proudly, looking powerful and majestic, in the middle of the tranquil forest, towering over the half-serpent, half-canine. Millie slowly walked over to Jupiter and hesitantly placed her hand on his soft nose.

"Thank you," she whispered, gratefully.

Oliver cautiously joined her at Jupiter's side. He hesitantly scratched Jupiter behind the ear.

Oliver smiled in surprise, "I think he likes it." He moved his hand through the coarse fur on Jupiter's strong shoulders to where the fur transformed into feathers. "You're amazing," Oliver whispered.

The sound of marching feet broke the silence of the forest. "Serperus! Serperus where are you boy!"

Jupiter turned and ran into the forest. Serperus began to stir.

"Quick go!" shouted Whartorlli.

They moved towards the portal, the glow flickered then grew bigger, spilling out of the hollow. Millie glanced back at Whartorlli.

"I'll be fine, just go! Go before anyone sees the portal!"

Millie climbed into the hollow followed closely by Oliver.

8

They clambered through the gateway between the two planes. Their hearts skipped a beat when they felt the cool air on their face and damp soil under their hands. The glowing fog cleared, revealing the leaves of the bushes in the garden. They jumped to their feet and waded eagerly through the hedges. Once they were out of the overgrown grass and bushes, they turned to watch the portal close, hoping nothing followed them through.

The glow slowly turned into a dull ember before disappearing altogether. They stood in silence as they watched the first light of dawn appear, indicating just how close they'd been to being stuck in Morendale, and more importantly; to losing their lives.

"Ophelia! What about Ophelia, and Whartorlli, and Jupiter!" Millie said, pained, as the fear subsided, and guilt took over.

"I'm sure they'll be fine; the soldiers were after us not them. And I think Jupiter can look after himself!"

"But they know we were in Ophelia's cottage! They'll go after her and use her to find us!"

"Millie, for all they know we're just some stupid kids that were hanging around her cottage. They don't know for sure we were in there!"

She nodded and tried to calm herself. Suddenly she remembered some damning evidence. "The teacups! There were four cups out! They'll know! We have to go back and see that she's alright."

"No!" Oliver grabbed hold of Millie firmly. The sudden visible fear on his face shocked her. "You can't go back there, ever! Are you listening to me? We almost died in there!"

Millie looked at him, speechless; overwhelmed with guilt, and knowing that Oliver was right. Her eyes once again filled with tears.

"I'm sorry about Ophelia, Mills, but honestly what can we do? You saw that *monster*; we wouldn't have a chance. Anyway, Serperus followed us so she'll be safe with the soldiers."

"Yeah and they probably took her to Hillontropa, and you heard Whartorlli – he said it's a horrible place – or even worse, they took her to The Queen! And it's all my fault – I sensed that I shouldn't have gone back there-"

"You didn't know there was an insane Queen, soldiers and a snake-dog! We didn't know any better, Mills," he said, desperate to console his friend. Millie had taken him there knowing in her gut how dangerous it was, but he was equally to blame; he knew she was consumed with fascination, and still he chose to go. Even when Whartorlli had told them of the dangers, they chose to stay, knowing that nothing good would come from overstaying their welcome in Morendale. "C'mon, we'd better get back to bed before everyone wakes up."

They walked slowly up to the door and let themselves in. Millie closed the door behind them and locked it, Oliver carried on into the living room. She looked out of the window back to the hedges, her mind running wild. The familiar jingle from Chris' collar sent another bout of worry and adrenaline surging through her. He appeared in the kitchen and wound around her ankles. Chris would keep going through the portal, and it was only a matter of time before the knowledge of its existence fell into the wrong hands.

Every night after being caught sneaking out of the house, Carla would climb out of her bedroom window, onto the garage roof, hop down and enter the garage through the side door. The garage was cluttered with old bikes, toys, tools and exercise equipment. It was the land of failed hobbies, no-one ever went in there, and so it was perfect for her newfound responsibility.

It'd all started five nights ago; Carla was woken suddenly by Millie pounding up the stairs and diving noisily into her bed. Carla had been surprised that she hadn't woken the whole house. Since she was wide awake and furious, she went down to the kitchen for a drink of water. She filled her glass and looked out of the window as she tried to subdue her anger that was ready to spill over. She resented Millie but she hated herself for it. She knew that Millie was going through a rough time at school, but she didn't understand why that meant nothing or no-one else mattered. When Millie had a bad day, everyone had to plaster on a false smile, regardless of how they felt. Everyone had to eat spaghetti and meatballs, even though they couldn't stomach another bite of it. Carla sometimes wished that she would have a bad day at school, just to see how her parents would react. She suspected that they would probably lock her sadness away up in her room, so it didn't add to Millie's unhappiness. Consumed with anger she forced herself to think back to when they were younger and smiled. She missed the time when they got along, when they'd play and laugh for hours every day and look forward to doing it all again the day after. She pushed the sadness of happier times away, knowing that they would never be the same as they once were. Things were too different now; *they* were too different. At that moment Carla thought to herself that everything would just be better without Millie.

As she sipped her water wishing hard for Millie's disappearance, she saw movement in the shadows in the corner of the garden. She leaned closer to the window and squinted into the darkness. She put her glass down on the counter and walked over to the door. She stepped out onto the dewy grass and walked towards the far corner of the garden. Halfway down the garden, she stopped near the wildlife patch and searched the shadows from a distance. She was still too far away to make anything out, so she edged closer and allowed her eyes to adjust to the darkness. As her eyes adjusted, she saw the small figure cower further into the shadowy corner. It was a fawn, almost camouflaged against the fence, apart from the smattering of white spots along its flank. It pressed itself against the fence, making itself as small as possible.

"It's OK," Carla said, in a quiet soothing voice as she edged closer. "Don't be scared." She noticed a fresh wound on the fawn's hind leg. "Wait here, don't move."

Careful not to startle the fawn she walked calmly back to the house. She went straight to the first aid box in the kitchen under the sink and then went to work finding the fawn some food.

"Hmm cat biscuits, nope. Crisps, I hope not. Bananas, definitely not. Carrots, hmm... carrots could work." She grabbed the bag of carrots, a bottle of water, a bowl, and the first aid kit; and put it all into a carrier bag. On her way out of the door she thought of one more thing; she turned back and crept into the living room, she picked up the large woolen throw that was folded neatly on the side of the sofa and placed it in the bag.

As she made her way back down the garden, she reached into the bag and pulled out a carrot. She knelt on the damp grass opposite the fawn and held it out in her palm. The fawn looked cautiously from the carrot to Carla and back again.

"Come on, you must be hungry. I'm not going to hurt you."

The fawn slowly edged forward, keeping his big brown eyes fixed on Carla. He slowly opened his mouth, he snatched the carrot and shot backwards into the shadows. She giggled at the sound of his eager munching.

"Ah, so I was right, you *are* hungry," she said, as she held out another, this time taking a step backwards.

Eventually the fawn hobbled unsteadily out from the shadows and took the carrot from her palm. After his fifth carrot, Carla had managed to lead him three quarters of the way up the garden. During his sixth carrot she managed to gently stroke the fawn's head while he ate.

"OK, good boy," she said, as she closed the bag of carrots. His large glinting eyes watched her and the carrots carefully. "Follow me," she whispered, as she dangled the bag in front of him and walked backwards towards the gate. The fawn followed while he tried to pull the bag from her grip. When she opened the gate, the fawn stopped still. "Come on," she urged. "I can't help you if you don't trust me." The fawn tilted his head, almost as though he was trying to understand. He made a small huff sound and then began to limp towards the gate.

Mark hid the garage key in the front garden; just in case they were ever locked out of the house. Carla carefully reached into the hanging basket near the front door and pulled the out from underneath the flowers. She opened the garage side door and turned on the light before she coaxed the fawn inside and closed the door behind them gently.

"Hello James, how are you feeling?" Carla asked rhetorically, as she walked into the garage during the early hours of Sunday morning.

The fawn was wrapped snuggly in the large warm throw she had taken from the living room. The garage was spacious, warm, dry and safe. Carla planned to keep him there while she nursed him back to health, then she would ask her parents for help when she released him back into the wild. The truth was she'd become attached to the fawn, it was a nice change to have something happy to see her, rather than want to leave a room on her arrival. She'd called him James on the second evening, for no reason other than she thought it suited him.

James stretched and yawned as he lifted his head out from under the thick blanket. He looked at her expectantly with his large ears standing to attention, and his bright eyes scanning her for evidence of snacks. She pulled off her backpack and placed it in front of her on the floor. James rose from his bed in anticipation. Carla unzipped the backpack and reached in while James watched. All four hooves danced excitedly on the spot; the injured leg faltered slightly. Carla slowly pulled out a bag of carrots, and after careful research, a bag of nuts. James made an excited gruff sound and clumsily trotted over to Carla, then planted his face into the treats. Carla refilled his water bowl and laid down some fresh sheets and a couple of large plump pillows before folding the throw up neatly.

James nudged her side to move her from his bed and lay down along the pillows. Carla rubbed his head lightly, then went to work changing his bandages. His wound was healing nicely, she worked quickly while James pulled at her hair and clothes inquisitively. They had established a routine almost instantly - food, water, make bed, change bandages; then snuggles.

Once James' wound was clean and freshly bandaged, she sat next to him in his comfortable bed and pulled the throw over him ready for his nightly cuddle. She noticed that the small white spots along his back were gradually fading; she made a mental note to look this up when she got back to her room. She ran her finger lightly over the hard stubs on his head near his ears, where his infant antlers would soon be. The stubs were becoming more prominent each day, she wondered how long it would be until his little antlers appeared, and suddenly felt irrationally sad about James' rapid growth. Carla cast her eyes over his back, on the first night she'd noticed something unusual about the fawn; near his shoulder blades were two definite stubs, similar to the ones on his head but somehow different. She'd researched it but hadn't found anything. Living in a rural area with woodland she'd seen lots of deer, but she'd never seen stubs like the ones on James on any of them before. She eyed the unusual stubs while she absently stoked the small white spots along his back, as he lay snuggled in his warm blanket.

When James' breathing was deep and steady, she quietly got to her feet and made her way to the door. She looked back at the sleeping fawn feeling maternal; he was warm, safe and full. "Sleep well, I'll come by in a few hours," she whispered, before closing the door behind her.

Millie woke to the smell of eggs, bacon and coffee. The autumn sun beamed through the gap in her curtains causing a bright stripe across her bed where Chris lay happily baking. Her stomach suddenly flipped as she remembered the details of the night. It'd been magical up until the moment reality came along in the form of The Queen's Army and their tracker, Serperus. She worried for Ophelia and hoped that Whartorlli would somehow get word to her that she was alright. She also hoped that he would get the memory-loss potion to her for Chris. She didn't know how she was going to keep an eye on Chris and keep him away from the portal every night. She knew that one way or another she would have to get the potion. She tried not to think of the consequences if she didn't get it before the portal was highlighted to the wrong people. If The Queen was as evil and as powerful as Whartorlli had said, then there was no telling what she would do if she discovered the portal. Millie's blood ran cold as she pictured soldiers flooding through the gateway into her garden, along with Serperus. In a sense Whartorlli was right, she thought, there wasn't anything special in Farnham like there was in Morendale; no-one had any magical powers and Farnham was dull and lifeless in comparison to Morendale. But she had the feeling that it didn't matter that Morendale and its people were superior in every way, they were different, and to The Queen, that would surely be a threat.

Millie pushed the thought from her mind. She needed to talk to Oliver, and she hoped that he had a plan. After she replaced the key in her parents' bedroom, she made her way downstairs and into the kitchen. Mark was stood at the cooker making breakfast while Jane sat at the table having a light conversation with Oliver, who was changed out of his ruined sheep-print pyjamas and looking exhausted.

"Morning darling, how did you sleep?" beamed Jane.

"Morning Mills," Oliver yarned.

"Morning love, sit down and I'll whip you up some breakfast."

"Thanks dad. I slept well," she lied. "Do we have to go to aunt Julia's today?"

"Yes Millie," Jane said, in a tone of warning.

Oliver smirked, knowing how much Millie hated going to her aunts.

Every Sunday Millie and her family would go to aunt Julia's for Sunday dinner. Aunt Julia was her dad's sister, and they never took it in turns to alternate between their houses each Sunday. Millie didn't really mind; she liked the drive through the quiet Sunday roads. The only issue Millie had, was her cousin, Dale; he was six years old and was spoiled rotten. Every week Dale would somehow get either Millie or Carla, or both of them into trouble. They couldn't even avoid him; Jane and Mark would always make Millie and Carla entertain him while the adults had their chats.

"Wanna come, Oliver?" Millie said, smirking back at him.

"Errmm-"

Jane raised her eyebrows expectantly. "Oh, you're more than welcome, Oliver."

"Errmmm, I-I'm seeing my nan today," he stammered, kicking Millie under the table.

Missing his blatant excuse to avoid joining them at aunt Julia's, Jane smiled. "Another time maybe."

Mark placed a plate of bacon in the middle of the table. "Here we go! Now, Jane - poached?" he pointed at Jane and she nodded. "Millie - scrambled?" Millie nodded. "And Oliverrr....poach-scrammm-friiie..." Oliver smiled and nodded at his last guess. "Fried! Yep, see I remember!" He reached for the tray of eggs and went back to the oven.

Millie looked over at Oliver and pulled her phone from her pocket, signaling she was about to text him.

Ping, 'We need to talk about last night.' *Ping*, 'Put your phone on silent you idiot!'

'Now on silent ☺ What do we need to talk about, we're not going back there!'

'Chris will keep going there!'

'That's his choice!'

'OMG Oliver how are you not getting this! It's only a matter of time until Serperus or a soldier sees the portal, then what will stop them from coming here?'

Oliver looked up from his phone, a small wrinkle formed between his eyebrows. Millie felt the worry rise from the pit of her stomach as she realised Oliver didn't have a plan. He stared at his phone in contemplation before he replied.

'Yup see what you mean, but we can't go back! We'll just have to block it!'

'How do you block a portal!'

'We don't need to block it; we just need to block Chris from it. Either way we're going to have to try Plan A through to Y before I go back there... Plan Z is going back if you didn't get that.'

'Ok I'll try to find something to block Chris later.'

Millie put her phone down on the table and looked over at Oliver, he looked back with hope in his eyes. Millie took a deep breath, she didn't want to let Oliver down, she hoped that she could put a stop to Chris' night-time wanders.

"Carla's sleeping in late."

"Teenagers need their sleep Mark," Jane sang distractedly, as she read the newspaper.

Millie and Oliver exchanged a look, they had forgotten that they'd seen Carla sneaking out through her window with a backpack. Millie felt sick with worry; either Carla was still in bed because she had been out all night, she thought, or she hadn't come home. She thought back to the size of the backpack and was then convinced that Carla hadn't come home. She looked over at Oliver with worry written on her face. He knew exactly what she was thinking and shook his head, silently telling her to be cool. Millie told herself that Oliver was right, she was overreacting. She couldn't just blurt out to her parents what they'd seen because that would put them in trouble too, and probably for no reason if Carla were upstairs in bed.

The anxiety got the better of her, she decided she would check for herself first before revealing any information. "Just going upstairs, I'll be right back."

"Well be quick your eggs are almost done."

Oliver turned to Millie with a look to say - 'Are you crazy?'

Millie carried on through the hallway towards the stairs, she hesitated and glanced back at Oliver sat at the table, his expression said, 'OK, you'll regret it.'

With her heart racing Millie quickly walked up the stairs. She stood outside Carla's room wringing her hands, not sure whether to go in and check her sister was home or to just listen to Oliver. She put her ear to the door – the room was silent. Overwhelmed with worry, Millie decided to go with her instincts. She burst into the room and to her relief, there was a large heap under the bed covers. Her relief was short-lived and was quickly followed by regret when the heap slowly began to rise. Millie was frozen in place, knowing she'd made a deadly mistake. The large lump was now fully upright. Slowly It pulled the covers from Its face, revealing a tired, messy-haired, furious morning Carla. Millie slowly retreated backwards towards the door, raising her hands in apology. Suddenly Carla jumped to her feet and charged at Millie.

"GET OUT OF MY ROOM!" boomed Carla.

"Agghhhhhh! I'm sorry-I'm sorry-I'm sorry!"

9

Millie sat in the back of the car watching the countryside go by in a yellow and green blur on the way to aunt Julia's. They'd just dropped Oliver off at home, leaving Millie alone with her thoughts. She felt a constant worry in the pit of her stomach. She worried for Ophelia and Whartorlli and felt enormous guilt. They'd left them in a mess that they'd caused, while they had returned to their untampered world, free of scaled dogs and evil Queens. She worried for her family and knew that only she could protect them. She felt disappointed in Oliver, that he didn't seem to care about Ophelia or Whartorlli. He reserved his concern for those closest to him, he worried only about what could come through the portal into Millie's garden, and harm her and her family. Consumed by her thoughts and close to losing her mind, Millie, not for the first time, tried to think a little more like Oliver. Thinking only of herself and of those closest to her was against her nature, she was caring and thoughtful; but she had to adjust, it was the difference between self-preservation and self-destruction. She focused her thoughts, the plan was to block Chris from the portal, and she had to do it before tonight. The thought sparked a new concern; she had no idea how she was going to block Chris from something so intangible. Her mind was working overtime when her phone pinged.

'HAHAHAHAHAHAHAHAHA!!! I can't stop seeing it!' said Oliver's text. She rolled her eyes in annoyance and began to type.

'It wasn't that funny get over it!'

'I'm literally still crying! Your face when you ran down those stairs was hilarious!! I knew you'd regret it!'

'I don't regret it! I had to put my mind at rest and check she was home.'

'Yeah seemed like she really appreciated it,' Millie read, looking over at Carla, who was looking angrier than ever with her jaw clenched and fists balled. 'Plan B - if blocking it doesn't work maybe we should send Carla in, give Serperus a run for his money!'

Millie didn't respond, she threw her phone down in temper and tried to clear her mind as they drove to aunt Julia's.

Mark, Jane, and Julia's husband, Grieg, sat in the living room after dinner, all in a food coma. To Carla's frustration, she was chosen to play video games with Dale up in his room, while Millie was asked to help clear the kitchen.

"Oh, bless you Millie, thanks so much for all your help clearing the kitchen!" aunt Julia said, theatrically. Aunt Julia was over the top, full of emotion, bubbly and loud.

"No problem aunt Julia."

Julia rinsed the suds off another plate and passed it over to Millie for drying.

"Is that your mum's necklace?"

"Yeah, she gave it to me," Millie smiled, placing her free hand on the small emerald.

"It suits you - brings out those beautiful green eyes of yours," she said, gripping Millie's face affectionately and leaving her with a frothy soapy beard from the ton of washing-up liquid she'd used.

Millie could sense her aunt was gearing up to something and instantly wanted to leave the room.

"Are them girls still bothering you?"

The truth was Millie had barely thought about Jamie and Mora, and now actually quite liked Jenna. She'd had bigger things concerning her during the past 48 hours.

"Well, they've been in isolation, so I've not seen them much."

"Your dad told me that you went to see the Headteacher," she said, raising her eyebrows, indicating that Mark hadn't left out any detail about Mr Wright. "Are you happy with what he said?"

"Yeah, I mean, we'll have to see what happens I guess."

Millie could almost hear her aunt's brain working overtime; she clearly had an agenda and was approaching each item cautiously.

"Do you think you can trust this *Headteacher* to handle it? Don't you think it'd be best to just transfer schools?"

There it was; this was her dad speaking. Millie knew that he didn't trust Mr Wright, he had made no attempt to hide what he thought about him. Mark knew if he spoke to Millie about transferring schools, it would go against what he and Jane had discussed; so, he got his sister to do it instead. Her mum and dad had always believed she could handle the situation at school, and that she was strong. Transferring schools was a last resort, for if things got out of hand. Hearing second hand that her dad thought it was best for her to run and back down didn't sit well with Millie. She suddenly felt furious, she wanted to march into her dad and tell him, 'Watch me handle it!' She gained her composure and reminded herself not to shoot the messenger.

"If Mr Wright doesn't sort it out, aunt Julia, I will."

Julia smiled, seeing the familiar gumption return in Millie that she respected, and hadn't seen in a long time. "Good for you."

"MUUUUMMMMMM!!!!! CARLA WON!!!!" Dale screamed from

the top of the stairs, startling Millie and Julia.

They heard the pounding of Carla's feet running down the stairs. Within seconds she was in the kitchen with a face like Millie's that morning, she held her hands up in surrender while still holding a controller, "I didn't mean to win I swear!"

Millie stood in the garden opposite the bushes holding a garden gnome in each hand. She huffed in exasperation; she'd been racking her brains all afternoon; thinking what she could put at the entrance of the portal to stop Chris. She looked down at the gnomes in her hands, these definitely won't work, she thought. Millie had told her parents she wanted to have a go at some gardening. They'd exchanged a bemused look but let her carry on. Every so often Jane would peer out of the kitchen window to check on her. Millie would wave and smile until she was gone and then put down the rake.

Millie put the gnomes back and picked up a spade. She began to work on the edges near the back of the garden while she thought about what she could use. The sun was setting, and she could feel the threat of rain. She didn't have long, as soon as the first drop of rain would hit the window her mum would be straight out telling her to come in.

She dug the spade into the mud, so it stood on its own, she crossed her arms over the top of it and rested her chin on her forearm while she scanned the garden for inspiration. It was only then that she registered the shed - it was full of junk. She cursed herself under her breath for wasting time and for not thinking of it before. Millie pulled open the soggy wooden shed door and was not disappointed. The shed was filled with half used fence paint, old hoses, more garden tools and the shell of their old pond. Near the back she spotted a large stone bird bath without its stand. It was perfect - it was heavy enough for Chris not to be able to move, the right sort of shape, although Millie wasn't sure what shape the portal was, but she assumed it was circular; and it would be easily concealed in the bushes.

She fought her way to the back of the shed and brushed the cobwebs away from the bird bath. As she rolled it out of the shed into the light, she thought to herself that she had no memory of ever seeing it in their garden. The bird bath was heavier than she'd expected, and she struggled to move it, but she was grateful that she was able to roll it along the grass. Millie moved as quickly as she could to the bushes, all the while keeping an eye on the house, just in case her mum looked out of the window. She leant the bird bath on the sturdy hedge so she could catch her breath before rolling the weight inside the pre-made tunnel.

Millie maneuvered the bird bath through the bushes to the back of the tunnel where it met the fence. She stared at the fence as she tried to pinpoint where she'd seen the light flicker when the portal opens. She had no idea where best to place the bird bath given that the portal wasn't something physical; it was a change in the atmosphere, an aura, a cross-over between two different planes. She reasoned that the end of the tunnel at the fence would be the logical place to put it. The tunnel was there because Chris used the route regularly, she hoped the bird bath at the end of it would be a deterrent. She heaved it in place and fought her way back through the hedges. Millie suddenly felt the familiar guilt she'd been feeling ever since she left Morendale. If the block was successful, she really was turning her back on Ophelia and Whartorlli. She reminded herself why she had to do it, without the potion Chris would never stop crossing through, and going back for the potion was not an option; blocking the portal was best for everyone. She cast one last look at the circular bird bath propped up against the fence, only the very top of it visible, and turned back towards the house. Just then, the first drop of rain landed on her nose and simultaneously, Jane was at the door.

"Come on in, it's raining... wow Millie you've worked up a right sweat!" she said, looking from Millie back to the unchanged garden.

It was a rainy Monday morning, and to Millie's dismay her first lesson was P.E. They all stood on the muddy field waiting for Mrs Turner's instructions.

"Morning ladies! Beautiful morning isn't it!" she shouted, "Luckily for you all, you're not made of sugar so you don't get out of P.E.!" she roared, marching up and down the line of girls like a drill sergeant.

Mrs Turner was always shouting, there was no difference between her indoor and outdoor voice. Millie suspected it had something to do with the fact that she was always on a field and her ears had become weathered.

"Right!" she barked, clapping her hands together, "we need two teams! Jamie, you're a captain.... *and* Jenna, you can be a captain... well come on girls, up you come."

Both girls weaved through the crowd to the front of the group and stood either side of Mrs Turner. She pulled a coin from her pocket and tossed it in the air before shouting, "Call it!"

"Heads," said Jamie, unenthusiastically.

"Heads it is, you pick first, Jamie."

Without missing a beat Jamie murmured lazily, "Mora."

"Jenna?" Mrs Turner encouraged.

"Erm, Amy."

"Keira."

"Millie."

Jamie's and Mora's heads snapped towards Jenna, she kept her eyes forwards, not wanting to see the look on their faces. Their expressions went from absolute rage to ultimate betrayal. Millie was grateful for the gesture but even she felt uncomfortable for Jenna. She was contemplating saying, 'No thanks, I'll wait till last like I'm supposed to – then not actually get picked, someone will get stuck with me, and then only I will feel the humiliation.' But that wasn't an option, Jenna had made a brave move to break the cycle of Millie's torture and she couldn't leave her out there alone. Millie moved forward and joined Jenna's team, stepping into the hot gaze of Jamie and Mora.

"Jamie, *hello*! Your turn!" Boomed Mrs Turner.

"Layla."

Mrs Turner had chosen rugby to be the game they played that day.

Millie believed it was because Mrs Turner found it funny for teenage girls who tried so hard to look perfect at all times to be diving headfirst into mud.

Jamie's team were winning by some margin, so Jenna called a huddle to review their strategy. Millie couldn't concentrate on what Jenna was saying, she was focused on the familiar devious looks that were being shot her way by Jamie and Mora.

Mrs Turner blew her whistle sharply - indicating that they were back in play. Millie ran to her position where she was being marked by Amy, a tall and wide girl who made sure that Millie could get nowhere near the ball.

The whistle blew once more, and they were off. Mud flew in every direction, the ball passed from player to player in a blur. The pep talk from Jenna had made no difference, Jamie's team completely dominated theirs. Just then, Annie intercepted the ball and clung onto it like her life depended on it.

"Run Annie!" shouted Jenna, exhilarated that her team finally had the ball.

Annie ran as fast as she could in a panic as the swarm of girls chased her down the field. She ran past Millie then unexpectedly threw the ball backwards towards her. To her disbelief, she managed to catch the ball and not drop it. Millie swerved around Amy and ran towards the line desperate to score a try. Suddenly Layla was in front of her, Millie bravely continued to plough forward towards Layla, knowing that she was about to have the ball taken from her.

"Millie!" Jenna called from behind, "pass it here!"

Millie threw the ball to Jenna before she reached Layla. Jenna caught the ball with ease, she had a clear run and sprinted all the way to the line, scoring a try.

Millie and the rest of the team ran to Jenna screaming at the top of their lungs. They were far from winning, but their first try of the game needed to be celebrated. They jumped around in a circle screaming like banshees.

"Nice, Jenna! OK, back to your positions!" called Mrs Turner, over their screams.

The girls began to disperse. Millie strolled back towards her position, she noticed a few of the girls stopping to look in her direction, including Jenna. Suddenly she felt a hard shove on her back and next thing she knew, she was face down in the mud.

"What do you think you're doing!" she heard Jenna shout, as she ran over to the scene.

"What are *we* doing, more like what are *you* doing?" said Mora, accusingly.

"I've had enough! Why are you doing this to her? What has she done to you?"

A squelching suction sound accompanied every limb that Millie pulled out of the mud. She didn't feel upset, she didn't want to cry, she didn't even feel embarrassed; all that she felt was anger, red-hot anger. She got to her feet and turned to face the girls, they stopped arguing and looked at Millie. Mora and Jamie took one look at Millie's muddy face and burst into fits of laughter. Jenna looked at them both, suddenly seeing them clearly, and seeing what she was associated with; and she didn't like it.

Without thinking, Millie bent down and grabbed a hand full of wet mud. "What's so funny?" she asked, as she pulled her arm back and fired the mud full force at Jamie's face.

The whole crowd watched, speechless and in shock. A few sneers escaped from the braver girls.

Jamie wiped the mud from her eyes and mouth. "It wasn't even me it was her!" she spluttered, pointing at Mora, who looked at Jamie with a mix of betrayal and horror.

Millie bent down to gather up another lot of mud, her eyes fixed on Mora.

"Don't you dare!" shouted Mora, backing away.

She soon realised that no matter what she said, Millie wasn't going to back down, so she turned and bolted down the field.

"Oi! Stop it!" Mrs Turner shouted, who had only just noticed the commotion from across the field.

Millie set off into a sprint, chasing Mora around the field with a heap of mud in her hand.

Mora couldn't outrun Millie, as she caught up her, Mora turned and tried to weave out of the way. "Stop! Stop! Go away! I swear if you throw that-"

Millie launched the mud directly at Mora's face, the mud mostly ended up in her mouth, cutting her off mid-rant.

Mora spat and gagged, she looked at Millie furiously. Before she had time to react Mrs Turner was next to them grabbing each one by their arm.

"What's going on? I turn my back for one minute and this is how you behave!"

Millie, Jamie and Mora sat in Mr Wright's office, covered from head to toe in mud. He had laid towels down that made a path leading through his office to three cream chairs, which had also been draped in towels.

"Sir, Millie started it! She threw mud in my face first-" Jamie said, pointing vehemently at Millie.

Mr Wright jumped as she flung her muddy finger in Millie's direction, and more importantly in the direction of his bookshelf of selfies.

"Ah! - there will be no quick movements, thank you!" he shouted shrilly. After seeing that no mud had left Jamie's finger, he took a deep breath. "Right," he said, regaining his composure and smoothing back the hair that'd fallen briefly out of place, "I don't care *who* started it!"

"But Sir! -" Mora moaned, edging forwards on her chair and placing her hand on his pristine desk.

"Don't touch my desk!" he shouted, jumping up out of his seat and brushing the spot Mora had touched with a tissue. "Don't. Touch. Anything!" He sat back down and straightened his tie before patting his hair again. "As I was saying, I don't care who started it. It always seems to be the same people - you three, and that other one with the red hair," he said, flinging his hand in the air dismissively. "The point is, I need to talk to your parents about your futures at this school." He looked directly at Millie, "And Mollie, I expected better from you."

"It's Millie, Sir," she murmured timidly, hanging her head in shame.

She hadn't wanted it to get out of hand, but after recent times it was only a matter of time before things had boiled over.

Millie sat at the dining table; Mark sat in the seat next to her with his arms folded while Jane paced the kitchen.

"Expelled! For a week! Millie, what were you thinking!" Jane shrieked.

"I-I-"

"You lowered yourself to their level!"

"I-I'm-"

"Mark, can you believe this!"

"Oh yeah, awful, awful behaviour Millie," Mark said, trying to look at Millie sternly and failing to keep the hint of amusement from his eyes.

"That's right! Terrible behaviour! Mr Wright *told* you, any more trouble from them and you go straight to him."

"I know, I jus-I just-"

"Can I go to Kendall's?" Carla interrupted, as she strolled into the kitchen obliviously.

"What!" Jane shouted, irritated by being pulled out of her focused scolding.

"Woah *calm down*, I just want to know whether I can go to Kendall's?"

Jane looked over at Mark - reading her dangerous expression, Mark quickly answered before she exploded, "Yeah, sure honey, just be back for dinner at seven."

"Ahhhh seven?"

"Carla," Mark warned.

Carla rolled her eyes; she turned and scuffed her feet all the way to the front door in protest.

"Mum, can I just explain-"

"I know all that I need to know, now go to your room!"

"But mum-"

"Now! Millie."

Millie stood from the table and made her way slowly to her room, she found herself imitating Carla and scuffing her feet in protest along the way.

When Mark heard Millie's bedroom door close, he let the smile spread across his face, "Jane you have to admit, the look on them girls' faces was pretty funny."

Jane tried her best not to let the grin appear on her face, "It's not funny, Mark."

Mark began to convulse in silent laughter. Jane couldn't help it, she let the grin take over her serious expression and began to laugh quietly along with Mark.

10

Millie lay on her bed as she waited for a response from Oliver. *Ping,* 'No way! I wish I could've been there to see it!'

'My parents aren't impressed!'

'They'll get over it! We need to celebrate! Stop over at mine on Saturday? I need to hear it in person, facial expressions and all! Joe's stopping at his girlfriend's so we won't have his moody face around either!'

'Sounds good... if I'm not grounded!'

'OK let me know. Did you block it?'

Millie closed her eyes as the familiar feeling punched its way back into her consciousness after a day spent distracted, 'Yeah, I did it last night.'

'Good, is it definitely blocked? Don't feel guilty, Mills. We had no choice!'

Millie walked over to her window and looked over to the bushes. Even though she knew that they had no choice, it didn't stop her from feeling guilty, but more than anything else, she felt concerned. She couldn't bring herself to tell Oliver that she had no idea whether the bird bath had blocked the portal, and she was too scared to test it. She'd seen no evidence that Chris had recently been through the portal, but if Whartorlli had been captured, then Chris wouldn't be chasing him; and wouldn't be sprinkled with his golden fairy dust.

She had no choice but to watch Chris. Being expelled from school for a week couldn't have come at a better time; this week she would have to become nocturnal. Millie needed to know for sure that Chris could never visit the parallel world again. She planned to start the surveillance that night, so she set her alarm for 2:30am. She picked up her phone and replied to Oliver.

'Don't worry it's sorted.'

The alarm sounded; Millie was wide awake and alert to her mission. She had to make sure she had successfully blocked the portal; it wasn't only her family's safety that depended on it. Millie knew that The Army wouldn't stop at her family, directly outside of the portal, they would continue through the neighbourhood and beyond. Butterflies flew around her stomach as the enormity of the responsibility sank in.

Millie sat in a chair at her window and watched. Chris was in the garden by 4:15am, he walked near the hedges that contained the portal but never actually went in. For the first time in a while she actually wanted Chris to go to the portal; the suspense was too much, she had to know one way or another. When he moved away from the bushes, she thought about going down and testing it herself. The thought alone made her feel sick, but she knew that if Chris went through the portal, then she would have to follow - only then would she jump to Plan Z. She had no other ideas and she knew that Oliver hadn't either. It would be the last time, merely to get the potion. As she made her peace with Plan Z, she hoped that the blockage would be enough, and that she would never have to visit Morendale again.

At 6:50am the sun spilled over the horizon, casting a spectacular orange light that spread across the fields and into the garden. It was an uneventful night, other than a strange sound at the side of the house at 5:00am that Millie quickly recognised as Carla ascending the makeshift rope back through her window.

Millie plopped into bed and closed her stinging eyes, she drifted off instantly.

"Breakfast!"

Millie walked behind Jane, pushing a shopping trolley loaded with groceries. Jane had insisted that Millie helped her with the errands and made herself useful during her suspension from school.

She followed her mum in silence, isle after isle, and she was beginning to lose the will to live. Even with the torture of errands and the many chores her mum had assigned to her, Millie didn't regret throwing mud at Jamie and Mora. She'd had enough, she knew that she could've handled it better, but in the heat of the moment Millie had acted without thinking. She could see in her dad's face that he was proud of Millie for sticking up for herself, and so was her mum, deep down – although she knew her mum didn't approve of the *way* she'd gone about it. It was unfortunate that it had taken a life-threatening experience for Millie to take the first steps in putting a stop to the bullies, and even more unfortunate that the experience may not be over. In fact, her whole perspective during the past few days had completely flipped; before really exploring Morendale, she would keep her mind occupied from Jamie and Mora by thinking about the portal. Now she would keep her mind off Morendale by thinking about Jamie and Mora.

They turned into the pet isle, Jane picked up two boxes of cat food, comparing his usual food to a new brand with searing concentration. Millie could hardly keep her eyes open. She had no idea how long she could keep up the night-time surveillance, it'd been one night, and she felt like she hadn't slept in a month. Exhausted and bored out of her mind, Millie walked over to the pet toys, deciding that they would be slightly more interesting than her mother's all-important decision with the cat food. She glanced at the small mice, none of which were the colour of a real mouse. She fumbled with the brightly coloured mice thinking to herself that they would never fool Chris, he was unfortunately too into the real thing. Then her eyes landed on something that caught her interest - the dog leads. The leads sparked an idea that would help with her all-night Chris-watch. She read the labels carefully then picked up the longest extendable lead.

Millie looked over her shoulder, Jane was still reading the descriptions on the boxes. She turned and casually strolled over to where her mum stood with the trolley. Keeping one eye on Jane she carefully placed the lead under a large bag of potatoes just in time before Jane made her decision and placed the winning brand into the trolley.

"Let's go," said Jane, none the wiser.

They walked over to the checkout where Jane began to unload her shopping onto the conveyor belt.

"Let me help you mum!" chirped Millie, too enthusiastically.

Jane eyed Millie suspiciously. "What are you up to?"

Millie thought fast. "Well, I know what I did was wrong, and I know you're mad. But I was hoping if I did lots of chores I could stop over at Oliver's on Saturday? Please?" she asked, hopeful that she would agree and hopeful that she'd thrown her off the scent of the contraband in the trolley.

"We'll see."

"OK well let me put the shopping out and pack it away," she said, sweetly.

"Alright, that will be a start," agreed Jane, stepping away from the conveyor belt and walking over to the cashier for a chat.

With her mum distracted, Millie began to pile on the rest of the shopping. She casually stacked the groceries, all the while keeping an eye on her mum and trying to decipher the right time. When they were in a deep conversation about the new cat food brand, Millie made her move. She hid the lead underneath a cereal box then quickly threw on the rest of the shopping.

"Millie, be careful with the eggs!"

"Sorry mum," Millie said, as she skipped eagerly to the other end of the checkout to pack the shopping away.

She waited with bated breath as the cashier leisurely scanned each item through, still nattering away with Jane. Jane grabbed blindly at each item and stuffed them into bags. Millie picked up the odd item, while keeping her eyes peeled for the one she couldn't have her mum notice.

The cashier scanned the broccoli, bag of potatoes, milk, then the cereal - leaving the lead exposed. The cashier reached over for the next item and to Millie's horror, she skipped the lead and went straight for the talking point - the cat food.

"This is the one, Pauline. See it's cheaper but looks just as good as the one I usually buy."

"*Oh* yes, I didn't know we had this in the store..."

The lead sat on the conveyor belt in the open. Millie waited anxiously for Pauline to continue scanning. She thought about walking over and knocking something else onto it, but that would look unnatural and then her mum would know for sure she was up to something. So, she decided to hold her breath, wait it out and hope for the best.

"You'll have to let me know whether he likes it, then I'll try it with mine," said Pauline, reaching for the lead and scanning it through.

Millie dived for the lead and grabbed it at the same time as Jane.

"Millie! What's up with you today?" she asked, looking puzzled at Millie with the lead in her hand, hovering over her bag. "I said I'd see about you stopping over at Oliver's, calm down a bit please."

"Sorry mum," she said, as calmly as she could as she noticed Jane's focus slip away from her and back to packing. Millie tried to distract her again, "Didn't dad ask for double chocolate chip cookies? You only got chocolate chip."

"What's the difference?"

"They're not double."

"Well maybe he'll prefer these," reasoned Jane, turning her attention back to packing.

"Doubt it mum," Millie said with certainty, and once again gaining her mum's attention.

"Fine, quickly run back and change them-"

"That'll be £54.20," Pauline beamed, who'd continued scanning while Jane had been distracted, causing a huge backlog.

Jane looked at the pile, flustered. "Oh-" She dropped the lead to search for her purse in her oversized bag.

"Ah sorry mum too late, I'm sure he'll like them. Let me help you." Millie said sweetly, grabbing her mum's half-packed bag and ramming the lead inside, then covering it with the rest of the groceries.

They grabbed a couple of bags each, Millie ensured one of hers contained the lead - and they made their way back to the car.

Millie changed from the nightdress she'd gone up to bed in, into her jeans and t-shirt she would sleep in - just in case she needed to go through the portal. She placed her trainers near the door then went over to her coat, hung on the back of the chair. Millie pulled the lead out of her coat pocket; she'd managed to sneak it away while she helped her mum unpack. She sat on the bed next to Chris and clipped the lead to his collar, he stirred slightly then rolled onto his back, settling again into a deep slumber.

She had a new plan, after one night of monitoring Chris she knew she couldn't keep it up; not only because of the lack of sleep, but because she couldn't bear another night of waiting for him to wake up, only to watch him prance around the garden and attack anything that moved. Millie had seen the lead and it'd sparked an idea - she would attach the lead to Chris' collar and attach the handle to her. The plan was perfect, with Chris being attached to her, she'd know exactly when she had to get up and she could sleep in-between.

For the first time in a while Millie didn't set her alarm. She pulled the belt out of the loops of her dressing gown and weaved it through the handle of the lead, then tied it securely around her waist. After taking one last look at Chris, she let her head hit the pillow and descended into an immediate deep sleep.

Millie stood alone in the dark and silent forest. She couldn't see a thing, not even her own hand in front of her face – and she knew instantly, she was in Hillontropa. Just then the extinguished lanterns high in the trees all set ablaze, flooding the forest with a dull light. It was then she saw Serperus towering over her. His slit pupils stared lifelessly; his snake-like tongue slithered through his jagged sharp teeth. Millie couldn't breathe, she knew if she dared to move his yellow eyes would flicker into life with joy. He circled her, building her fear ready for the moment he chose to lunge. She closed her eyes but could still feel his hot breath and his dry porcelain-like scales brushing against her arm.

Just then something grabbed her t-shirt. She opened her eyes, it was Oliver. A relieved whimper escaped her as he pulled her into a full-blown sprint out of the light of the lanterns and into the darkness. She could hear the pounding of Serperus' heavy paws as he gained on them, getting closer and closer. She ran blindly, guided only by Oliver's tight grip on her t-shirt. She couldn't keep up, she suddenly felt like she was running against a force that was pushing her backwards. Oliver pulled on her t-shirt, trying to pull her to safety. He pulled desperately as Millie pumped her feet on the ground and leaned forwards against the force pushing her backwards. He pulled and pulled-

Millie gradually woke in a sweat feeling dazed and confused. She could still feel the pulling - as sleep wore off, she lifted the covers and saw the dressing gown belt around her waist. The sight of the lead brought her back into consciousness and she sprang out of bed, remembering with a jolt that Chris was on the other end.

She found Chris in the kitchen; the lead had just stopped short of his bed near the dining table - which he never usually used. She let the lead extend so he could curl up in his bed. It was a drizzly night and Millie had suspected Chris would spend it indoors sleeping.

She felt the familiar anxiety rise at the thought of spending another day of not knowing whether the block had worked, and once again having one of her reoccurring nightmares featuring Serperus. She preferred it when he had been a faceless creature - people always say the thought is usually worse than the actual thing, she thought, but not in this case. Millie could never have imagined anything more terrifying. She suddenly remembered a Greek Mythology class in primary school, Millie and Oliver had found it fascinating. She cast her mind back to Cerberus, the three-headed dog that guarded the gates of the Underworld, and wondered whether Serperus was a descendant of his, and had kept to the family business. But instead of guarding the Underworld Serperus brought the Underworld to the picturesque kingdom of Morendale. She tried to look on the positive side; she was now able to get some sleep, she checked her watch - 6:30am, if she hadn't had the lead, she would've been sitting awake since 2:30am.

She pulled Chris' bed closer to the kitchen door so the lead would reach back to her bed. She knelt to give Chris a brief fuss before getting up to leave the kitchen. She made a mental note to set her alarm for 6:50am, so at sunrise she could release Chris and put his bed back in its proper place. As she padded towards the door the kitchen was suddenly illuminated by the familiar green light. Millie turned quickly and ran to the window, her eyes locked on the hedges. She looked away briefly to check that Chris was still in his bed and not in the garden. The portal was now brighter than ever, the autumn season had kicked in, leaving the bushes almost bare and the portal exposed. She waited tensely, willing Whartorlli to emerge from the fog with news from Ophelia and holding a vial of memory-loss potion.

After a minute of nothing but blinding light, she knew that it couldn't be Whartorlli. He would've been through by now, she thought, this had to be someone or something else. She looked around the kitchen for anything she could use for protection, and grabbed the closest thing to her, a plastic spatula. Millie ran to the door to make sure it was locked. A sudden image of the powerful dog filled her mind as she looked at the feeble wooden door. She scanned the kitchen in a frenzy for anything that could keep Serperus at bay. In a panic she pulled all the chairs from the table and pushed them against the door.

Millie darted back to the window with the spatula held in both hands. Slowly the glow dissipated, plunging the garden and kitchen into darkness. Without looking away from the hedges, her hand rummaged blindly for the torch in the kitchen draw. Pushing aside odd batteries and screws, she finally found the torch. She fumbled for the switch and shone it unsteadily out of the window, flicking it frantically from the hedges to the darkest corners of the garden, to the door and back to the hedges.

Once the adrenaline subsided, she put down the spatula and replaced all the furniture, then sat at the table and waited.

Daybreak came on cue at 6:50am. Millie stood with purpose, she unclipped the lead from Chris and untied her belt, putting it safely in the cupboard along with the lead behind the mop bucket. She moved towards the door, this time with a rolling pin in her hand. Luckily, her parents had stopped hiding the key - Carla sneaking out of the house was old news compared to Millie being suspended. She unlocked the door and stepped into the cool damp garden. She took a steadying breath before she cautiously approached the hedges. With the rolling pin ready to swing she peered in through the hedge tunnel. The thickness of the leaves had reduced significantly with the onset of autumn and she could see right through to the back without having to crawl through. She scanned the mass of hedges from end to end - it was completely clear. Millie's eyes fell on the bird bath, still in place - of course it was, she thought, they'd crawled beyond the fence. How could they've thought that they could block Chris from the portal? The portal was intangible, it wasn't a block-able object, Chris only had to get close enough to activate it – it didn't matter what was around it. Millie knew she'd have to tell Oliver what had happened. She hoped that even though she had told him that the portal had been successfully blocked, that he still would've worked on a Plan B - just in case. Just then something caught her eye, something that stood out from the autumnal browns, oranges and reds of the garden. Something small and white lay on the floor in front of the bird bath. She looked quickly over to the house to check no-one was up before she scrambled through the bushes. It was a small scroll, roughly the size of her index finger, and it was tied neatly with a little rope. She quickly put it in her pocket, shuffled backwards out of the tunnel and ran back to the house.

11

Millie pushed her breakfast around the plate with her fork, she'd taken the small scroll to her room and read Whartorlli's words carefully –

'Dear Millie, I hope you're OK. I'm sorry I didn't write sooner! There have been soldiers patrolling everywhere! I thought with the extra patrols it would be best that I left this note for you rather than come to see you and risk getting caught on the way back through.

Ophelia's being watched closely, but she managed to make a batch of the potion. She visited her friend, Mr Lawfus, in the village; she has left the potion with him so it can be collected away from the watch of the soldiers.

I went there earlier today to collect it and bring it to you, but I couldn't fly with it! Walking back from the village to the portal with the vial would take me days! Ophelia was clear not to tell Mr Lawfus about the portal, otherwise I would've asked for his help. I'm sorry Millie, but you need to collect it.

I can take you to Mr Lawfus and get you back to the portal, I'll wait for you... I just hope you get this message soon! From Whartorlli.'

Millie knew she had no choice but to meet Whartorlli on the other side of the portal, and soon. She'd thought about posting a note back saying, 'No thank you', but then nothing would be resolved. Millie even considered trying to convince her family to move to a new house, but that would never happen, the house meant too much to them and held too many memories. She was glad to hear that Ophelia was safe, and if she stayed away The Army would soon relax their patrols, which was one worry off her mind. But this did little to console her, she wished that she had another option other than going back to Morendale, but there wasn't. She had dragged Oliver along into danger and had put Ophelia and Whartorlli in harm's way. Now it was her *cat* that was keeping the danger alive. She needed to meet Whartorlli as soon as possible – it had to be tonight.

Before she'd received Whartorlli's note, she'd planned on telling Oliver the outcome of Plan A and that they needed to collect the vial; but she'd created the problem, and decided she was the one who had to fix it. She thought about texting Oliver to let him know what she planned to do, but she knew that he would somehow stop her, or try to go with her; so, she decided against it.

Millie, Mark and Carla sat around the dining table. Millie had once again spent the day with her mum. They'd gone to the Post Office in the morning and then to see her nan for the afternoon. It wasn't much of a punishment; Millie was actually enjoying the time with her mum.

Jane placed a steaming bowl of fajita mix in the middle of the table next to the fresh wraps. Millie smiled as she watched Carla's face light up at the sight of her favourite meal laid out on the table.

"OK guys dig in," announced Jane.

Carla was first in, spooning heaps of the mix into her wrap. Millie hadn't seen Carla this happy in a long time.

Life on her side of the portal was finally coming together, she had stood up to the girls who made her life a misery, her parents were treating her like less of a victim; and they were paying more attention to Carla, which made her less hostile. As she sat at the table with her family, she wished that she'd never discovered the portal; her old problems paled in comparison to her now life-threatening problem that she'd brought on herself and others. At that moment she felt more determined than ever to end the connection with Morendale. She had to be brave, not just for herself, but for her family and for Oliver.

Mark turned off the TV, signaling bedtime for the family. Jane stretched and hoisted herself off the sofa.

"Come on girls, bedtime. We'll be up in a bit," she said, planting a kiss on top of their heads.

"Night girls," Mark said, squeezing them tightly.

Millie and Carla made their way up the stairs and along the landing to their rooms.

Carla stopped in her doorway. "Millie!" Millie tried to suppress her surprise before she turned to look at Carla. "People are still laughing about what you did to Jamie and Mora," she giggled.

Millie laughed, "Night Carla."

"Night Millie."

Millie left her door open a crack, as usual. She placed her clothes neatly across her chair and set her alarm for 2:30am. She clipped the lead onto Chris' collar and picked up her phone once more. The urge to text Oliver was overwhelming, it felt wrong keeping this to herself. But she refused to pull him into it again or even worry him; so, she put her phone down and recited to herself that she would be back within an hour or two, no-one needed to know.

Millie was awake by 2:15am, Chris hadn't moved from the bed. She dressed quickly and unclipped the lead. She picked up her phone and stuffed it in her pocket, hoping that if she needed help, she could get signal in Morendale. She stepped out onto the landing and silently closed her bedroom door, careful not to wake Chris. She needed to keep him away, she couldn't risk leaving him alone with the possibility of him using the portal when Morendale was on such high alert.

She made her way through the house without a sound and once again stood at the foot of the tunnel at the edge of the hedges. After taking one last look at her house she knelt down and started her crawl. Just before she hit the bird bath the glow emerged, it shimmered away along with the leaves and branches into the hazy light. Just as before, she felt the sickening fear right before a burst of excitement washed it away, leaving her feeling giddy, and struggling to stay alert. She surged forwards expertly, fighting the spellbinding feeling as she crossed planes from Farnham to Morendale, forcing herself to stay grounded and focused.

Millie jumped down from the hollow, her entire body felt alive with the buzz of the Morendale atmosphere. She fought the urge to bask in the spectacular feeling and view of the forest, which once again, felt like the first time she'd seen it. She dived behind a tree and waited silently, hoping that she'd entered undetected.

"Millie! Hi! I'm glad you got my message, how have you been?" asked Whartorlli, as he floated down from a tree and hovered in front of her face.

"Did anyone see me?"

"No, we're all clear," he answered cheerfully. "Glad you didn't bring Oliver!"

"Whartorlli, I can't stay long," she said hastily, and ignoring his swipe at Oliver. "I need you to take me to collect the potion."

"OK, we need to keep off the paths, that's our best chance," he whispered. "This way."

They weaved through the dense forest amongst the shadows, far from any lanterns that dotted the forest. They came to an area that was well-lit, so they moved through the bushes – like in Farnham, the bushes had also thinned with the seasonal change into autumn. The forest had transformed so much since her last visit just four days ago; the colouring had changed from its bright summer palette to deep rich autumn hues. It still maintained its powerful allure which made Millie want to leave the shelter of the shadows and bushes and explore. She'd always found it difficult to resist the charm of Morendale, and this visit was no exception; making it hard for her to concentrate on her mission. Whartorlli held up his hand, Millie waited as he scanned the area outside of the bushes. He turned to her and signaled that they were safe to walk in the open. As they left the bushes, Millie was once again captured by the beauty of the new remote and eerie area of the forest. Whartorlli flew next to Millie in silence, nervously eyeing the stretch of forest ahead of them. Millie was about to ask him for one of his guided tours of the area to put him at ease when they heard something in the distance.

"Quick hide!" Whartorlli whispered, pointing to a bush nearby.

They jumped in and crouched low. Millie's heart raced, she scolded herself for even thinking about distracting Whartorlli, he was helping her and trying to keep her alive – she had to stay focused.

As the noise got closer, they could make out the sound of gallops and intermittent shouts. She pictured the soldiers hot on Serperus' trail, who had picked up her scent - she moved deeper into the bushes. Whartorlli hovered in front and moved one leaf aside, making a tiny spyhole.

"What is it?" Millie asked.

"I can't see... here," he said, pulling away another leaf for her, big enough for one eye.

She shuffled forwards to look out of the makeshift peephole.

They waited patiently in silence. Suddenly the galloping took a turn down the path adjacent to the bushes they were hiding in. The sound of hooves got louder and so did the shouting. As it got closer the shouting became mixed with screams and the gallop became frantic.

"AAAAAGGGGGGHHHHHHHH!!!!"

"What is that?" Millie whispered, as she tried to grab hold of Whartorlli's tiny arm for comfort.

Just then, something whizzed past in a cream coloured blur, followed by another more colourful blur.

"AAAGGGGGHHHHHH- LEMY!! STOP- AAAAGGGGHHH!!!"

"Oh! Of course, I'm so jumpy these days I didn't even recognise the sound of Mr Gnomello taking his pet llama, Lemy, for a walk!" Whartorlli chuckled, as they rose from the bushes just in time to see Mr Gnomello being dragged along effortlessly by an excitable llama.

Millie winced and wondered how Mr Gnomello was able to keep hold of the lead without his arm being pulled off.

"Come on, we need to go," said Whartorlli, flying low into the next bush, then popping out again irritably. "I said come on! We've not got long you know! Then we've got to find it!" he said, rolling his eyes before diving back into the bushes.

"Find it?" Millie asked, puzzled.

He appeared from the bush once more. "Don't start with the questions," he said, with an exasperated look.

Millie did as she was told and followed Whartorlli through the bushes that lined the path to Morendale Village, hoping that along the way she would get the opportunity to ask her question again.

"How am I supposed to get *there* without being seen?"

They stood at the very edge of the forest looking out onto a large stretch of open field. The vast opening was lit brightly by the full moon. Millie could see everything clearly in the silvery moonlight, and there was nowhere to hide. Across the field was a small stone bridge that arched over a shallow stream, connecting the field to the small old-fashioned village of Morendale.

"You'll be fine," Whartorlli said, unconvincingly. "You just need to get to the bridge - it's not far."

"What do you mean, *you* need to get to the bridge? You're coming with me."

"Well I can just direct you - once you're over the bridge you take the first right down Brickargan Lane-"

"I don't think so, you don't want Chris coming here as much as me, so you're helping me put an end to this world cross-over situation!"

Whartorlli suddenly looked subdued. "You're right, I don't really care for Chris *or* Oliver. But the thought of not seeing you again makes me sad," he said, earnestly. "I mean sure you ask *way* too many questions, you interrupt, you're quite rude, you're not very bright - but in spite of *all* your flaws, I like you and I'll miss you."

Millie couldn't help but laugh at the backhanded compliment. She also had a list of flaws for Whartorlli, but like Whartorlli, despite them all - she was still really fond of him and would miss him terribly.

"I'll miss you too," she said, with a sincere smile.

"Right, let's get you to Mr Lawfus!" Whartorlli said, triumphantly, while he discreetly wiped away a tiny tear from his cheek.

"OK, how?"

"We're going to have to run for it - on three."

"Seriously?"

"1..."

"You haven't got a better plan?"

"2..."

"Are you sure about this?"

Whartorlli stopped and looked over at Millie, "Any more questions?"

"Erm, no."

"Good! 3!"

They were off - Whartorlli flew effortlessly through the air in front of Millie, leaving her literally eating his fairy dust. She pounded forwards, her heart raced as she ran blindly, unable to see a thing through Whartorlli's panicked blasts of golden fairy dust that came in waves behind him. Choking and spluttering she flung her arms in the air, trying to disperse the dust. Losing the battle, she weaved left and right to avoid it.

"We're nearly there!" she heard Whartorlli shout over the loud pounding of her heart.

A second later Millie tumbled down the bank and landed in a heap at the edge of the stream.

"How did you not see this? Why didn't you stop?" asked Whartorlli, confused, looking down the side of the bridge at her, sprawled out on the floor.

Millie picked herself up off the ground and stared at him, her hair in disarray and covered from head to toe in gold glitter - looking like she'd been beaten up by Midas.

"Oh, woops, sorry that kindda happens when I'm nervous!"

She brushed the fairy dust off her face, clothes and hair, and climbed back up the bank towards the stone bridge. Whartorlli went first and gave her the nod that the coast was clear. She pulled herself up onto the foot of the bridge, and what she saw took her breath away. In the far distance stood Morendale Castle, set on a hilltop overlooking the forest and village. The castle glowed in the moonlight, highlighting its intricacy. Towers and turrets stood tall at different levels with hundreds of candlelit windows twinkling like stars. The view of the castle sent shivers through her entire body, giving her goose pimples; her chest swelled with brimming emotion. She'd never seen anything more beautiful and spectacular in her whole life.

"Millie, come on we've not got much time."

Millie jogged across the bridge, Whartorlli fluttered next to her. She cast one last look back at the castle before she disappeared into the streets of Morendale Village.

The streets were cobbled like the paths through the forest, but they were lined with odd houses, each fronted with a small, neat garden; all unique and incredibly charming. They moved quickly and carefully through the village; just as Whartorlli had said - they took the first right onto Brickargan Lane where the path opened into a large square that Millie recognised as the village centre. The square was lined with little shops, Millie noticed a large bottle green sign above the shop closest to her, with 'Pet Shop' hand painted across it in gold. She was intrigued, if Whartorlli had no idea what a cat was, then what would the people of Morendale consider to be a pet – a scaled serpent-like puppy, a winged deer, or a llama that took *you* for walks. She walked over to the bay window and pressed her nose against the glass. She squinted into the darkness, hoping to get a glimpse of the extraordinary assortment of pets.

"What are you doing!"

Millie snapped her attention back to the mission and ran to catch up with Whartorlli.

A few streets later they were outside Mr Lawfus' house. The house was old, narrow and five-storeys high. Compartments protruded from every floor, all sticking out from the main structure of the house without support. Every house along the street was in darkness.

"Is he in?" she asked, concerned.

"Of course he's in it's 3:40am, he's asleep!"

"Oh, right," she said, suddenly aware that time was running out.

Whartorlli flew to the door, Millie followed. He grabbed hold of the solid iron door knocker and beat his small wings, pulling the knocker backwards then letting it go, causing a single feeble knock. When there was no answer, Whartorlli flew towards the door again.

"Let me." Millie reached in front of Whartorlli and knocked the door a few times with ease.

A single light from the house flicked on. No sound came from the house, but they felt the presence of someone standing behind the door, watching through the peephole. Whartorlli flew upwards to place himself directly in front of the peephole to identify himself. Suddenly the door swung open, a hand shot out and grabbed Millie firmly by the arm then dragged her into the house. Whartorlli swooped in after her, before the door closed behind them.

Millie pressed herself against the wall, looking from the man to Whartorlli, who didn't seem alarmed. The man was still surveying the street from the peephole. He was tall with a big build, which made Millie feel instantly intimidated. He turned away from the peephole to look at her, kindness radiated from his hazel eyes. He was about a century younger than Ophelia, which placed him in his seventies. He had a full head of snowy white hair and a handsome friendly face.

"Can never be too careful these days! Looks like yuh've not bin followed. Ophelia said yuh'd come, I'm Mr Lawfus, bu' yuh can call me Bob," he said, holding out his hand.

Millie peeled herself away from the wall and shook his proffered hand, "I'm Millie."

"You've never said *I* could call you Bob!" said Whartorlli, crossing his arms.

"Millie! I understand yuh've got a curious cat! Never sin a cat... shame I din' get tur see 'im b'fore 'is mem'ry-loss potion!"

Millie nodded in agreement. "Yeah he's very curious."

Bob stared at Millie with a smile plastered on his face, she smiled back. After a few seconds they were still smiling broadly at each other. She fidgeted uncomfortably, then she noticed he was mirroring her perplexed expression.

"Erm, do you have the memory-loss potion?" she asked, politely.

"Oh yeah the potion! Sorry, follow me." He walked towards the stairs and caught a glimpse of Whartorlli still sulking. "Fine yer can call me Bob too!"

Whartorlli beamed and followed them up the stairs.

Bob moved from staircase to staircase, from room to room, and every so often they would come to a dead end.

"Nope not 'ere," he would say, then turn and walk in the opposite direction. Millie no longer needed to ask Whartorlli what he'd meant by - *then* we have to find it. Bob clearly needed his own batch of potion, but to gain memory rather than lose it. She wondered whether Ophelia had trusted Mr Lawfus because if he was ever questioned, he'd forgotten everything he knew anyway. She checked her watch anxiously - 4:00am.

Suddenly Bob stopped mid-staircase between the third and fourth floor, he turned to look at Millie and Whartorlli with uncertainty in his eyes.

After a few seconds Millie realised. "The memory-loss potion," she reminded.

"Oh yeah! G'dness me! Back down we go! Don' get old!" he chuckled.

Millie and Whartorlli exchanged a frustrated look and followed him back through the labyrinth-like house.

Eventually they found the potion, it was on the ground floor in a cabinet next to the front door.

"Well I don' 'member puttin' this 'ere!" he laughed, handing the potion over to Millie, who wasn't surprised that he hadn't remembered putting it there.

"Thanks," said Millie, relieved to have finally found it. The vial was a long cylinder, around the same size as Whartorlli, and was filled with a purplish pink liquid, capped with a cork.

"Now listen tur me," Bob said, fixing her with a serious look. "Don' linger 'round! I don' know where yer've come from, an' I don' wanna know, bu' jus' ge' back quick! I'd 'ate ter think of anythin' bad happenin' ter yer!"

He looked over to Whartorlli with concern written on his face, silently asking him to look after Millie. Millie understood why Ophelia had trusted him with keeping the potion safe. Mr Lawfus knew that Millie was *different,* yet he hadn't probed for more information. They trusted each other without needing an explanation, it reminded her of her friendship with Oliver.

Whartorlli nodded in response to Bob then looked at Millie. "We'd better get going."

12

They made their way back to the portal less cautiously, aware of time and anxious to complete the mission. Millie clutched at the pocket that contained the vial of memory-loss potion.

She recognised where they were, they'd been there just an hour or so before, where Mr Gnomello had been pulled along by his llama. The harsh tracks in the grass had now gone, Millie could only assume that it was down to the work of the wood nymphs.

"Not long now Millie. It's just through that next row of bushes."

With the finish line now in sight, Millie crawled faster through the bushes. She planned to go straight to her room, armed with Chris' favourite new brand of food, laced with the potion.

Finally, the familiar layout of the forest where the portal was concealed came into view.

Millie turned to Whartorlli, "Thank you so much for everything."

"It's been my pleasure. And who knows, one day we might see each other again!" Whartorlli said, hopeful.

She smiled. "I hope so."

Whartorlli flew forcefully at her face and embraced her in a tiny hug.

Millie chuckled fondly and gave him a kiss on his small cheek, "Until next time."

She crawled out from the bushes and headed towards the hollow. As Whartorlli watched her leave, his cheeks flushed pink and his bright blue eyes glazed with tears.

As she walked, sadness swelled inside of her; she knew she'd never see Whartorlli or Morendale again. She'd been so preoccupied with getting the potion, and consumed with fear and determination, that she'd forgotten to take the time to absorb the beauty and enchantment of Morendale for the last time. She looked up at the inky blue night sky, barely visible behind the millions of twinkling silver stars. The moon was so large she felt that if she climbed a nearby tree, she could touch it. One more step and the portal would be aglow, she stopped and looked over her shoulder to see Whartorlli's face one last time. She saw the fear in Whartorlli's eyes before the powerful blow knocked her to the ground with so much force the vial flew out of her pocket and smashed on the ground.

"No!" screamed Whartorlli, as he flew over to her.

Millie's vision was blurred, she'd took a heavy blow to the head. She rolled onto her back and watched helplessly as Serperus swiped his large paw at Whartorlli, sending him flying backwards into a bush and out of sight. She shook her head, trying to regain consciousness; her legs were unstable, and her ears rang, the stars that were once above her now surrounded her. Millie curled up on the ground and waited for Serperus to strike. Suddenly she felt vibrations on the ground, over the ringing in her ears, she heard the familiar sound of soldiers marching.

"What is it, Serperus?" a voice shouted, as his footsteps grew closer. "What have you got there boy!"

Millie felt Serperus retreat and his presence replaced with the soldier, "Sergeant, Quick!"

A crowd formed around her. Slowly her vision focused and the ringing subsided, but Millie continued to play dead. She was close enough to the portal to make a run for it, but she couldn't; she had to keep its existence secret to protect her family, no matter the cost.

"Hmm what do we have here then?" said the sergeant, as he walked confidently through the crowd, stopping at Millie.

"Shall we load her up and take her to Hillontropa? We're making a trip there tomorrow, Serg."

"No! *Look* at her," the sergeant said, curiosity in his voice. "This is the one that was here the other night. We need to take her to The Queen."

Mark and Carla were sat at the table waiting for their pancakes, while Jane did her usual dance around the kitchen.

"Mark can you call Millie again please."

"She's not in school Jane, let her sleep."

"She's coming with me to the garden centre this morning, she needs to get up."

Mark put down his paper and walked to the foot of the stairs. "Millie time to get up!" He waited for the familiar sound of Millie rising from her pit. "Millie!" Hearing no movement, he huffed and made his way up the stairs. "Millie, get up, your mother has to go to the garden centre and apparently you're going with her!" He walked across the landing and opened Millie's bedroom door; Chris shot out of the room through Mark's legs, nearly tripping him up. "Chris!" Mark scanned the room. "Millie?"

Mark watched his wife scrubbing the already clean kitchen sides.

"Sit down, love."

"I can't, there's always something to do," she said, her catchphrase sounding unsteady and weak.

Mark stood from the table and went to her; he stopped her hand mid-scrub and prised her fingers from the sponge. He guided her over to the table and helped her into a seat.

"Jane, they *will* find her," he reassured, trying to make eye contact to solidify his statement. He pulled Jane closer and rocked her back and forth. "We need to stay positive."

The police had concluded that Millie had ran away. After searching her room they'd found her nightdress left neatly on her chair, and noted that her jeans, t-shirt, shoes and phone were missing. They'd questioned Oliver and her friends at school; Jamie and Mora had claimed that Millie was a good friend of theirs and insisted on being interviewed. Jane and Mark had gone over every detail of the last few days; nothing seemed different about Millie, in fact to their short-lived relief, she'd seemed more like herself again. Jane blamed herself for being so hard on her after the incident at school, Mark had tried his best to comfort her and reassure her that she'd done the right thing. But no matter what Mark, the police, or anyone said, Jane still felt responsible.

Carla sat up in her room listening to the muffled distressed voices of her parents. She wiped at her swollen sore eyes, then to distract her mind, she hauled herself off her bed to tidy her room. Carla also felt guilty, she couldn't count the amount of times she'd wished for her little sister to disappear. Like Jane, she blamed herself; at the time, she'd meant it – she had wanted her sister out of the picture. Whenever they'd had spaghetti and meatballs – she wished it. Whenever Jane had asked her to keep an eye on Millie at school – she wished it. When Mark asked her to be nice to Millie at home – she wished it. She'd wished it, and she'd been granted it; and now, she'd give anything to have her sister back. She would eat spaghetti and meatballs for the rest of her life. She would spend the whole day at school watching Millie, making sure she was happy and safe; and cherish her at home. She gave up tidying her room and sat back down on her bed; no matter what she did she couldn't distract her mind. She thought about all the times she had been in that exact spot on her bed, wishing for her sister to disappear. Now she sat there wishing as hard as she could for her sister to come home.

Oliver rode up to the gate, he propped his bike against the fence and jogged to the front door.

Ding-dong.

Oliver waited anxiously. He had no idea what to say but knew anything he did say he would feel guilty for, because most of it would be lies. The police had questioned him, and he'd answered the best he could, without mentioning the unbelievable truth. He'd cleared all his messages from everyone, including Millie, hoping he could pass it off as a regular thing he did. But it'd only raised suspicions with the police, and Oliver knew that they suspected that he knew more than he was letting on. He'd gotten the impression that they took the disappearance less serious once they'd suspected he knew where she was and thought that he may have been in contact with her before erasing his messages.

Suddenly the door opened. "Oliver, come in mate," beamed Mark, as he stepped aside to let him in, joy spreading on his face at the sight of Millie's friend.

"Hi Mr Shepherd, I just wanted to come and see you all."

"Of course, you're welcome here any time - you know that."

Oliver nodded. "How's Mrs Shepherd?"

"Not good," he answered, nodding towards the kitchen.

Oliver walked to the kitchen, followed by Mark. She was sat at the table; her eyes were red and puffy. Tears streamed down her cheeks silently as she held one of Millie's t-shirts to her face.

"Hi Mrs Shepherd."

"Oh Oliver, hi!" she said, jumping to her feet and hugging him tightly. "Can I get you anything?"

"No, I just wanted to stop by and see you all."

"I'm so glad, here... sit down."

Oliver sat. "No news?"

"No, nothing. I just can't think where she would be."

"Me either," his first lie.

"I know, you've been a great help to the police – thank you. It must be really hard on you."

Oliver looked down, he didn't care how hard it was on him, he'd do anything to get his friend back – even Plan Z.

"She will come home, I know it," his second lie. He knew where she was, and he knew that he was the only one who stood a chance of saving her, but whether he could was another story. Serperus' snarling face came to the forefront of his mind, he shook the thought from his head and hugged Jane. "Is Carla home?"

As he climbed the stairs, he played his speech repeatedly in his head. He was going back for Millie, but he couldn't do it alone; he needed Carla's help. Millie had proved to him that *she* wasn't crazy, which had taken a lot of planning. As he planned what he was going to say to Carla, he realised that convincing her that *he* wasn't crazy in such a short time and under the circumstances was near impossible.

He took one last deep breath before knocking Carla's door.

"What?"

"Carla it's me, I need to talk to you."

"Go away."

"Nope."

A frustrated growl came from inside of the room followed by pounding footsteps before the door swung open. "What do you want?"

"Can I come in?"

Carla stared at him viciously.

"Please, I've got a bigger and badder version of you at home, you don't scare me," he said, as he squeezed past her into the room, thinking his brother would've kicked him backwards over the banister by now if he'd tried this with him.

She slammed the door behind him.

"OK...." he said, pacing the room, "I've got something to tell you that you're not going to believe, but I need you to be open minded." He looked at Carla, trying to read her expression – nothing. He felt an inner smile spread within him as he thought back to the similar conversation with himself and Millie, but now he was on the other end of the conversation. "I know where Millie is."

"What! That's great – have you told my parents... or the police?"

"No! They can't know."

"Why not? What are you talking about, we need to get my sister!"

He raised his hands, pleading with her to lower her voice. "I know we do, and when I say *we,* I mean me and you."

Carla tilted her head perplexed.

"Look - aggghh – this is hard to explain." He paced frantically. "Millie found something - something she shouldn't have. We went there and there are bad things there." He paused, waiting for Carla to absorb the first part of information. "We both promised we would never go back there again... but we had to block it to stop anything from coming out because stupid Chris kept going back!" She looked at him like he'd gone mad. Reading her expression, "Yeah you're right I'm making no sense... OK," he said, sitting on the bed and taking a moment to compose himself. He took a breath and started from the beginning, "There's a portal in your garden. It leads to a parallel world, like some crazy magic. Trust me I didn't believe Millie either, but she showed me – it was amazing, you come out of the portal into this huge forest - but not like a normal forest – there are fairies and nymphs and stuff. But there's a mad Queen, she's seriously paranoid and she's got soldiers patrolling the forest - they nearly caught us, with their weird tracker dog; luckily, we got out of there in one piece. Stupidly I believed Millie when she said she wouldn't go back. She told me she'd sorted it and had blocked the portal - but clearly it wasn't sorted! I think she went back for the memory-loss potion..." Carla stared, speechless. "For Chris... he keeps going through the portal - he's a cat, he doesn't know any better. So, what I'm saying is we need to go and get her.... tonight!"

Carla stood motionless, unable to form words.

"I know it's a lot to take in, just take your time."

"Get out."

"What? Carla-"

"I said get out," she repeated in monotone.

"We need to do this Carla; we've not got much time!"

"My sister is missing, and you come to my house and make up a ridiculous story like that! This isn't a game!"

"I'm not making it up! Why would I make it up! Just trust me!" he said, raising his voice in frustration.

"I don't want to hear anymore! Get out! Get out! Get out!" she shouted, pushing him backwards out of her room onto the landing and slamming the door in his face.

Oliver leaned on the banister outside of Carla's bedroom, defeated, and wishing that he had more time to convince her that he was telling the truth. But he was going to do this tonight, with or without Carla; he couldn't wait for her to come around. He had to get home and prepare and be back for 2:30am. He made his way back downstairs, readying himself to explain the commotion to Mr and Mrs Shepherd before he left, which would be his third lie.

As Oliver cycled home, his mind raced; Millie was in trouble and he had to go back to a place that terrified him to find her. He hoped he could find Whartorlli and find out what had happened to Millie. Oliver knew that if she was alive, she would be in Hillontropa – 120 miles from the portal. He couldn't make the journey there, find Millie, and be back to the portal before dawn - he would be gone for a few days. He pictured Mark and Jane with their distraught faces, and his heart ached. He planned to leave his parents a note, hoping it would ease their worry when they found him missing.

"Hey! Aren't you Millie's friend?"

Oliver turned, Jenna was sat on a wall outside of a house, mid-text. Her face flushed red as he looked at her. She got up awkwardly and walked over to him.

"Yeah, and you're Jenna, Millie's 'friend' from school," he replied, using air-quotations to punctuate the sarcasm. "Waiting for your other delightful friends?"

Jenna looked down guiltily, "Listen, I know you don't like me, but I genuinely liked Millie and I'm sorry-"

"What do you mean *liked*, you're saying it in the past tense, like she's gone for good!"

She looked at him sympathetically.

"Don't look at me like that, she's fine! Don't worry about Millie, I'll bring her back," he snapped defensively.

"Bring her back from where?"

He got back on his bike. "Doesn't matter, you'll think I'm crazy."

"No, I won't," she said, grabbing hold of the handlebars to stop him. "Tell me."

Oliver looked her in the eyes, he didn't care what people thought anymore, or who knew about the portal; they'd taken his friend so why should he keep their secret, he thought.

"There's a magic portal to a parallel world in her back garden, that's where she is. I'm going back at 2:30 tonight to go in and bring her back."

She looked at him hurt, she let go of the handlebars and stepped aside. "Fine, don't tell me."

Oliver shook his head and rode off, he felt furious and frustrated, and alone. He focused on what he needed to do before tonight. He needed to find something compact that he could fit in his backpack that he could use to protect himself, he also needed shelter and food. His mind suddenly flicked to his note, it needed to be as light as possible to minimise his parents worry - 'Gone to get Millie, be back soon!' no, he thought, what if he *couldn't* bring Millie back. He racked his brains - 'Gone out, be back in a few days.' no, what if something happened to him and he couldn't get back. His mind clouded with the pressure and responsibility he felt with both bringing Millie home and ensuring his parents weren't left in limbo. He let his mind go blank as he rode the way home. The cool evening air sent chills up his bare arms leaving goosebumps in its tracks. He rode along the quiet path that took him to his town, the rays from the lowering sun strobed through each tree that lined the path. When his thoughts calmed, it came to him - 'Gone to find Millie. Love Oliver.' It was simple and to the point and made no promises in bringing Millie or himself home safe.

13

Millie awoke on the small thin mattress in her cell. As she sat up her head pounded, she rubbed her temple where Serperus' paw had landed. She wasn't sure if it'd been the blow that had knocked her unconscious, or the force she'd hit the ground. She counted herself lucky, even though she had been marched by the soldiers to the castle with Serperus snapping at her heels, things could've been a lot worse.

She could hardly remember the journey through the forest, partly because she'd been terrified that Serperus was going to ignore the instructions of the soldiers and drag her off into the forest; but mostly because she was still fuzzy from the blow she'd taken from Serperus. One thing she remembered clearly was the feeling she'd had when they'd arrived at the edge of the forest. As the trees had cleared, she'd seen the castle perched proudly on the hill in front of them, breathtaking in its enormity and magnificence. The sun had just peered over the horizon, casting the open land and castle in a hazy orange glow. The very sight of the castle had filled her with awe and intrigue, and in that moment, there was nowhere else she would've rather have been. Once they'd arrived over the drawbridge she had been blindfolded and guided through the castle and pushed into a cell smaller than her bedroom – she'd passed out almost instantly.

She was now rested and the fuzziness she'd felt was no longer there, but her pounding head was a constant reminder of the force that she'd been hit. Now her vision was clear, Millie scanned her cell; the floor, ceiling and three walls were a cold black stone, one wall had a small, barred window. The front of the cell was closed off by bars, the cell looked out to a narrow walkway, beyond the walkway was an identical cell opposite. She picked herself up off the mattress and walked over to the window, she pulled herself up to sit on the ledge of the deep stone of the castle. She was small enough to be able to pull her knees up to her chest and sit comfortably in the frame. She looked out between the bars beyond the castle grounds to the forest, hoping to see Whartorlli. She worried for him, they had both been hit with some force and even she was finding it difficult to recover - she was only just able to focus her vision and the fog that clouded her head had only just cleared. Millie thought about her parents, she knew they'd be worried sick. Her thoughts jumped to Oliver, he was the only one who knew where she was, but she wished that he didn't; she couldn't bear the thought of anyone else getting hurt because of her. Millie knew that Oliver would come back to Morendale, and she hoped that he would be more cautious than she'd been. She also knew that he would assume she'd been taken to Hillontropa. She recalled trying to text him before one of the soldiers had taken her phone, but her phone had had no signal. She scorned herself for thinking that she may have been able to get signal in a parallel world when she could barely get it in Farnham. Whartorlli had said that those that were extradited were sent to Hillontropa – she hoped that once The Queen had questioned her, she would be sent there, and hopefully have more of a chance of escaping and intercepting Oliver. Millie thought back to Whartorlli's fearful expression when he'd mentioned Hillontropa. Either way, she thought with uncertainty, no matter how awful Hillontropa was, it had to be better than being locked away in a cell.

Just then Millie heard the squeal of the unoiled metal hinges of the dungeon door as it opened. She jumped down from the ledge and walked to the bars at the front of her cell. The guard marched down the stairs, gradually revealing his feet to his head as he descended each step. He wore brass steel armor that left only his lifeless face exposed. He marched robotically through the narrow walkway lined with cells and stopped outside of Millie's.

"You!" his voice boomed through Millie's cell as it bounced off the walls surrounding her. "The Queen wants to see you."

"Why?"

He didn't respond, he took the ring of keys from his belt and stepped towards the cell.

Millie backed away from the bars. "What does she want with me?"

He ignored her while he examined the keys. When he found the right key, he opened her cell, reached in and pulled Millie out effortlessly by her arm. He closed her cell and shoved her towards the stairs.

She moved forwards hesitantly, knowing she had no other choice. She glanced into the cells as she passed them, they were all empty apart from the very last cell closest to the stairs. She could just make out the silhouette of a woman in the far corner of the cell. Millie squinted as she tried to see if it was Ophelia.

"Keep moving!" the guard groaned, pushing her up the first step.

Millie climbed the stone stairs. When she reached the top, the guard nudged her out of his way against the wall as he reached to open the door. Millie cast a look back to the cell where she'd seen the woman. Relief washed over her as sparkling amber eyes peered back at her - it wasn't Ophelia. The woman stared at Millie inquisitively as she moved out of the shadows towards the front of her cell. Millie could see her presence had caused the young woman to briefly forget her situation. The stairs led out of the dungeon to an elaborate corridor, the ceiling was higher than Millie could fathom. The walls were a warm sand coloured stone, and were dotted with candles, giving just enough light for her to see the deep red carpet with golden edging that ran all the way to a single door at the very end of the corridor.

The guard marched Millie along the corridor and through the door. The enormity of the hallway they entered stunned her into stillness. He pushed her forwards and shut the door behind them. The sound echoed through the vast room and far into distant rooms until it was barely audible. The hall was the grandest room she'd ever seen. The deep red carpet spilled out of the corridor and opened out to cover the entire floor. Archways made from the same warm stone from the corridor punctuated each opening to a new room. Large, detailed tapestries and portraits of monarchs wearing extravagant clothing, jewels and crowns lined the walls. A huge chandelier with hundreds of intricate gold candleholders all holding bright flickering candles hung from the ceiling. The circumference of the chandelier spanned across most of the room and lit it in a warm subtle light that made the room feel cosy rather than sparse and cold. The foot of the main staircase started in the centre of the room underneath the chandelier and was as wide as her entire house. It curled around the chandelier to the next floor, then broke off into several staircases that curled above them and out of sight through the archways.

As the guard marched her across the opening to the grand staircase, the feeling she'd felt when she'd seen the castle from ajar returned. The same feeling she'd felt when she saw the castle for the first time with Whartorlli, and again with the soldiers; the feeling of consuming awe. The feeling left no room for Millie to feel anything else, even the severity of her situation. Her mind was focused on the magnificent castle, and all the places she wanted to explore where the echo had reached.

When they reached the top of the staircase another guard stepped forward from the room he was guarding. The guards exchanged a nod before the first guard turned and made his way back down the stairs. Her new escort was even more serious than the last. He reached for her and seized her arm, then guided her to the room he'd been guarding. The doors were as high as the ceiling and he strained to push them open. He pushed her inside where another guard waited near the door. The room was blindingly bright, she squinted and waited for her eyes to adjust. It was dramatically different to the rest of the spellbinding castle; the room made her feel empty and cold. The room was long, rectangular and sparse; floor to ceiling windows lined the pale lilac walls and the floors were grey and white marble. A thin red carpet ran down the centre of the room, all the way to the other end and up two shallow steps to a risen platform where a throne stood; on the throne sat Queen Naleem.

Millie buzzed with nerves and curiosity as their eyes locked across the room. The Queen rose from her throne, and glided down the steps and along the carpet, never taking her eyes off Millie. As Millie watched The Queen walk towards her, she could see what Whartorlli had meant when he said that her kind were basic. The Queen was poised yet exuded power. Millie couldn't put her finger on it, The Queen had an aura about her, something intangible that made her different to herself and the people she knew. She radiated the electric buzz Millie felt when she crossed over the threshold into Morendale. The same feeling she'd felt around Ophelia and Bob, but more intense; she could feel the importance, the royalty, the power, and the magic.

The Queen was laced in diamonds and was dressed in navy blue and black robes. Her crown was encrusted with diamonds and sapphires, yet it was understated, and sat perfectly on her chocolate brown glossy hair. She strode towards Millie with her head held high, oozing importance and authority. She broke eye-contact briefly to glance over to the guard beside Millie. With no words exchanged he grabbed Millie's arm roughly and moved her along the carpet towards The Queen. As the gap closed between them, Millie felt overwhelmed with awe and fear, but above all - curiosity. She wanted to meet The Queen but knew she should try to run. She scanned the room, a guard stood in every corner - even if she did break free, she wouldn't get far.

The Queen stopped midway along the carpet. The guard continued to drag Millie forwards; her heels dug into the floor, but the guard pulled her along effortlessly despite her resistance.

The guard released her arm a couple of feet away from The Queen then walked back to his post at the door.

"Don't be frightened," she smiled, the smile didn't quite reach her eyes. "I won't harm you. I'm Queen Naleem, ruler of this kingdom. Tell me your name."

Millie fought to speak. She'd never seen anyone so beautiful, but through the beauty Millie could see a cruelty; an evil that knocked the curiosity out of her, leaving room for fear to flow through her.

"I'm Millie- I'm nobody," she rambled, desperate to let The Queen know she didn't pose a threat.

"Where are you from, Millie," she demanded.

"I-I'm from here- well, near Thatchly Market," Millie lied.

"Thatchly Market you say. Tell me.... which part?" The Queen eyed her suspiciously, her dark eyes searched Millie's for hidden answers.

Millie didn't know what to say, a fog descended on her brain. The usual armor enclosed her, the same armor that stifled her when confronted with the girls at school.

"Is it a secret," smiled The Queen. "We don't keep secrets in this kingdom, little one. Keeping secrets gets people hurt."

She clicked her fingers; the guard in the far corner jumped to attention and opened the door nearest the throne. Serperus prowled into the room, he padded over to the throne and sat next to it - obedient yet restless as he waited for The Queen's instruction.

Millie's heart pounded against her ribs, she never dreamed she could feel more fear than what she'd felt the night Serperus had chased her and Oliver. Now she was face to face with an evil Queen and the scaled dog from her nightmares who was ready to attack on command.

"I'm from all over really, we don't stay in one place for long," Millie reeled off clumsily.

"Hm." The Queen eyed her. "I can't put my finger on it, but there's something about you. Something.... *different,*" she said, emphasising the word like it wasn't quite the word she wanted; but was the most fitting she could think of at the time.

"I'm not different," Millie said, panicked, "I-I'm just like everyone else, please let me go... please."

Adrenaline flooded her body; the sight of Serperus and the sinister coldness of The Queen was enough for her to know the ending to the encounter before it had even happened. The Queen enjoyed the fear that Millie now freely displayed. She enjoyed tormenting her prisoners before sending them to Hillontropa or allowing Serperus to finish what he'd started.

"Why were you in the forest?"

"I was just walking, I went for a walk," she answered, her voice trembling.

"My soldiers have informed me that they've seen you there before."

Millie didn't answer, her heart pounded, and her legs became unsteady as she struggled to think.

"I will ask you one more time," The Queen said, lifting her hand. "Why were you in the forest?"

Millie couldn't think of anything she could say. She couldn't mention Whartorlli or Ophelia – the fairies were already on The Queen's radar, and Ophelia was being watched. Disclosing either of their names would bring with it a death sentence to them all. She searched her brain for something, anything plausible to tell The Queen; but it was no good – her mind was paralysed with fear. She didn't respond, she had to protect her friends at all costs, even if it meant sacrificing herself.

"Have it your way," said The Queen, wicked joy spreading across her beautiful face. The air went cold, then began to move around her. The Queen kept her hand held out to her side. Millie's gaze was suddenly pulled to a flicker in The Queen's palm - Millie watched, unable to peel her eyes away. Gradually a blue flame rose from the centre of her palm. It grew bigger and bigger until The Queen held a roaring ball of blue fire in her hand. It grew higher and higher until the flames licked the ceiling. Millie flinched away from the blistering heat of the inferno that raged in front of her. The guards that lined the room were just as terrified as Millie. Serperus tucked his tail between his legs and hid behind the throne. The Queen watched the trembles around the room, bursting with pride. She turned her attention back to Millie, then without warning the flames fired towards her. She screamed and fell backwards onto the floor, shielding herself from the ball of fire. An icy blast rolled over her skin, blowing her damp hair away from her face and drying her tears. She opened her eyes shakily, The Queen smiled down at her triumphantly with wild eyes. The Queen clasped her hands gracefully in front of her. "Now, are you ready to talk?"

Millie trembled uncontrollably on the floor, fighting back her sobs. "I told you! I was walking! Why would I lie! What do you think I was doing!" she shouted through her sobs, tired of The Queen's relentless questioning and intimidation.

"Do you know of the fairies? Of the perytons? And all the other ingrates in that forest who conspire against me?" she hissed, her eyes now blazing with rage. "You are one of them, aren't you?"

"No no! I'm loyal to you, Queen. I would never-"

"Quiet!" The Queen demanded. The Queen thought back to the communication devise confiscated from Millie, displaying a failed message –

'Oliver, they haven't sent me to Hillontropa, they're taking me to The Queen. This isn't looking good so please don't come looking for me. Thanks for being an amazing friend! I love you! Tell my mum, dad and Carla I love them too. I'm so sorry.'

"There was a boy with you. Where is he now?"

"I only met him that day, he said he was from the village."

The Queen had already made up her mind, the questions were pointless. She'd had her fun and now wanted to conclude with a deadly sentence. Even though Millie was just a young girl, she was far too unusual, and it made The Queen nervous; so nervous that she didn't care whether she had all the information she could possibly extract from her. The Queen wanted her out of the picture permanently, and as soon as possible.

The Queen clicked her fingers; Serperus jumped to attention. She stepped away from Millie before she signaled for Serperus to deliver the deadly verdict. Serperus moved slickly away from the throne and down the steps towards Millie. Millie didn't have the energy to run or scream, she lay on the floor exhausted and defeated. Her thoughts transported her; with Carla giving her the silent treatment, and her dad sat at the table with his face buried in the newspaper while her mum sang in the kitchen. She thought about Oliver and felt helpless knowing he would come looking for her and there was nothing she could do to stop him. Tears streamed down her cheeks, she couldn't believe the damage that had been caused and was about to be caused because of her reckless choices.

The Queen watched in content as Serperus stalked towards Millie. She watched Millie quivering on the floor, absorbing her from head to toe, from her dirty trainers to her scuffed muddy jeans and grass stained t-shirt. From her dull blonde hair and milky complexion, to her vivid green eyes and the thin silver chain around her neck with the emerald stone that matched her eyes perfectly.

The scaled dog crouched low to the ground, his lethal teeth exposed, and his rattlesnake tail vibrated with excitement.

"Stop!" called The Queen, holding up her hand to signal Serperus away. His ferocity subsided in disappointment and confusion, he turned away hesitantly and walked back towards the throne. "Guards! Take her back to her cell." The guards exchanged a look of disbelief. "She needs time to think about her situation and reconsider her story."

The guards seized Millie and dragged her backwards towards the door. The Queen watched with contemplation; the hint of a hidden thought escaped her eyes, which Millie couldn't quite identify. She turned back towards the throne just as Millie was pulled from the room.

On the way back to her cell she had been less occupied by the beauty of the castle and more focused on her encounter with The Queen. Once the guard had secured Millie back in her cell, he'd walked back towards the stairs and stopped at the last cell. Even though he'd had to drag the young woman kicking and screaming out of her cell and up the stairs, she'd still managed to compose herself long enough to get a final lingering glimpse of Millie.

Millie sat on the window ledge in her cell and looked out between the bars. She watched as a herd of perytons flew in the distance over the mountains and down into the forest. The sun was setting, casting everything in a pinkish haze and forming elongated shadows across the vast castle grounds. She watched the guards circulating the grounds while Serperus and the soldiers gathered behind the drawbridge in their formations, ready to commence their patrols. Another group of eight soldiers surrounded a large wagon with narrow barred windows at the very top. She knew that the wagon would be used to transport prisoners to Hillontropa, and she hoped to see the young woman. Suddenly a soldier marched from one of the castle doors, followed by a line of prisoners. Millie scanned each of them as they filtered out of the door, hoping that the woman had been sentenced to extradition. Just then the young woman appeared, Millie's heart leapt, and she smiled inwardly. The woman craned her neck towards Millie's cell window before one of the soldiers pushed her into the crowded wagon and closed the door. The wagon jumped into life and rolled away over the drawbridge without assistance. As Millie watched the wagon roll across the land separating the castle and the forest, she wondered what was so different about her. In her eyes, she was the same as the people of Morendale, just duller - in every aspect.

Millie heard shuffling behind her. "Hey! Girl."

She turned to see a young man in his late teens in the cell opposite. She hopped down from the window and walked over to the bars. She could tell that he'd been in his cell for a while; he was covered in dirt and his clothes hung loosely on his thin frame, yet he had that same aura that all Morendale people shared.

"Did you just see The Queen?" he asked, with a frown.

"Yeah," Millie said, still shaken.

He sat on the floor cross-legged. "Wow, so you must be *the* girl they've been looking for. I've been in this cell for well over a week, they've put everything on hold because they've been searching for you! I can see why, you look so-"

"Different, yeah I know," Millie snapped.

Sensing he'd offended her he moved away from the subject, "They usually question prisoners straight away and then, well, you know."

Millie nodded, not really knowing what 'you know' meant, but she didn't care.

He tried again to make conversation, "So, you're going to Hillontropa then? Strange that they've brought you back here, normally they just load you up and drop you off during the patrol."

"I'm not going to Hillontropa," Millie said, defensively. "They're taking me back for more questioning."

The boy looked confused. "What? When?"

"I don't know, when The Queen gets bored probably."

He stared at her, trying to find a reason why The Queen would keep her around.

"What are you looking at!" Millie shouted.

"Nothing," he said, as he tried to look away but didn't quite manage it. "It's just that The Queen never questions anybody twice." Millie looked at him, now paying attention. "She only questions people once - at most! Sometimes people just get sent straight to Hillontropa, or they get the other thing."

"The other thing?"

"Erm, sentenced to death," he answered hesitantly, not wanting to scare Millie but not wanting to lie.

"Oh. The Queen called Serperus into the room just now. Is he... the one who? You know?" she asked, as a chill made its way down her spine.

He looked at her sympathetically, he knew that neither of them had a chance.

"That's the best way to go, it's quick!" he said, sincerely. "The worst is when she uses her powers - of course no-one's ever lived through either of them to confirm the theory but that's what people say."

Millie nodded, suddenly desperate to be alone and out of the boy's inquisitive gaze.

"I'm Thomas, by the way."

"Millie."

"Nice to meet you."

Millie smiled weakly, she felt sick. She knew Thomas was just trying to console her, but he wasn't particularly good at it. The truth was there was no way she could be consoled in the situation. She'd nearly been on the receiving end of both Queen Naleem's powers, and the jaws of Serperus during her questioning. Millie could only hope that The Queen had sent her back to her cell so she could reconsider her sentence. She envied the prisoners that had been packed into the crowded wagon and sent to Hillontropa. Even if it was as awful as Whartorlli had said, it still couldn't be worse than the alternative.

14

At 2:30am, Oliver was outside of Millie's house. He'd dumped his bike half a mile up the road and ran the rest of the way with his backpack strapped securely to his back. He'd camped often with his dad and brother, so he knew the essentials he would need; a sleeping bag, a small tent, a torch, a water canteen and filter, fire starter, first aid kit, rain jacket and snacks. He'd also brought something that wasn't on the essentials list for a camping trip - a small wooden baseball bat for Serperus. Oliver had left the note on his pillow, he'd wanted to leave a letter just in case the worst should happen; but he decided against it – he wasn't going to write himself off before he'd even tried.

He stood at the gate, determined, and ignoring the fear flipping around in his stomach. He opened the gate and stealthily tip-toped through the shadows to the fence that separated the front and back gardens. He took off his backpack and, keeping hold of the strap, he heaved it over the fence and lowered it soundlessly to the ground. He placed his foot on a protruding panel and lifted his other foot off the ground.

"So, you *are* serious about this huh?"

Oliver jumped and fell from the fence. He looked over to the gate where the voice had come from.

"Jenna? What are you doing here?" he asked, irritably.

"You said you were going to find Millie here tonight. When you left you seemed really annoyed that I didn't believe you, so I thought I'd see for myself."

"Well, now you know I *am* serious - go home!"

"I can help-"

"I don't need *your* help," he said, as he turned back to the fence and prepared to climb.

Jenna felt a wave of embarrassment and walked away quickly.

Oliver needed help, even if it was from a girl that had assisted in making Millie's life a misery.

He took a deep breath. "Wait," he called after her, she turned expectantly. "Actually, I could use some help."

Jenna smiled as her embarrassment slipped away. "You could use some *help*......" she said, playfully.

Oliver gritted his teeth, already regretting his decision. "I could use some help, *please* - now get over here we haven't got much time!"

Oliver climbed the fence with ease and waited on the other side for Jenna. After a few seconds of scratching and laboured breathing from the other side of the fence, it suddenly went quiet.

"Everything alright over there?" Oliver asked, impatiently.

"Erm, not really, I've never done this before."

"Well, not *many* people have gone through a portal to a parallel world. Just get over here and we'll go through fast - like ripping off a plaster!"

"No, I mean I haven't climbed a fence before."

Oliver put his hands to his face. What had he gotten himself into, inviting this girl along, he thought. He was used to Millie, who was good at most things - apart from bowling. He considered telling her to turn back and go home, but he needed help. He swallowed his annoyance and willed himself to be patient.

"Right, just... put your foot on the panel sticking out and pull yourself up."

"OK."

He heard her hurl herself at the fence. After more scrambling and exaggerated huffs, her head popped up above the fence.

"Good... now just pull yourself up and fling your leg over, so you're sitting on top of the fence."

Using all her effort, Jenna heaved her torso on top of the fence. She had a brief rest before taking three attempts to swing her leg over.

Oliver watched with his arms folded and frowning in disbelief. "Wow, you made that look hard. Now just jump down."

"Jump? No, it's too far," she said, perched on the fence and shaking her head while accessing the distance to the ground.

"It's really not, I've just done it and *look*, I'm still walking – jump."

"I can't," she said, frozen.

"1, 2, 3... jump!"

She didn't move. Oliver turned his back to her to hide the exasperation on his face. He thought about knocking her down with his backpack but instead he took a deep breath to calm himself down.

"OK Jenna, let's try-aagghhh."

Jenna jumped and misjudged her landing; she stopped herself from hitting the ground by landing on Oliver and pushing him over. She flushed red as she watched him jump to his feet. Oliver recited in his head, 'She's down from the fence, that's all that matters.'

He picked up his backpack. "Right. Good. Let's go," he sang stiffly, his cheery tone not matching his furious expression.

Oliver walked over to the bushes, he saw the bird bath leaning against the fence, and his heart sank; he'd failed his friend, he was angry with himself for not being there to support her when blocking the portal.

"So where is it?" Jenna asked, joining him at the foot of the tunnel.

Oliver nodded towards the bushes. It suddenly dawned on him what he was asking of Jenna.

"Listen, Jenna, you don't have to come with me, it's dangerous."

"No, I want to."

"You don't understand, it's dangerous like - we're probably not going to be coming back kindda dangerous."

"Look, I feel bad for how my friends made Millie feel, and you were right, I did nothing to stop it... I just want to make things right."

Oliver could see the desperation in her eyes; the need to put a stop to the inner torture she'd been putting herself through. He thought about trying to deter her again, but he knew it would be pointless - she would follow him no matter what he said.

"Sure?"

"I'm sure. What's your name anyway?"

"Oliver," he answered, warming to Jenna. He threw his backpack into the bushes. "Ready?" She nodded in response. "Follow me."

Oliver crawled through the bushes, followed by a hesitant and squeamish Jenna. Just before they bumped into the bird bath it dissipated along with the fence as the portal activated. He heard Jenna stop and gasp in amazement, he reached back to pull her along. They crawled through the green haze, the further they crawled the more the mud beneath them solidified. Oliver could hear Jenna fidgeting behind him; he crawled faster, all the while trying to keep the warm feeling he'd had about Jenna before they started their crawl. Suddenly he felt the tingling of Morendale's atmosphere prickle at his face, he ploughed forwards.

Oliver heaved himself out of the hollow into the forest and landed in a superhero-like crouch. He stayed in the position, only using his eyes to scan the forest thoroughly. When he was satisfied the area was safe, he reached through the hollow into the glow and grabbed hold of his backpack; he pulled the strap and both the backpack and Jenna fell out of the hollow. She hit the floor then shot to her feet instantly, dancing round while flicking her hair and smacking herself.

"What are you doing?" Oliver hissed, irritably.

"I think there's a spider on me! Get it off! Get it off!" she shouted, aiming the top of her head at Oliver.

"There's nothing there," he said calmly, wishing he hadn't pulled her along with him when she'd stopped in the portal.

"There *is* I can *feel* it!"

Oliver rolled his eyes and pretended to pick something out of her hair, "There you go, you're safe – that was a close one, just about escaped with your life."

She smiled at him sarcastically.

Oliver looked for signs of Millie as he walked towards the path. Jenna followed, twitching while looking around in awe. Something caught Oliver's eye near the edge of the opening, he jogged over to it; it was the broken vial. He stared at the shattered glass as he tried to form a positive scenario in his mind. The smashed vial proved that Millie had been there and had gotten the potion. He imagined how relieved she would've been when she had the potion, and then had been so close to home. He hoped that the soldiers had intercepted her at the portal, and not Serperus.

"What is it?" asked Jenna, as she looked over his shoulder, still randomly smacking invisible bugs on her arms.

Oliver wiped his eyes roughly. "Nothing."

Fueled by determination, Oliver marched towards the path, Jenna walked quickly to keep up. They took a right towards Thatchly Market and stopped at the sign pointing along the path to Hillontropa. Oliver set his backpack down on the ground at the junction and opened it up.

"Oliver! What took you so long?"

Jenna turned first, she screamed and smacked Whartorlli out of the air.

"Jenna no! He's a friend!" Oliver shouted, too worried to enjoy the sight of Whartorlli getting a smack.

"I'm sorry! I'm scared of moths!"

Whartorlli sat up and rubbed his face. "I'm not a moth, I'm a fairy! Wow Oliver, I thought *you* were dumb."

Oliver knelt to where Whartorlli sat recovering. "Whartorlli, where's Millie?"

"They took her, I'm so sorry. We had the potion and we made it back to the portal, then Serperus came-"

"Serperus?" questioned Jenna.

They ignored her.

"He knocked her to the ground, then knocked *me out*!" Whartorlli continued. "When I woke, she was gone."

Oliver looked down at the ground, devastated.

"No, Oliver, I think she's OK! I wasn't out for long; the sun hadn't even risen by the time I woke! The soldiers must've gotten to her, otherwise things would've been... messier. They must've taken her to Hillontropa!"

Oliver sighed, relieved. "Alright, Whartorlli, you stay here and watch the portal. Knowing Millie, if they've taken her there, she'll be trying to escape. If she makes it back to the portal, get word to me... somehow," he directed, assertively and with renewed hope.

"The perytons are always flying around the kingdom, I could get a message to you through them."

Oliver nodded in appreciation, then looked over to Jenna, who was still staring at Whartorlli.

"Hey, take this." He threw her the bat and then pulled the torch from his backpack.

As they approached the first bend along the path to Hillontropa, they cast a final look back to the slight silhouette of Whartorlli, before they turned the corner into darkness. Oliver shone his camping torch along the dark footpath. The route was different to the others he'd seen; it was overgrown, wild and eerie, and not in the endearing way the rest of the forest was. Oliver wondered why it wasn't lined with lanterns like the other pathways, and why the nymphs had left this patch without care. He could barely see more than a few metres in front of him, he felt as though they were being watched by millions of eyes that were dotted along the outskirts of where the light touched. His heart raced and his skin prickled with heightened senses; his hearing became acute as he tuned into the forest.

A firefly dipped from a tree and bounced in the air towards them, shining light beyond the beam of his torch; to Oliver's relief the next few feet looked clear of threats. The firefly danced closer, Jenna swung the bat and just missed Oliver by an inch.

"Woah! Watch what you're doing with that!"

"Sorry, I don't like things that fly," she said, holding the bat close.

"Jenna, I hate to say this, but that bat is meant for something far scarier than a fly!"

"What's it for?" she asked, jittering with nerves.

"I hope you never find out, but you'll know if you see him," Oliver answered, trying not to picture Serperus' terrifying face, or even mention his name; scared it would somehow summoned him.

They walked cautiously along the dark path in silence, watching their footing on the uneven cobblestones. After a couple of near misses with his nose, Oliver was less occupied by the invisible eyes along the pathway, and more alert to Jenna and her sporadic bat-swinging. He considered taking the bat away from her, but then after considering the alternative of her screaming-slapping dance routines, he decided a broken nose was the lesser of the evils.

Oliver moved his torch from the path to the bushes either side of them, the beam fell on a purple ladybird on one of the leaves. He smiled as he thought back to the first few minutes in the forest with Millie, when he'd been delighted to see a ladybird just like it in the bushes instead of the *then* faceless beast.

"Look!"

"It's only a ladybird don't swing!" he shouted, shielding his face.

"No - look! Is that light?"

Oliver looked straight ahead to where Jenna pointed. All tension left his body when he saw the light at the end of the dark path where the forest once again opened. He charged towards the opening; Jenna grabbed hold of his hand to keep up. In normal circumstances he would've shook his hand free, but he didn't care; he was exhilarated to see the light and couldn't wait to be out of the darkness. His purposeful stride broke into a jog, he gripped Jenna's hand tighter to pull her along with him.

They breathed in the open air as they came out from under the canopy of trees and into the moonlight. The forest was darker than the area near the portal, and wildly overgrown; moss covered most of the footpath, making it barely visible. There wasn't a lantern in sight; the forest was lit solely by the moon and stars, which cast the forest in a silvery filter. Oliver spotted a battered sign ahead of them that read 'Hillontropa'; it pointed along the moss-covered path, which ran alongside a wide lake. At the far edge of the lake was a tall steep mountain, where a waterfall trickled down into the water.

Oliver suddenly realised Jenna was still holding his hand, he subtly pulled it free and heaved his backpack off onto the floor to put the torch back inside.

He looked at Jenna, she was still clutching the bat. "Think I'll take that," he said, plucking it from her grasp.

They walked along the path towards the lake in silence, feeling more comfortable now that everything was in view, and taking in the peacefulness and beauty of their new surroundings. The waterfall trickled gently from the face of the mountain and splashed softly in the lake below. The dark water glittered as the ripples grew outwards throughout the lake towards the shore, shattering the reflection of the large bright moon and millions of sparkling stars.

Oliver let the tranquility wash over him, allowing himself to briefly forget his worries and doubts. He looked out across the lake; something caught his eye that caused him to stop in his tracks and grab for Jenna's hand. Startled, she looked at Oliver, he stared across the lake; she followed his eye-line and searched the shimmering lake. When her eyes found what Oliver was seeing, her breath caught, and she gripped his hand tighter. Floating just above the surface, in the centre of the lake, were luminous mint green eyes and the top of a magenta haired head. They stared in shock as the eyes stared back at them. Mesmerised, Jenna tried to move forward but Oliver pulled her back by her hand and held her tightly in place next to him.

The head rose slowly out of the water, revealing her face, and its ghostly grin. Suddenly she sank beneath the surface and reappeared within a second at the shore, the force and speed sent waves over the grass. The water rolled from her hair like it was made of feathers, leaving it completely dry. The pink hue fell luxuriously around her shoulders, the colour enhanced the shocking shade of her eyes. She floated near the shore, watching them rigidly, like they were skittish animals ready to bolt if she moved. Then, almost as though she felt they were now comfortable enough for her to do so, she lifted her arms out of the water onto the grass; like she was about to heave herself out. They gasped and stepped back instinctively. The woman giggled and leant on her elbows, she tilted her head to the side, enjoying their shocked expressions. Then, playfully, she arched a mother-of-pearl-coloured tail out of the water, sending a small wave through the air that landed at their feet. Her tail curled and settled gracefully behind her head; scorpion-like.

An awe-filled smile spread across Jenna's face, "Wow, she's a mermaid."

Jenna tried to move forward again. The mermaid smiled and reached her hand out to Jenna. Oliver pulled her back, and out of reach. The mermaid eyed him and settled back into the water patiently. Jenna tried to pull away from Oliver, but he held on tight, remembering what Whartorlli had said.

He grabbed hold of her shoulders and turned her towards him, but her gaze never left the mermaid, "Listen, mermaids are dangerous, you can't trust them."

"Who told you *that?*" asked the mermaid, amused.

"My friend."

"I'm afraid to tell you that your friend lied to you," she said, a smile never leaving her lips and her mint eyes never blinking.

"We're looking for our friend," said Jenna, remembering why they were there. "She's about my height, pale, blonde straight hair to about here.... have you seen her?"

"Yes, I have, I believe you'll find her in Hillontropa."

"Great, thank you!" beamed Jenna.

"But you won't get there in time. It's too far.... best way is by boat," she said, casting an eye towards a tethered boat further along the shore.

"But isn't this a lake?" asked Oliver.

"Oh no, this isn't a lake - it opens out to the river just up there." She corrected Oliver, pointing into the distance. "I could help you; I can swim quite fast and I can push that boat along easily."

They looked back over to the boat just in time to see an orange mermaid tail disappear beneath the surface next to the boat. Jenna looked at Oliver, comprehending the danger the mermaids posed; there were more of them lurking, watching, and waiting.

"No thank you, we can make our own way," Jenna declined, politely.

"Are you sure? Your friend is in danger, and I could help you take days off your travel."

"We said no," Oliver said, firmly.

The mermaid stared at them, unblinking, her smile faltering and her body ridged. Suddenly she launched herself towards Jenna. They jumped backwards; the mermaid missed Jenna's foot by an inch. Her whole torso was on the ground, she clawed along the grass towards them until only the lower half of her tail was in the water. They bolted back to the path, knowing the further away from the water they got the safer they'd be. When they reached the path, they didn't stop running. Oliver glanced to his side at the river, the mermaid glided through the water at speed. She followed them until the water no longer ran parallel to the path. Just before she hit the edge she turned harshly, sending the water gushing over the shore. When they were far from the edge of the river, several sets of eyes emerged from the water, and glared as they ran along the path into the forest.

They'd walked for three hours and had covered around ten miles. Oliver set up the tent so they could rest before they started again in the morning.

Oliver lay on his back on the lining of the tent. "So, you'll swing a bat at a fly and scream, but a mermaid that wants to drag you into water and kill you - you'll happily talk to."

"I didn't know she wanted to kill me!" Jenna shouted, from inside the sleeping bag at the other side of the tent.

"She wasn't *blinking*, she didn't exactly look friendly!"

"She was smiling!"

"Yeah, because she was happy that she'd found someone as gullible as you!"

Jenna sighed in frustration. "I'm *so* sorry that I'm not as skeptical as you and choose to see the good in people!" she ranted. "People aren't *all* bad you know! Fine, I've made some bad choices with the friends I have, and I've hit a fairy, and spoken to a mermaid; but I'm not a bad person! You treat me like everything about me is bad and I'm sick of it!"

"Jenna, that was a great story - can you tell it again? But first, can you throw me the popcorn? It's in my backpack."

Jenna rolled over in temper, to face away from Oliver.

Oliver could only think about Millie, he had no room for guilt for how he was treating Jenna. He had no idea where his friend was, he could only assume that she was in Hillontropa - but something didn't feel right. He had to find Millie, but he worried for his and Jenna's safety after learning that Serperus wasn't the only threat in the forest. He closed his eyes to try and get some rest, but he already knew he wouldn't sleep.

15

Jane put down the phone and sat on the sofa, new tears brimmed in her eyes. The front door opened and closed - Mark was back from the shops.

He popped his head around the living room door, his greeting smile faded from his face, "What's wrong?" He rushed to her side.

"That was Oliver's dad. He's gone."

"What do you mean he's gone?"

"He left a note to say he went to look for Millie. They found his bike not far from *here*."

Jane was devastated, but she was ashamed to admit that she was secretly hopeful. She felt that if anybody could find Millie, it would be Oliver.

Mark looked at his wife, and he knew; he felt the same way, but wouldn't dare say the words.

"I was just in the shop and overheard someone saying that a girl who lives just down the road is missing too." Jane stared in disbelief. "A Jenna Morgan? Isn't she in Millie's classes?"

"Yes, she is.... what's going on, Mark?" Jane asked, not expecting an answer as she leant her head on his shoulder.

• • •

Carla listened from the top of the stairs. Her mind whirred as she tried to digest what she'd heard; Oliver and Jenna were now missing too. She wished she'd taken Oliver more seriously, even if she had thought he was losing his mind. If she had, she would probably know where he was now, and possibly even Millie, she thought. She had the overwhelming feeling that if she'd gone with Oliver to find Millie, she would've been able to protect them, and bring them home. Since Millie had gone missing, she'd felt an all-consuming guilt. Now that Oliver was missing too, she felt an entirely different level of guilt – a guilt that came with knowing you could've made the difference. She desperately wanted her sister and Oliver back, she saw him as a little brother, and she felt she'd failed them both. Oliver came to her asking for help, and she screamed in his face. She thought back to the conversation in her room, and she wondered why she'd been so adamant he'd made up the story; she knew he wasn't a malicious person. Even if she thought the story was ridiculous and that he was insane, he needed her help, and she'd refused. She knew then that she had to give her parents all the information.

Carla plucked up the courage and walked down the stairs, then through to where her parents were in the living room. Jane looked broken, leant on Mark and staring into thin air. Her face was motionless as tears streamed down her cheeks. Since Millie had gone missing, this was her natural disposition; her face was always sad. Mark also stared lifelessly, teetering on the edge, grasping hold of any bit of strength he could find to prop up his family. As he consoled his wife, thinking no-one was watching, Carla could see just how lost he was.

They hadn't noticed her enter the room. Carla took a steadying breath before she spoke, "Mum, dad... I need to tell you something."

Mark and Jane turned towards Carla; hope flushed their faces. Carla's heart sank, she knew she didn't have the information they were hoping for, but they had to know *everything*.

"Yesterday, when Oliver came to my room, he said something

strange. He was talking about going to get Millie, but he said she'd found something dangerous. He said it was a portal, I think - in our garden.... he asked for my help," she said, looking down at her feet, ashamed of what she was about to say. "And I told him to get out of my room. I thought he was just messing with me or going crazy - I didn't know what to think," she gushed, hating herself for letting him down, and hating herself more as she tried to defend her actions. "Now he's gone, and his bike isn't far away," she continued, looking down to conceal the emotion swelling. "Anyway, I thought you both should know."

Mark and Jane stared at Carla with gaping mouths. She waited, unable to read their thoughts. Jane's face suddenly crumbled. Carla had never witnessed anyone as broken as her mum was at that moment, and it made Carla's heart ache. Mark's expression transformed from shock to pure rage.

"Go to your room," he whispered, barely able to conceal his anger.

"What? Dad, I'm just telling you what he said-"

"Carla, please just go," he hissed, as he held Jane.

Carla turned and ran up to her room. She closed the door quietly; a trail of hot tears ran down her face as guilt overwhelmed her. She hated herself for telling her parents the ridiculous story and causing them more pain. Nothing good was going to come from it, she thought, they'd think either she was losing it, or that Oliver *had* lost it, and then gone on a crazy misinformed search for Millie. She closed her eyes and could see her mum's distraught face after she'd finished her story; a story that was so far from what they'd expected to hear. A fresh wave of tears flooded and spilled from her eyes. She curled up on her bed feeling hopeless and alone, wondering how her family would survive. Even if they did survive, she thought, their family would never be the same.

Jenna crawled out of the tent and stretched as she breathed in the crisp early morning air. She felt refreshed and had forgotten about her spat with Oliver. Oliver crawled out after her, feeling groggy and tired.

They sat in silence, eating fruit packs Oliver had packed in his backpack. After breakfast, Oliver went to work dismantling the tent, while Jenna sat on a nearby log examining her ruined manicure.

"Ew that's disgusting."

"What is?"

"My nails, I need to find somewhere I can wash."

"Well, after last night I won't be going anywhere near water, but you go ahead."

Jenna thought back to the mermaid, with her lifeless hypnotic eyes, and decided she would have to smell for a few days.

"OK," said Oliver, after he'd successfully folded away the tent and sleeping bag and had hoisted the backpack onto his back. "We need to go that way," he pointed.

Jenna stood and followed promptly. The forest was so different in the light of day; it was even more alive than it was at night. The sun beamed through the thinned autumn leaves, casting abstract shadows along the grass. Birds sang happily and creatures rummaged purposefully around the bushes and through the trees. The fear Oliver had felt the night before had no place in the forest during the day. He'd never seen the forest in day light, he marveled at the contrast. The day had brought with it a sense of security. He knew how naive he was to allow himself to lower his guard in the forest, but he welcomed the break, so he let himself enjoy the relaxed morning.

They walked leisurely in silence along the overgrown pathway. The path ran underneath a canopy of burnt orange leaves which provided shade from the warm autumn sun. They walked single file as the wild bushes closed in on the path and made it narrow. Oliver led the way, moving back the branches to allow Jenna through. She gave him a grateful smile and followed closely. He was trying his best to be patient with her, but he knew if a branch was to so much as graze her arm, it would send her into another nervous fit; which would only trigger him to say something else that he would later regret. They waded through the bushes and came to an opening in the forest where there was a vast pool of water. The water was still, like a mirror; it curled around some land that jutted out from the perfect semi-circle that encased it. Unable to see the mass in its entirety, they eyed the water cautiously. Jenna made a move forward.

"Wait," Oliver whispered, putting his arm out to stop her.

"It looks safe. Look, you can see the bottom over there," she said, brightly.

"We can't risk it; it could open into a river around that corner. We need to make sure that this is actually a lake."

"Does it matter?"

"Yeah it matters," he replied, measuredly, careful not to snap at her. "Lakes are closed off, so mermaids shouldn't be able to enter," he clarified, as he started to walk around the edge, leaving a large gap between himself and the shore. "You go that way and see if there's anything leading off it."

Jenna walked around the semi-circle shore in the opposite direction to Oliver. The view was stunning; Oliver investigated the crystal-clear water, between the delicate light pink water lilies, to the light grey pebbles that lined the bed. The sun and trees reflected off the undisturbed water. Suddenly in the reflection, something floated by behind Oliver. He turned quickly, a beautiful woman wearing a pale blue flowy dress glided elegantly into the water and disappeared. The woman hadn't disappeared under the surface like the mermaid – it was as though she became the water. Remembering his words, Oliver smiled and silently thanked Whartorlli; he had just seen a water nymph, the rarest of all nymphs. As Whartorlli had said; the mermaids had driven them to the far corners of the waters, and so he knew the water was safe.

"Jenna!" he called across the lake. "It's OK, it's safe!"

"How do you know?"

"Just trust me!"

She stared at the water, he could see her scanning and deciding for herself whether it was safe or not. He left her to it, he was glad to see that she was becoming a little more cautious.

She made her decision, "Turn around!"

Confused, Oliver did as he was told.

Jenna folded her jumper and jeans neatly on the ground, then took a run up and dived into the lake, "*Wahoo!*"

The splash alerted him she was in, he turned to see Jenna swimming happily.

"Get in it's *so* refreshing!" she shouted, while poking at a water lily.

Seconds later, Oliver cannonballed into the water, "Aagghhhh it's cold!" He swam over to where Jenna floated leisurely and grabbed her foot. "Mermaid!"

She jumped and thrashed around frantically, searching the water. When she saw Oliver laughing, she sighed in relief. "You think you're funny?" she said, as she drove her arms through the water and splashed him, wiping the smile from his face.

Jenna was feeling herself again - clean. She squeezed the excess water out of her hair and watched as Oliver refilled the water bottle, then popped in a couple of purification tablets. It hadn't occurred to her to bring a thing for the journey, although she hadn't expected there to actually be a portal. She was impressed by Oliver's commitment; he'd anticipated being in the parallel world for a while and had planned for it. He was sharing everything he had, which she was grateful for, but it cut his supplies in half. She had no idea what supplies he had in his backpack, but she knew that there wouldn't be enough to get them both to wherever they needed to go and back again. She wondered whether they were doing it all for nothing. A sinking feeling suddenly came over her; Oliver wouldn't stop until he either found Millie, or knew what had happened to her, and she wondered if she had the same commitment.

He tucked the bottle in a side pocket on his backpack, then flung the bag onto his back. "We need to make up time, so we're going to have to move a bit faster."

Jenna didn't move.

"C'mon, we need to go."

Jenna looked at Oliver, unsure how to say what she was about to say, "What if we're doing this for nothing? Our families are worried, we're not even halfway to Hillontropa, and she might not even be-"

"Don't even think about saying it," Oliver warned.

"Come on, Oliver, you can't say you haven't considered she might be-"

"I said-don't say it!" he shouted, as he stormed off along the path, then turned back around to face her. "Look, if you don't want to carry on then *go back!* I don't need you!"

"I'm sorry I mentioned it!"

"Just go away!"

"I said I was sorry, what more do you want?" she said, genuinely, moving towards him.

"What more do I want? Maybe I wasn't clear... I want you to *go away!*"

"Fine!" she shouted, turning to march away then turning back to him in a rage. "You know what... I don't know why I thought I could talk to you, why did I bother! You're mean, you're stubborn, and you're rude!" she listed.

"Oh, I'm sorry - go away, *please!*"

"I forgot you're also sarcastic!" she shot before she turned and stormed back in the direction they came from. She'd had enough, she wanted to find Millie as much as he did, but she had to be realistic. They'd been in Morendale less than twenty-four hours, and already they'd nearly been killed, and they were quickly running out of supplies.

As Oliver watched her go, the familiar feeling of guilt washed over him. Jenna was right, he just couldn't face the fact that Millie might be dead. He also couldn't bring himself to tell Jenna that deep down, he thought Whartorlli was wrong about Millie being in Hillontropa. But without an alternative in mind of where to look for her, he had to hold onto the hope that Whartorlli was right. When she ploughed through the overgrown bushes without so much as a flinch, he knew she wouldn't come back. He took a cleansing breath, preparing himself to go after her and apologise. He knew if she went back alone, she wouldn't make it, but he wasn't willing to go back with her; they needed to carry on. The encounter with the mermaid had brought with it clarity for them both. Oliver now knew that nothing would deter him from his mission to find Millie; not Serperus, the mermaids, or anything else Morendale had to throw at him. The encounter had also forced Jenna to re-evaluate her decision to follow Oliver into the parallel world; it'd made her recognise that she didn't share the same devotion as Oliver did to the mission.

Oliver heard marching in the distance and his blood ran cold. He sprinted along the path to catch up with Jenna. He flew through the bushes and along the narrow path. He saw Jenna in the distance, frozen and listening to the sound echoing through the forest.

When he reached her he grabbed hold of her arm, "Quick we need to hide."

Jenna didn't question him, the look on his face told her everything. The anger she'd felt moments earlier dissipated and she nodded in compliance.

He directed her towards some bushes, far back from the path. She hesitated and looked at him anxiously.

"Trust me, spiders are the last thing you need to worry about," he said, his face marred with dread.

She did as she was told and crawled in.

They waited in silence as the marching grew closer and voices became clear. The soldiers came into view, eight of them accompanied a wagon full of prisoners. It rolled along on its own, magically, with two soldiers at the back, two at each side, and two at the front. Oliver breathed a sigh of relief when he saw that Serperus wasn't with them.

Jenna grabbed Oliver's shoulder. "Is that wagon rolling along on its own?"

Oliver frowned, "You saw a *mermaid* last night - how has *this* shocked you?"

Jenna nodded, reminding herself that she was in a parallel world. "Do you think she's in there?"

"I don't know," he answered, weaving his head as he tried to find an angle in the leaves where he could get a good look through the barred windows of the wagon; in hopes he'd get a glimpse of blonde hair.

"Did you hear what happened?" said one of the soldiers from the front of the wagon.

"Care to be more specific?" chuckled another.

"With The Queen and that girl."

"Which girl?"

"That girl we've been looking for... you know, the one that kept turning up in the forest?"

"Oh yeah, I didn't know she'd been caught!" one of the soldiers from the back said, in surprise.

"Yeah, lucky girl – Serperus found her, apparently George got there before Serperus could do his thing."

"*Very* Lucky."

The soldiers continued to march along the path towards Hillontropa, and away from Oliver and Jenna. As the path narrowed, the two soldiers at the front pulled out their swords and swung the blades at the overgrown branches. "I'm sick of the wood nymphs, thinking they can stop The Queen from sending people to Hillontropa by leaving the path to grow wild!" the soldier called over to the other as they hacked away at the bushes, making the gap wide enough for the wagon to pass through.

Oliver turned to Jenna, "Follow me - and keep quiet."

They moved through the bushes to keep up with the soldiers and listen to their conversation.

The soldiers holstered their swords. "Anyway - The Queen questioned her," the solider continued. He glanced back at the others to check they were listening intently. "Apparently the girl was put back in her cell half an hour later."

Shock rang through the other seven soldiers. "What? Why?"

The soldier shrugged, "Nobody knows."

"Rumour," stated a soldier from the side of the wagon. "Nobody comes out of that room alive, unless they're loaded into here," he said, smacking the wagon.

"Maybe you're right, but I heard it from David - said he was in the room during the questioning."

"David told you! Maybe it *is* true."

The soldiers continued their speculations as they walked along the path towards the lake. Oliver and Jenna waited until they were out of sight before they came out of the bushes.

"I knew it!" Oliver said, smiling broadly.

"Knew what?"

"That she wasn't in Hillontropa, I just knew it! She's in the castle!"

"Hold on, you've dragged me all this way and all along you knew she wasn't in Hillontropa?" she said, with simmering anger.

Oliver gave her an apologetic look, unable to keep the smile from his face. "Erm, well, it was just a feeling. I didn't know for sure that she wasn't there, so I had to go with what Whartorlli said."

Jenna was furious, she marched past him in the direction of the portal.

"I'm *sorry!*" he called after her, as he tried to suppress his laughter.

"Hey, Millie? You awake?"

Millie had been awake most of the night, she rolled over on her mattress to face Thomas.

"Morning!" he beamed.

She smiled. Even though Thomas said the wrong thing most of the time, she was glad he was there. Millie had been locked in her cell for what felt like an eternity, and she was beginning to feel like she was going crazy. Thomas had been in his cell for over a week, and she couldn't imagine how he felt.

She got up and stretched. She went over to the window and stuck her nose out between the bars as far as she could and took a deep breath of fresh air. During her sleepless night she'd decided that she could no longer think about her parents, Carla, or Oliver. She refused to spend any more time dwelling on things she couldn't fix. She couldn't put a stop to her parents' torturous worry. She couldn't stop Oliver from looking for her in Morendale. She was being held captive in a cell, and there was nothing she could do about it. Millie had to think solely about herself, and how she was going to escape. She had to focus and prepare for every scenario, every opportunity, and hope for the best.

"How did you sleep?" Thomas asked, interrupting her thoughts.

Millie looked over her shoulder at Thomas, he was sat cross-legged near the bars, facing her. She grabbed her mattress and pulled it close to the bars, then sat mirroring Thomas.

"To be honest, I didn't. How did you sleep?"

"Same," he answered, still wearing his positive smile. "Too scared to sleep."

"Me too," Millie admitted. She noticed the smile waiver from his face. "So..." she said, brightly - his smile returned. "You never said what you did to get yourself locked up in here?" She tried to channel Oliver, and sound light-hearted.

He laughed, "Well, I was really stupid."

She laughed too, "Why, what did you do?"

"One morning I was on my way to work, and I saw an old man struggling with his shopping. I was running late but I couldn't leave the poor guy – so I helped him to his house. He lived on the edge of the forest, not too far from the village – I dropped his shopping off and ran back to get to work," Thomas explained. "By the time I got to work, I was fifteen minutes late, and the patrols had started.... I walked in and straight away the soldiers questioned me about where I'd been. I told them - I'd helped an old man home with his shopping." He shook his head, like he'd made an obvious mistake and couldn't believe his stupidity. "I told them he lived in the forest, and that was it.... they took me."

"Huh?" Millie asked, confused.

"They like to keep an eye on everyone, if you go to the forest and you don't live there, The Queen believes you're conspiring against her."

"But why the forest? It can't just be because of the creatures there – I've seen her powers and they wouldn't stand a chance... there has to be something more," she said, to herself rather than Thomas.

Thomas shrugged, not attempting to make sense of The Queen's insanity.

Millie recalled Whartorlli saying that the fairies are against The Queen, and The Queen herself had eluded to the fact she also didn't trust the perytons. It made no sense to Millie why The Queen was so threatened by them. Maybe she was just crazy, and it was as simple as that; there was no reason or logic. Or maybe The Queen was concerned about something else, something that *did* pose a threat. She wondered how long she was going to be kept in the cell, and what information she could use to her advantage when she was questioned again.

In the garage, Carla sat on the floor next to James' bed. He was making progress but still had some way to go until his wound was fully healed.

He lay on his large soft pillow on the brink of sleep, while Carla lightly bushed his fur with her hand from head to toe. She still couldn't get the distraught looks on her parents' faces out of her head – she hated herself for upsetting them so much. Her parents knew that over the last few months, Carla and Millie hadn't had the best relationship, but she hoped that they also knew that she loved her sister and missed her.

She was now crying uncontrollably. She looked up and began bargaining with a higher-being that she wasn't sure even existed. In desperation, she listed everything she would do, and everything she would give up, just to strike up a worthy trade that would bring her sister home. She looked down at James who was now in a deep sleep. She stilled her hand and let it rest on his side. Concentrating hard on Millie's face, she screwed her eyes closed and reiterated her deal in her mind. Silent tears rolled down her cheeks, the hole in her chest ached as she pictured Millie in detail.

Just then, she felt a warmth growing from her palm. She opened her eyes and looked down at the hand that rested on James – a white light seeped from underneath her palm. She pulled her hand away from James, startled. She held her hand at a distance and stared at it in disbelief. Using her other hand, she checked through James' fur where her glowing hand had been. There was no damage to his skin, she looked at his leg curiously, then slowly reached for his bandage. She unraveled it gently, careful not to wake him. The bandage fell away, her hand flew to her mouth to stop the scream from escaping. His wound had completely healed, there was no sign it was ever there. She wondered whether she'd bandaged the wrong leg and glanced to his other leg – it was also wound-free. She cast her mind back to just fifteen minutes before and recalled changing the bandage, she'd seen the wound with her own eyes – healing, but very much still there.

An hour later Carla was still sat on the garage floor, trying to think of logical explanations. She gave up and slowly rose from James' side, leaving him curled up asleep in his bed. She couldn't make sense of it; she'd gone through it repeatedly in her head. She left the garage, deciding she needed to sleep on it, hoping it would become clear in the morning. A wave of relief came over her as she calculated the amount of sleep she'd had over the past few nights. With caring for James and Millie's disappearance, she'd barely slept at all. She'd heard of people hallucinating through lack of sleep and stress. She climbed the side of the fence onto the garage roof, she grabbed hold of the rope that dangled from her bedroom window. She was about to pull herself up when she was blinded by a blast of bright green light. Shielding her eyes, she sank to the ground and curled up in a ball on the roof. She waited until the light dimmed enough for her to be able to see. She crawled to the edge of the roof and squinted into the garden as her eyes adjusted to the light. She saw a figure standing in the garden.

"Mum?" she whispered.

Jane crawled into the bushes and disappeared into the light. Carla thought she might faint, she gripped tightly to the edge of the roof to steady herself. In the space of a few days her world had been turned upside-down, and now she was losing grip of reality. She wondered whether she'd brought Oliver's story into her hallucinations. Millie and Oliver had disappeared, and she'd now seen her mum disappear into a blinding light in the back garden, just as Oliver had said. The light slowly began to fade and retract. Carla picked herself up and moved quickly.

16

Oliver and Jenna sprinted back in the direction of the portal, giving the river a wide berth as they past.

Suddenly, the forest lit up as if the sun had instantly risen. They looked up to see a meteor shower shooting across the sky in bursts of brilliant white light. Oliver and Jenna couldn't help but stop and watch, spellbound. They'd never seen anything so beautiful; never ending sparks of light showered across the night sky like millions of sparklers.

Jupiter flew across the sky towards the portal, casting a winged antlered figure along the forest floor. The sight pulled Oliver out of wonderment and he pulled Jenna back into a run.

"What was *that?*"

"*That* was Jupiter!"

Whartorlli sat high in a tree on a wide branch, watching the meteor shower as it arched streams of white light across the royal blue sky. He'd had an unusual few weeks; finding a portal and meeting some unusual characters, and now the celestial display was in keeping with the recent strange events. He'd sat guarding the portal on the instruction of Oliver and Jenna for almost twenty-four hours. He felt useless, he worried for Oliver and Jenna, but he couldn't go looking for them; Oliver had asked him to stay near the portal in case Millie made her way back.

He watched as the magnificent light shot across the sky endlessly like silent fireworks. His attention was pulled away from the sky by the familiar glow of the portal that now regularly emanated from the hollow in the tree opposite. He jumped to his feet and watched anxiously. An arm suddenly appeared from the portal, and blindly felt its way through the hollow. It grasped frantically for something to grab hold of. Her head emerged, she found a nearby branch and pulled herself out of the portal. The woman stumbled out of the tree hollow and landed on her hands and knees. Her distressed eyes searched the forest, she scrambled unsteadily to her feet and moved purposefully towards the path.

She looked different to the others that had come through the portal, and Whartorlli was hesitant to let her see him. He flew silently to the next tree so he could get a better view of her. She reached the signs on the cobblestone path and stopped - she looked left, then right, and then continued along the path straight ahead towards the castle.

Whartorlli heard the familiar rhythmic beating of large wings growing closer. A gust of wind sent him flying side-wards, pinning him flat against the branch he was spying from. The winged stag came into view, he soared through the trees as he descended towards the woman. She backed away, shielding herself from the powerful blasts of his wings as he came to a halt. He landed elegantly and folded his wings against his body. Jupiter stood tall, facing the woman. She slowly lowered her arms as Jupiter lowered himself to the ground. The woman approached the peryton cautiously. She stroked his powerful wing delicately, then expertly climbed onto his back. Jupiter rose and began to gallop through the forest. The woman clung tightly to the mane of fur that ran along his neck. He spread his enormous wings and beat them forcefully. Moments later they left the ground and soared high above the trees among the last of the sparkling surge of the meteor shower.

Whartorlli began to move in their direction. The portal once again became aglow; he turned to watch in disbelief. A young girl tumbled out of the hollow and landed flat on her back, with her eyes closed tightly. Whartorlli flew down to the girl and hovered above her face as he studied her.

"You must be Millie's sister?"

Carla opened her eyes to find herself face to face with Whartorlli. "Oh - you're a fairy, you really are a fairy. I didn't actually believe it - I thought Oliver was just being Oliver, you know," Carla rambled.

"Yeah, totally know what you mean, Oliver is a bit dumb, I don't blame you for doubting him."

Carla stared up at Whartorlli in shock. She sat up suddenly as she remembered why she was there. "Have you seen my mum? She came here a few minutes ago, I need to find her."

"*Oh,* that was your mother! Well, she *was* here - then Jupiter came and took her off that way," he pointed to the sky in the direction of the castle.

"Who's Jupiter? And did you mean to point up?"

"Yes, I did – sorry, Jupiter's a peryton," he clarified.

Carla looked at him, clueless.

"Honestly, your education system is horrific! A peryton is a deer with wings!" he said, as if it was obvious.

Carla instantly thought of James, and the small lumps near his shoulder blades.

"Where did he take her?" she asked, as she jumped to her feet and brushed herself off.

"They were flying towards the castle," he answered, with concern in his voice. "If your mother's here to find Millie, I think she's in Hillontropa - Oliver and Jenna are on their way there to find her."

"*Hillontropa?*" Whartorlli opened his mouth to answer. "Never mind – I have to help my mum." Her heart ached as the words came out of her mouth, she had to help her mum, whether she was looking for Millie in the wrong place or not, even if that meant letting Oliver down again.

"If your mother is right and Millie is in the castle, I don't hold out much hope - Queen Naleem is evil, it's dangerous to even go near the castle."

"I don't care, you need to take me there, *now*! I can help!" she said, urgently, hoping that she could somehow help her mum with what she'd discovered she could do. As she stood on the other side of the portal, she no longer had doubts about what she'd seen. She hadn't been hallucinating; she *had* healed the fawn. She now knew that James was a peryton, and the lumps near his shoulder blades would soon sprout wings. As Oliver had said, there *was* a portal in her back garden, and she had crawled through it and crossed into another world. Carla didn't know *why* this was happening to them, all she knew was that it *was* happening.

"I can't take you all the way, but I can take you as far as the edge of the forest. We better get moving if we're going to keep up with Jupiter!"

Millie lay in the cold dark dungeon, staring at the ceiling of her cell. Suddenly, the cell was lit in a bright white light. She lifted herself off the mattress and moved quickly over to the window. The extraordinarily beautiful sight of the meteor shower took her breath away. It blotted out the moon and stars yet illuminated the castle grounds and the forest with its light.

"Thomas, look out your window!"

He woke with a jolt and scrambled over to look out of the bars, "Woah!" he said, rubbing his eyes. "Amazing," he whispered.

"Have you ever seen anything like it?" Millie called from where she was perched on her window ledge.

"Never in my life! Feels like the atmosphere's buzzing!"

Millie watched the display in silence, contemplating Thomas' words. She could always feel the buzz of Morendale's atmosphere, although the longer she was there, the less she felt it. She couldn't understand why Thomas was now suddenly feeling it. Thomas was just as in awe as she was of the display from the extravagant meteor shower. Millie wondered, if this wasn't a regular occurrence in Morendale, was it linked to the portal.

The metallic sound of the heavy door echoed through the dungeon as it opened. Millie and Thomas moved away from their windows and walked apprehensively towards the front of their cells.

The guard marched down the stairs and along the walkway between the cells. "It's time," he said, as he fumbled with his keys between the two cells. He didn't look at either of them; Millie didn't know who the guard had come for, but she would be devastated no matter who he took. She couldn't imagine being in her cell without Thomas' friendly innocent face opposite, checking in on her. And if it was her time, she would be shipped off to Hillontropa, or worse. The guard found the key he was looking for - her heart sank as he turned towards her cell.

Carla was focused and determined, she sprinted through the forest, her feet pounded along the path. Whartorlli flew behind her, barely able to keep up.

Carla stopped abruptly as they reached the edge of the forest. They watched as Jupiter circled above the castle, then glided overhead, back over the forest. Carla strained her eyes across the open land and across the drawbridge, she saw Jane slip stealthily through the doors into the castle.

"Are you sure you want to do this?" asked Whartorlli.

"I'm sure," she said, as she took a step forwards out of the forest. She looked back at Whartorlli. "Thanks for your help," she said, earnestly, before she sprinted tirelessly across the land towards the castle.

Whartorlli had never met Queen Naleem, but he'd heard enough horror stories to know that he'd probably never see Carla or her mother again. A tear spilled down his cheek as he watched Carla run across the land to her deadly fate.

Oliver came to the forefront of his mind, he had to get word to him that Millie's mother and sister were in Morendale and had gone to the castle looking for her. He beat his wings ferociously, propelling himself towards the portal and leaving a golden trail in his path. He hoped he'd done the right thing in sending Oliver and Jenna to find Millie in Hillontropa. He hoped Millie's mother was wrong about her being in the castle. He'd never heard of anyone coming out of the castle alive, unless they were sent to Hillontropa, and even then, they were never seen again. The situation was hopeless, but he had to stay hopeful, for Oliver's sake.

The castle was dark and eerily quiet, only a few candles lit the grand hallway. The drawbridge had been down, and there wasn't a guard in sight. Jane walked slowly across the vast room, her eyes darted from door to door, not knowing where to turn. Her eyes rested on a portrait on the wall, of a man and woman dressed in royal gowns and jewels.

A noise from the second floor refocused her. She walked eagerly towards the staircase. As she climbed the stairs, she heard rustling from the room directly opposite; her eyes fixed on the room at the top of the stairs. When she reached the top step, she saw that the door was ajar.

Jane pushed the door with all her strength, it opened just enough to allow her to squeeze inside. The long room was only half lit by candles, leaving the farthest half of the room in darkness.

"Mum?"

Jane's head snapped in the direction where her daughters voice had come from. Where the dark half of the room met the light, Millie stood gripping the bars of a stand-alone cage. "Millie? Oh Millie!" Jane sobbed, as she ran towards her.

"Mum!" Millie cried. "How did you know I was here?"

"Don't worry about that. Are you hurt?" Jane asked, reaching through the bars and stroking her daughters tear-soaked cheek while inspecting her from head to toe.

"No, I'm fine. Mum listen, you shouldn't be here, it's dangerous – you need to go!" Millie said, desperately.

"I'm not going anywhere without you." Jane said, fiercely, while she fumbled with the lock on the cage.

"I don't know what's going on, Mum! They've brought me here from my cell and left me in this cage - I don't know what they want with me!"

Jane pulled at the lock and the bars with all her strength, desperately trying to free her daughter.

"Jainella."

Jane's eyes widened, she looked into the shadows behind Millie's cage to where the voice came from. A small glint shone from the darkness from The Queen's crown as she rose from her throne.

"Mum - it's The Queen, you need to go!"

"Millie, just stay calm," Jane consoled, as she peered through the bars into Millie's eyes a little longer than usual as she played the ending in her mind before it'd even taken place.

"I'm so happy to see you," said The Queen, as she sauntered along the carpet towards them. "I've been worried sick. It wasn't nice of you to leave without telling anybody. People thought you were dead." She let out a brittle laugh. "But not mother and I, we knew better.

"We knew your pathetic parents had so many faithful followers, that they could and would easily conceal you in the forest. And you were constantly around those disgusting fairies and perytons – they'd help to keep you hidden without question." Her eyes darted around the room in anger and frustration.

A smile spread across her face as a pleasant memory came to her. "We started the patrols almost instantly. And then when Serperus was introduced into the patrols, we covered twice as much ground. We also enlisted the mermaids to be our eyes in the waters." Sadness washed the smile from her face. "But after my mother passed away, and we were *still* no closer to finding you, I began to think - maybe something terrible *had* happened to you. Thousands of people have been questioned, and yet, no-one has ever confessed to concealing you. I was so close to giving up hope," she frowned, contemplating her thoughts as if they were new, feeling her disappointment over again.

"You took no pictures with you, no clothes, no food," she stated, calmly. "The only thing you took was a family heirloom - just one item," she said, raising a single finger. "Then one day, I was informed of some unusual activity in the forest." She looked over to Millie. "A girl that kept reappearing in the forest, a girl that didn't look *quite* right. Some time went by, and then she was brought to me." A wicked smile flashed across her face. "You can imagine my surprise when I saw the very heirloom you had taken all those years ago, around her neck." Millie clutched at the emerald that her mum had given her. She looked over to her mum as she recalled Ophelia's story, and it all fell into place; her mum was Princess Jainella.

"Did you really think we'd let you disappear? Especially after what needed to be done with your parents and brother. We couldn't risk you coming back, we had to make sure none of you could ever rule this kingdom." Naleem eyed Jane, enjoying the look on her face as she tried to suppress her upset. Jane had always known that her aunt had murdered her parents and brother; but this was the first time she'd heard it as fact and not speculation. "I've been searching for you, Jainella, now here you are, all grown up. But now that you're here in front of me, with your *unusual* looking daughter, I don't think you were ever in the forest, were you?" She tilted her head in curiosity. "You look almost, *alien.*"

Jane stared speechless; her mind raced.

"Oh, come on Jainella, speak to me. Haven't you missed me?" The Queen said, standing where the light met the darkness.

Jane fought back tears as she looked at her cousin. When she'd last seen Naleem, they'd been innocent children. Now they were grown, and Jane could see that Umelle had managed to sink her toxic claws into her daughter; Naleem hadn't stood a chance. She stood in front of Jane, humanity devoid from her eyes, and only an empty lifeless evil left.

"You don't have to be like your mother, Naleem. You don't have to hurt people. She murdered my parents because they were good people, and my brother because she was threatened by him."

Naleem flinched, "She murdered your parents because they were weak, and your brother would've been a weak leader too. His powers would've been wasted - he didn't deserve them! You're the same, Jainella. I can't allow you to rule this kingdom."

"I'm sorry, Naleem. I'm sorry that your mother poisoned you, and that I couldn't help you," Jane said, sadly.

"Careful Jainella," Naleem warned, through gritted teeth.

"Just let my daughter go and we will leave, you'll never see us again."

A devilish smile returned to her face. "You didn't answer my question. Where have you been hiding all these years?" Naleem probed, ignoring Jane's request.

Jane stared at her defiantly, ready to take the knowledge of the portal to the grave. She glanced over to Millie. She hadn't been able to save her parents, or her brother, and it had haunted her since the day she left Morendale - the day she ran in defeat. Jane knew that this time, she wouldn't run. The love she felt for her daughter was so powerful, she knew she'd do anything without hesitation to protect her.

"Oh, come on Jainella, you can tell me – we're family."

"My name's not Jainella anymore. Release my daughter *now*, Naleem," Jane said, fiercely.

Naleem smiled darkly. "Make me."

"I didn't want it to come to this."

Millie looked from The Queen to her mum. Jane stood deadly still, her eyes fixed on The Queen. Millie watched as the panic left her mum's eyes, leaving them simmering with rage while her face remained calm and composed. Suddenly, the air began to move, it whistled through the bars of Millie's cage, and whipped her hair around her face. As the air picked up speed, Jane's appearance subtly changed. The aura Millie felt around The Queen, now surrounded her mum too; not only the aura of someone who belonged in Morendale, but the aura of a powerful being. Her blonde curls glowed almost gold, and her eyes sparkled like clear emeralds. Millie's breath caught as she watched her mum transform into not only a person of Morendale, but a Queen, and a magical being. The air vibrated as energy absorbed into Jane with force. Naleem waited, barely able to contain her excitement.

The air stopped moving abruptly, and the vibrations ceased, plunging the room into silence. Jane lifted her trembling hands gracefully. She looked at Naleem with regret before she thrust her loaded hands towards her, sending concentrated, green-tinged energy rippling visibly through the air. It hit Naleem with such force it sent her flying backwards into the shadows.

Jane ran over to Millie, she waved her hand and energy shot at the cage, leaving a cloud of green smoke around the dismantled lock. Millie stayed inside the cage while she studied the woman in front of her, she was her mum, only not. She was other-worldly, and lethally powerful; not only through her royal status, but her magical capabilities.

Jane knelt outside of the cage. "It's alright, Millie," she coaxed. Millie burst out of the cage and threw her arms around her mum. Jane held her tightly. "Let's go."

They walked towards the door, hand in hand. A rush of energy pulled Jane backwards out of Millie's grip, sending her skidding across the room.

Millie bolted towards Jane. "Mum!"

"Stay back, Millie!" Jane shouted, raising her hand.

Naleem appeared from the shadows. "You haven't lost it Jainella, I'm impressed."

Jane got to her feet unsteadily. The women glared at each other, determinedly; one driven by power, and the other by love. They pulled back their arms simultaneously, then lunged them towards each other. Blasts of green and blue energy shot through the air. They collided and rebounded outwards towards Millie. Millie dived out of the way and crawled to the edge of the room. The continuous pulses radiated from their fingers and met with equal force in the middle. Jane winced as she strained to keep Naleem's power at bay.

Their powers were equally matched, but Naleem conserved her power expertly, whereas Jane used all her energy with every blow. Naleem had nurtured her powers, and Jane had suppressed them. Jane knew she couldn't overpower Naleem, but she could hold her off long enough for Millie to make a run for it to the portal.

"Millie, go! Run!"

"No, I'm not leaving you!"

"Go, *now!*" Jane shouted, feeling a love so powerful she found the energy within herself to drive Naleem backwards, so Millie could escape.

Millie had to go; she knew she was distracting her mum; Jane needed the peace of mind that came with knowing Millie was safe. Millie tore her gaze away from her mum and sobbed as she ran towards the door.

"No!" Naleem screamed. "Serperus!"

The far door burst open; the sound of eager paws pounded through the dark room. The bright snake eyes appeared from the darkness, then his shining bared teeth, and scaled powerful body as he padded into the light towards Millie.

"Millie! Get behind me!"

Millie ran towards Jane. Serperus weaved and blocked her path and herded her towards the door. She considered running into the hallway, but she knew he would catch her before she even made it through the door. Jane managed to free one hand briefly and divert her power. She shot a small blast of energy at Serperus and knocked him to the ground. Jane hoped he would turn his attention to her, but there was no breaking his focus. His gaze never left his target as he stumbled to the ground and rose to his feet again in one fluid motion. Jane tried again to break her hand free, but she couldn't. She couldn't divert her power long enough to keep him on the ground for Millie to make a run for it; all her energy was barely keeping Naleem at bay.

Millie edged backwards, her back pressed against the door. She couldn't believe what was happening, and what was about to happen - she closed her eyes and waited.

She felt the door behind her shift. It nudged her forwards as Carla squeezed through the gap.

"Millie!" she shouted, relieved.

Her relief drained as she registered Millie's horrified face. When she saw the snarling creature in front of them, she plastered herself against the door next to Millie. Her eyes focused on the magical battle taking place between her mum and The Queen behind the scaled dog. The Queen propelled powerful rippling blows that forced Jane backwards to her knees.

Carla shifted herself in front of Millie. "Stay behind me!"

She planted her feet and held out her hand towards Serperus. He bared his fangs gleefully.

Jane spotted Carla across the room, between Serperus and Millie. "Carla! Go! Take Millie! You need to leave!" Jane pleaded.

Carla ignored her. She mirrored Jane and thrust her hand forwards in determination, willing something to happen. Tears of terror rolled down her face as the beast moved closer.

"No!" Jane screamed, she broke her hand free and pulled Serperus away from them. He clawed at the marble floor as he wrenched himself away from the force pulling him back from his prey.

Naleem charged forwards, and with a violent thrust of her arm, she delivered a blow that pinned Jane to the wall. When the force subsided, she dropped limply to the ground.

"Mum!" Millie choked.

The Queen looked euphoric as Jane lay motionless on the marble. "Now that's taken care of... Serperus, would you mind."

Serperus turned rigidly towards Millie and Carla. He let out a high-pitched yelp of excitement as he launched into a powerful run.

Millie and Carla held each other tightly. Carla closed her eyes and pushed her hand outwards again in one last attempt. As Serperus' hot breath touched her palm, a blast of energy spurted out clumsily, sending him skidding backwards. Millie gaped at Carla in awe. Serperus shook his head vigorously. He cowered to the ground and snarled as he retreated into the shadows.

"No," Naleem whispered, as she shook her head in disbelief. "No, no, no!" Tears of anger flooded from her eyes. "You're about to join your grandparents, uncle and mother," she spat viciously, as a blue flame rose from her palm.

Carla turned hastily to Millie. "Put your palm up and keep hold of my other hand."

The Queen pulled the flame back and launched it towards them. Without hesitation, Millie lifted her palm to mirror her sister's. Instantly, a stream of blinding white light erupted from their palms and joined in the middle, dousing the fireball that hurtled towards them. Millie turned her palm to her face in amazement.

The Queen shook with rage. She reached for the ground with her claw-like fingers. Flames rose from the marble and surrounded her. Carla and Millie raised their hands again in unison. Feeble waves of energy spurted from their palms, aggravating the blaze.

"Your mother should've taught you how to use those powers properly, it could've saved your lives." The Queen boomed over the roar of the inferno.

With a twist of her clawed hand the flames surged towards them. They were hit by a cloud of smoke. As they realised the flames had been extinguished, they opened their eyes. Their eyes stung from the smoke that filled the room.

"Step away from them Naleem."

"Mum!" they shouted.

Naleem glared blindly around the room. A gust of wind dispersed the smoke. A shadow of fear swept over Naleem's face as she saw Jane standing strong. Naleem screamed and shot a deadly blast at Jane. With a swipe of one hand, Jane deflected the blast, while the other fired three sharp bolts to The Queen's chest. She fell backwards to the floor and lay unmoving.

"Is she dead?" Carla shouted, from across the room.

Jane stood over Naleem. "No, she's not dead." Jane closed her eyes and lifted her hands, she weaved them in a circular motion as energy spun between her palms.

"Mum no! Don't do it," shouted Millie.

Jane smiled lovingly at Millie. "Don't worry, I'm just binding her powers and putting her into a long sleep until we figure out what to do with her."

Carla frowned. "What *are* we going to do with her?"

"I don't know, but we can't leave her here. We need to take her back with us, it's the only way to be sure the people here are safe."

Millie visibly relaxed. Jane was better than Naleem and Umelle, she would never lower herself to their level; she wasn't a murderer. Millie watched in admiration as her mum carefully administered her magically induced sleep. Even with the power Jane possessed she was still moral, despite what Naleem and Umelle had done to her family and her people.

With her powers, she gently lifted the sleeping Queen into the air. Naleem floated behind them as they left the room. They eagerly walked towards the stairs. They froze as a low growl came from a dark corner in the hallway below; yellow eyes glared up at them.

Millie stepped in front of her mum and Carla. It was now or never, she thought, she had to face her demons. She knew that if she didn't, Serperus would always haunt her. She reached back for Carla's hand and raised her palm towards him in warning. Terrifying eyes stared back, they darted nervously from Millie to the door. Millie smirked and lowered her hand. "Serperus. Out. Now!" she demanded, as she swiped her arm across her body, opening the castle door weakly with her powers. Serperus scuttled out of the shadows and through the door. Millie frowned at her palm. "We're really going to have to work on this," she said, to Carla.

"I'm so proud of you both." Jane said, swelling with pride.

Jane looked back over to the painting that'd caught her eye when she'd entered the castle, the portrait of her mother and father. She had nothing to remember them by other than the necklace, her memory of them had faded over time. When she'd left Morendale, she'd left everything behind, her name, her life, and her people. But she was never able to leave behind her regret and sadness. Despite being a young girl fleeing from danger, she had always felt cowardly. As she looked into the eyes of her parents, her memories of them became alive. Clarity suddenly filled her mind, like she'd been consoled by her parents. She knew that she hadn't been cowardly; she'd done what she needed to do to survive. She had returned to Morendale stronger and had avenged the murder of her parents and brother. They were at peace; and now, so was she.

Oliver appeared in the doorway, frantic and out of breath. When he saw Millie he sighed in relief, "You alright?"

She walked down the stairs towards him. "Yeah, I'm fine. Thanks for coming back for me," she said, gratefully.

"I didn't, I came to see Whartorlli about booking one of his tours," he teased. She chuckled and rolled her eyes. "You would've done the same for me."

Millie flung her arms around him and hugged him. It was only then she noticed Whartorlli and Jenna behind him.

"Whartorlli!" she beamed, tears prickling in her eyes. "I thought Serperus had-"

"I'm OK, just a bump on the head," he smiled. "If I hadn't been OK - these two would *never* have found you! They'd still be on their way to Hillontropa."

Oliver shook his head but allowed the white lie.

"Jenna, what are you doing here?" Millie asked, astounded.

Jenna was as white as a ghost. She stared at Millie, speechless and blinking rapidly.

Oliver glanced over at her, "Jenna? You OK?"

Her head jolted towards him, "Wha- tha- it- huh-" she babbled, incoherently.

"It's OK," he said, patting her on the shoulder. "Jenna's just met Serperus," he said, in explanation. They all nodded in understanding. "We saw the flashing lights from the castle all the way in the forest. When we got to the castle grounds, Serperus came running at us! He ran straight past us; those lights must've scared the life out of him."

Millie smirked. "Guess so."

Oliver eyed Jane cautiously. "Hi Mrs Shepherd."

"Hi Oliver. Thank you for everything," Jane said, appreciatively with a warm smile.

He smiled, then turned his attention to Carla. She anticipated his next words and rolled her eyes.

"So, Carla, you didn't think I was completely crazy after all."

Whartorlli flew in front of Oliver, authoritatively. "One obvious question," he said, glancing back at Oliver irritably. "*Where* is The Queen?"

With a subtle flick of her finger, Jane shifted Naleem to the front of them.

"What the-"

"Oliver!" Millie warned.

Jane followed the levitating Queen down the steps. "Come on, we'll fill you in on the way back."

Millie hesitated. "Mum, there's something I need to do first," she said, as she rushed to the far door that led to the dungeon, and to Thomas' cell.

17

'Hey Mills! I know you said to come over for dinner at six, but would you mind if I came over straight after school? I'll help you pack!'

Millie replied to Oliver's text, 'Sure! I'm so excited. I can't believe this is my last day at school! ☺' Millie hit send and continued getting ready for school.

For the first time in a long time, the thought of going to school gave her butterflies of excitement rather than anxiety.

Ping, 'OK great. I know, I'm excited too! It'll be like old times - seeing you every day again! Don't get too emotional saying goodbye to Jamie and Mora, I know how much they mean to you.

Say hi to Jenna for me! See you later!' Millie giggled and rolled her eyes.

Ping, 'Hi Millie! Can't wait to see you today, it's been ages since I last saw you! See you at school! X." Millie smiled at the message from Jenna.

Millie couldn't believe what Jenna had done for her; she'd put herself in danger to help find her. Millie would forever be grateful to Jenna, and envious that she'd seen a mermaid.

The morning they'd arrived back from Morendale, Jane pulled Millie and Carla out of school - once she'd explained everything to Mark, including the sleeping woman on their sofa. That morning, Mark had been startled, not only by Naleem, but by his wife and children. He'd woken to them all looking a little different; they had an aura about them - a glow.

Jane began from the very beginning – how she'd been born into royalty, and her memories of growing up in Morendale Castle, in a parallel world. She told him how she and her family possessed powers that were rare in her world; powers that no-one from his world could fathom. She told him how her aunt had murdered her parents and brother and had taken the throne. She cried as she relived the last time she'd seen her brother - the night he came to her, panic-stricken, after an errant spark had emanated clumsily from his palm in front of Umelle – indicating to her that he'd come into his powers; a death sentence. She told Mark, without guilt, how she'd feared for her own life and had fled her home through a portal. A portal that she and Ophelia had created through powerful magic, which allowed her to cross into other planes of existence. He listened as she told him how she'd crawled through the portal years ago, into a garden which was now theirs. The garden had belonged to a man and woman who'd found Jane - scared, confused, and alone. They adopted her and gave her a wonderful childhood, one with joy and without fear. She explained how the portal could only be activated by those with knowledge of its existence.

Naleem was more difficult to explain; not only why she'd kidnapped their daughter, but why she was unconscious in their home. Jane told Mark how her cousin had been corrupted by Umelle and had been threatened by power that could challenge her own. She explained that Umelle and Naleem had never accepted her disappearance and had searched for her in hopes that they would one day find her and eliminate the threat. When Naleem saw that Millie wore the family heirloom, she knew Jane was alive, so she used Millie to entice her back to Morendale. Jane explained to Mark that she needed to keep Naleem close until she figured out what to do with her. And that leaving Naleem in Morendale was dangerous, even without her powers. There were people, like Ophelia, that were not naturally gifted with magical powers, but studied the art - who were able to undo the bind.

It hadn't been until Carla had told them about the peryton fawn in the garage that Jane had realised that it had been Jupiter who had activated the portal. As a fawn, Jupiter had watched Jane, with Ophelia's help, create the portal - an escape. Jupiter had saved his fawn by sending him through the portal, and out of Serperus' reach. Millie recalled Whartorlli's story, how he'd seen Jupiter and his fawn running from Serperus just before he'd discovered the portal; and had thought that Jupiter had been frightened by its light. The knowledge of its existence had grown from there; passing from Jupiter to Whartorlli, from Whartorlli to Chris, from Chris to Millie, and from Millie to Oliver, Carla, and Jenna.

Mark thought it was all an elaborate joke and had laughed uncontrollably - until Jane stunned him with a few magic tricks. After that he'd sat with his mouth gaping for hours.

When Mark was able to form words, they concocted a story. One that explained the disappearance of Millie, Oliver and Jenna; and ensured that Naleem would no longer be a threat to their family, or anyone else. Once they had their story figured, Jane called the police. With urgency in her voice, she told them that Millie and the others had managed to escape and had made their way to the house. She told them that a few minutes later, their kidnapper had come looking for them, and had forced her way into the house.

When the police arrived outside the house, Jane woke Naleem from her slumber. The police kicked open the door and found Naleem in deep concentration, with her palms outstretched towards the family and their friends. It'd taken her a while to notice the officers; but when she did, she turned her hands towards them. Her face had contorted with fury as she tried and failed to inflict harm on them. In her efforts her hands had curled and resembled talons. When she started to scream in frustration, and ask what had happened to her powers, they restrained her and took her away. Naleem had a psychiatric assessment, which led to her being sectioned. Even though this had been Jane's intention, she was distraught. She remembered them both as children - untainted and innocent. Jane had decided, she would always remember her cousin as the innocent child she'd known, and not the menace she'd become.

It took a few days for Mark to ask the many questions that clouded his mind after her story, and the incident with Naleem. It took a while for him to comprehend it all, and longer to feel fully comfortable with it. Jane asked Millie and Carla to keep their magical inheritance to themselves until Mark had fully recovered.

"Come on girls! You'll be late for school!" Jane called from the kitchen.

Millie put her phone in her bag and skipped to the stairs. As she walked down the steps, a soft dusting of glitter fell like snow from the air. Millie smiled and looked up to see Carla leaning over the banister, making a swirling motion with her hand as flurries of sparkling glitter appeared from her palm and floated down onto Millie.

"One of you better clear that up," said Jane, from the bottom of the stairs. Millie smiled at her playfully and clicked her fingers; the glitter vanished instantly. "Show off," she said, trying to keep a serious face as she pointed to the kitchen where Mark was sat.

"What've you both done?" Mark said, feigning exasperation as he joined Jane in the hallway, and giving her a kiss on the cheek.

Carla walked down the stairs and stood beside Millie, "Nothing, dad."

Mark looked mildly confused, then shrugged. He gave them a tight hug and kissed Jane again before he left the house for work, "See you later, ladies."

Millie and Carla walked to school together - chatting, laughing and discreetly practicing magic. They were half of their father; a regular yet extraordinary man from one side of the portal. And they were half of their mother, a powerful magical princess from the other side of the portal. Together they were the best of both; together they made a whole. They'd lost their bond as sisters, and it'd taken Carla to lose Millie to awaken their bond, and their powers. Their sisterhood was the key to their powers; their sisterly bond connected their magical halves. When they left Morendale, their powers had diminished; they were only able to move small objects, and only while being in physical contact with one another. They discovered that the growing strength in their relationship reflected in their powers. As their bond and their powers grew stronger, they only had to think of one another to ignite their magic. On one occasion they tried doing their chores using only magic. It'd started off well; but due to their inexperience the magic took on a life of its own. The broom, mop, and vacuum cleaner turned on them, and chased them up to Carla's room and pounded on the door while the duster kept watch. They'd had to barricade themselves in until Jane came home and saved them. They were now closer than ever, and neither of them had to actively think of one another anymore to activate their powers.

Millie and Carla said their goodbyes at the school gates and joined their groups of friends. Millie's group was significantly smaller than Carla's – consisting of just Naomi and Jack. Millie had been out of school for three weeks, and neither Naomi nor Jack had contacted her. As they rambled through their excuses, Millie noticed the signature flame red hair in the crowd bobbing towards her. They followed

Millie's line of sight and scattered to a secluded area of the grounds, with a clear view of the action.

"Hey!" Jenna squealed, as she threw her arms around Millie. "I've missed you!"

Over the past three weeks, Jenna had contacted Millie every day; they'd become true friends. Millie was grateful to finally have made a real friend, other than Oliver; and to have one fond memory of Farnhall Academy.

After the incident, Mark and Jane had decided to move house. They had pulled Millie and Carla out of school so they could recover from their experience, while Mark and Jane made arrangements for the move. Millie and Carla had decided to attend school one last time before the move. They wanted to say goodbye to their friends and teachers. After Millie had faced Serperus, he no longer haunted her dreams. Millie now made it a point to always face her fears, but Jamie and Mora were no longer one of them; she'd encountered worse monsters and had beaten them. She was strong and courageous, and always had been she'd just lost sight of it. She couldn't leave Farnhall Academy being remembered as the girl who ran.

Jenna pulled back from the hug to look at Millie, "How have you been? How's your sister? How's your mum? How's Oliver? Has he asked about me?"

Millie held her hands up, "Woah, one question at a time!" she giggled. "Everyone's great, and Oliver said hi," Jenna beamed at the mention of Oliver. "How have you been?"

"I've been good, just hard to get back to normal after what we've seen," she answered, lowering her voice. Millie looked around anxiously. "Don't worry I've not told anyone; they wouldn't believe me even if I did!"

Millie laughed and nodding in agreement. "I haven't had chance to thank you in person," said Millie, earnestly.

"Thank me for what?"

"For risking your life for me."

Jenna shrugged as if to say, 'It was nothing'.

Millie smiled, "Even though you probably did it initially because you've got a thing for Oliver!" Jenna blushed and they giggled. "But honestly, I'm lucky to have you both as friends."

Jenna smiled and linked her arm as they walked to their first class.

"Has he said anything else about me?"

"Oh, hi Millie! It's wonderful to have you back!" chirped Mrs Carpenter, as Millie walked into Art class, closely followed by Jenna.

Millie smiled broadly. "Thanks, Mrs Carpenter, it's good to be back."

Millie and Jenna sat at an empty desk. Mrs Carpenter couldn't help but look twice at the unlikely friends. She noticed the new air of confidence Millie was exuding; a similar confidence she'd noticed in Jenna, but somehow different – an aura. An aura which, unbeknownst to most, had been ignited by her other-worldly heritage.

When Jenna had returned to school following her disappearance, she'd distanced herself from Jamie and Mora. She gradually cut herself out of conversations and then chose to sit by herself in classes and at lunch. Her lonely spell hadn't lasted long; once she'd broken away from Jamie and Mora, she made other friends – friends she was proud of. It became apparent to Jenna that most of the school disliked Jamie and Mora. She felt guilty for abandoning her cousin; but it was Jamie who had made the choice to be a bully, and Jenna couldn't be a part of it anymore. Jenna had to make her own choices, the right choices. She could only hope that one day her cousin would make better choices too.

The class gathered around their desk to give Millie their well wishes. A few of them asked questions about the kidnapping; she knew they'd heard the half-fabricated story from Jenna just a few weeks before, so she kept her answers vague.

The door flung open and slammed against the wall, everyone jumped and turned to face the door. Jamie and Mora lingered in the doorway with faces like thunder.

"Awww look Jamie, Millie's fifteen minutes of fame must've come to an end, so now she's come back to school to bore everyone with her annoying story."

"It really is pathetic," Jamie added, as she laughed cruelly.

"That's enough! Now both of you sit down and be quiet unless you want detention!" raged Mrs Carpenter.

"It's OK Mrs Carpenter," Millie said, calmly, with an air of authority and wisdom. She gave Mrs Carpenter a reassuring smile before she focused on the girls. "First of all, I think it's awful that you'd make fun of a situation like kidnapping. If my sister were here, I wouldn't be responsible for what she'd do to you – don't worry I won't tell her what you said, I wouldn't wish Carla on anyone." Jamie opened her mouth to speak and was met by Millie's raised hand that instantly silenced her. "And second, I think you two are the ones who are pathetic. Look around you, nobody actually likes you, not even your own cousin, Jamie." Jamie glanced at Jenna and looked away shamefully. "You make people feel bad about themselves to make yourselves feel better. My advice is to change now, before it's too late and you're out in the real world - and you're forced to change."

Everyone in the room was speechless, including Jamie, Mora, and Mrs Carpenter.

Jenna clapped her hands together out of awkwardness and brought everyone out of their trance-like state, "Well said Millie. Mrs Carpenter, over to you!"

"Yes," Mrs Carpenter said, shaking off the shock. "Yes, we should get on with the lesson – everyone, go to your seats and let's begin." They all walked leisurely to their seats, apart from Jamie and Mora who took a seat instantly, looking embarrassed and perplexed. "OK, we're continuing with pop-art!" she continued, as she glanced over to Millie proudly.

At the end of the day, Millie and Jenna chatted enthusiastically as they waited for Carla by the school gates at the back of the school. They decided to take the quieter more scenic route for their last walk home from school – mainly so they could show Jenna their newly refined magic skills.

Millie peered at her watch, "Wonder where she is."

"She's probably still saying bye to her friends at the front gates."

Millie was about to suggest meeting Carla at the front gates when she felt a tap on her shoulder. She saw Jenna's face drop and knew *they* would be behind her when she turned around. She looked over her shoulder, and to no surprise, Jamie and Mora were behind her.

"Listen, if you're here to beat us up - Millie's sister will be here any minute!" Jenna rambled, panicked, as she realised they were alone.

"Calm down," said Jamie, in exasperation. "We're not here to *'beat you up'*, we just wanted to say sorry." Jamie visibly winced when the words came out of her mouth, as though it had physically hurt her to apologise. "I didn't realise we'd been that bad to you, we thought you'd take it as a joke." Not even Jamie looked convinced by what she'd said. Mora loitered behind Jamie, hanging her head in shame.

Millie laughed, "I don't believe you thought I'd take it as a joke. I think you two had fun though." Jamie's eyes darted around as she tried to avoid Millie's glare. "But I appreciate the apology anyway."

Jenna spotted Carla walking towards them over Jamie's shoulder. As she passed Jamie to join Millie and Jenna, she bumped her shoulder and knocked her off balance. Jamie's face went from furious to passive as soon as she saw Carla.

"W-we were just apologising to Millie." Jamie blurted out.

"Good," barked Carla. "What are you waiting for? A gold star? Go!"

Jamie and Mora scrambled through the school gates. When there was a decent distance between them and Carla, they turned to look at Millie maliciously. They smirked and giggled before they walked away through the field.

Without warning, the sky turned from a bright crisp autumn afternoon to pitch-black and stormy. Jamie and Mora stopped in the middle of the field and looked up at the rolling clouds. The wind whirled around them, whipping their hair into their faces and swirling the fallen autumn leaves into mini tornadoes. The leaves floated upwards purposefully and fell into a formation as Jamie and Mora watched in confusion. The leaves weaved themselves into one another, and stabilised in mid-air as they formed a terrifying autumnal structure. They stared in disbelief as the leaves shifted themselves into place, and the formation became recognisable as a full-sized raptor. Lightning flashed where its eyes should be. The raptor jolted into life. It took a deep breath before it thrust its head forwards and opened its mouth to let out a deafening clap of thunder. The girls screamed and ran; the raptor lowered its head and bolted after them. Rumbling thunder escaped its jaws as it chased them across the field. Jamie reached the end of the field first, she launched herself over the fence and bolted - leaving Mora behind. Mora was there a second later; she tried to climb over the fence, but she slipped and fell to the ground. She heard the frenzied pounding of the raptor's feet behind her. As she turned the raptor lunged at her. Mora screamed and shielded herself with her arms. A wind with hurricane-force knocked her back against the fence as the leaves exploded out of the raptor form and whipped against her skin. She peeled her arms away from her face and watched as the leaves floated to the ground gently, and the clouds rolled away - leaving the sky bright blue and cloudless. Haunted with fear, she glanced across the field to where Millie, Carla, and Jenna watched from the gates. She scrambled to her feet and climbed the fence, then ran until she was out of sight.

"Carla!" Jenna scolded.

"Don't look at *me*!" Carla laughed, nodding towards Millie.

Jenna turned to Millie in astonishment.

"What? They deserved it!" she shrugged, feeling uncomfortable under their gaze, and slightly guilty. "OK, fine - it was a bit dark, but they *did* deserve it."

They all nodded in agreement as they walked into the field.

"A *dinosaur*?" Carla asked.

"First thing that came to mind."

Millie and Oliver spent the evening packing. While they worked, she entertained him with magic and told him about her day, including the storm infused raptor she'd conjured out of leaves for Jamie and Mora - which earned her a standing ovation from Oliver.

The door knocked. Mark came into her room and grabbed a suitcase in each hand, "It's time."

Millie and Oliver followed him, each with a smaller case, down the stairs through to the kitchen. Jane was sat at the dining table next to a stack of suitcases, and Chris in his carrier. Carla was trying to keep James under control, as he pulled at the handles on the kitchen cupboards.

"Ready?" asked Mark.

They nodded hesitantly as they looked around their empty home. Just hours before, the walls in the hallway had been filled with memories; now they were bare, with only the patchwork of faded wallpaper as evidence that they were ever there.

"This is intense," Oliver sighed, as his own memories flooded his mind.

Millie's lip quivered, "I didn't think it'd be this hard."

Oliver put his arm around her shoulders. "Things will change for the better. Look on the bright side, we'll get to see each other every day."

"How is *that* a bright side?" Carla teased.

"Each to their own," Oliver smirked.

Jane's eyes glazed over with tears. Mark pulled her into a hug and kissed her temple.

"We'd better get going. Oliver, we'll drop you off home," Jane said, as she composed herself.

They each took one last look at their old home as they filtered out through the back door into the garden, each pulling a case behind them. They stood opposite the wildlife patch, which Jane had encouraged Mark to nurture years before. She'd thought by concealing her escape route, it'd help her to forget her past-life. The bushes had been there for over fifteen years, and to anyone other than Jane, they'd been nothing more than bushes. Now, to them all, they were much more; they'd concealed a portal which had given each of them what they'd needed. The portal had allowed Jane to confront her demons. She had not only avenged her parents and brother, but many others who had been executed due to Naleem's madness. Jane had freed the kingdom from a tyrant; the kingdom was now at peace, but without a leader. She had a destiny that she thought she'd never fulfil; it was her place to take the throne and continue her parents' legacy. Mark hadn't needed much convincing; his joy came from the happiness of his family, and he was more than happy to leave his job behind. The hope of a more fulfilled venture nearly had him agreeing instantly; but it'd been his daughters who had made his decision an easy one. He saw how happy the idea made Millie and Carla, so he agreed to the move wholeheartedly, and without doubt.

The second Millie had felt the buzzing atmosphere of Morendale, she'd felt at home; she was drawn back regardless of the dangers. She had found an escape and had grabbed hold of it with every ounce of her being. Morendale had helped Millie to grow, and find herself, and her strength again. It'd helped her to love her life, and no longer see it as something she needed to escape from. Morendale was where she belonged, and she couldn't picture herself anywhere else. In Morendale, she could he herself; magic could be used freely, and she loved that fairies, perytons, nymphs, and mermaids were real, and not a myth. Millie had chosen to live in Morendale, not because she wanted to escape, but because it felt like home.

"Just one question - sorry for my ignorance, but how are we dropping Oliver home?" asked Mark, who was still new to the concept of the parallel world and portal travel.

"I've got my own portal outside your front door through to the cupboard in my room," Oliver said, with self-importance. "Mrs Shepherd created it! It was amazing - you should've seen it!"

Mark nodded, still none the wiser.

"Just one more thing before we go," Jane said, as she turned to look at her daughters, with love and pride that was palpable. She held out her hand and smiled at Millie. Millie didn't need to hear the words;

she knew what needed to be done to make things right. She took off her necklace and placed it in her mum's hand. The necklace rose slowly from her palm, until it was at eye level. They watched in silence as it twirled in the air; the precious stone sparkled in the sun, and the silver chain glistened. Jane closed her hand into a fist and the gem split into two identical halves. The thin chain doubled in size, then split in the middle. The chains fastened themselves to the emeralds. The necklaces floated down; Millie and Carla opened their hands to allow the necklaces to float into their palms. Millie felt elated as she gazed from the necklace in her hand, that now held so much more meaning, to the look of gratitude and joy on Carla's face. Oliver watched the ceremonial exchange in awe. Mark smiled as he breathed deeply through the dizziness he felt every time he witnessed magic.

"OK, ready?" Jane said, flashing a playful smile. She stepped towards the hedges and raised her hands above her head. As she parted her hands, a sliver of brilliant green light shone through the bushes. It grew brighter until a rush of green dust spurted out, signaling the portal was open fully. Jane led the way through the shrubs and through the portal, closely followed by Mark, Carla and James, then Oliver. For the final time, Millie stood, with Chris in his carrier, at the foot of the tunnel. She glanced back at the house once more and smiled fondly.

"Come on Chris, let's go."

Thank you for reading.
Keep up to date with new releases,
www.kerrytaylorwrites.com

Printed in Great Britain
by Amazon